MARKED

Chronicles of Calan, Book III

I0671914

Written by Nikki Moore

Cover and Illustrations by Ryann Armstrong

MARKED, Chronicles of Calan: Book III
Copyright © 2018 by Nikki Moore.

Moore Enterprises. All rights reserved. Published in the United States of America. No part of this book may be used or reproduced in any manner whatsoever without written permission except in the case of brief quotations embodied in critical articles and reviews.

This book is a work of fiction. The characters, incidents, and dialogue are drawn from the author's imagination and are not to be construed as real. Any resemblance to actual persons, living or dead, businesses, companies, events, or locales is entirely coincidental.

For information visit the author's website: moore-books.com

Cover design and all illustrations: Ryann Armstrong keylligraphyink.com

FIRST EDITION
ISBN 978-0-9982380-6-7 (print)

To Wendi, for giving me the push I needed to start this journey

The Realm of Nowles

(more commonly known as the Old Kingdoms)

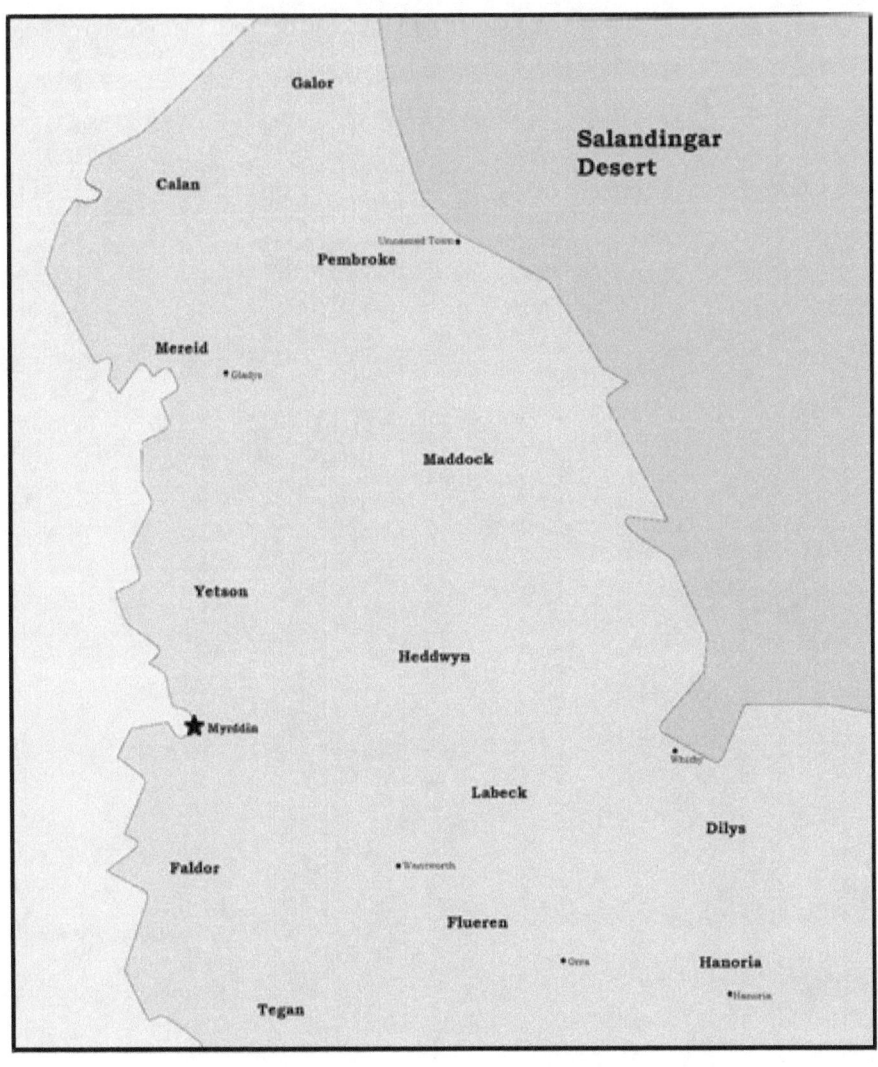

Chapter 1

He came to her in her dreams. When she woke, she could never hold onto more than a few fleeting impressions—sparkling green eyes, laughter rumbling in her ear, whiskers tickling her skin—but the knapsack beneath her cheek would be damp from her tears and the ache upon her heart renewed. Only when she slept could the memories seep into her mind. Upon waking she packed them away, struggling throughout the day to keep thoughts of Lang at bay, always dreading the arrival of evening when she would once again have to close her eyes for sleep.

Though she could have easily traveled it in less time, her journey from the lone oak, where Kyreen and Rhun had parted ways, to the small, unnamed village on the edge of the desert took five days. Aren had promised to stall the ascension ceremony until Spring Festival, at which time Kyreen would need to be present to formally abdicate the throne. This gave Kyreen until spring to complete the task of finding her twin. In order for her cousin to ascend to the throne, Kyreen must either confirm Quillan's death or bring him back to also complete the abdication ceremony. She felt no need to rush. She could afford to travel at a leisurely pace, to permit the fog in her mind to descend, to give the gelding free rein to set his own pace.

When the sun's decline lengthened the shadows, she would halt the gelding, dismount, groom him, and release the animal to graze with hours of summer light left. Then she would go through her daily meditations over and over again, until her muscles ached and her clothes stuck to her body with perspiration, her breath ragged and loud in her ears.

Once the sun settled behind the western horizon, the direction in which she headed, where the Salandingar Desert, and the elf lands beyond that, waited, she would practice the handful of spells that Brigit had taught her. She knew that eventually, with enough work, the smell of magic would no longer trigger a reaction. For now, she battled the terror welling up inside, her body reacting to her time with Sten, to those encounters still locked away from her conscious thoughts, unlike her memories of Lang which pressed at her, vying for her attention at every waking moment. Then and only then, in the deep of the night, with her body and mind exhausted, could Kyreen sleep, falling into a deep slumber, though when her eyes opened in the grey dawn, she never felt rested.

Cresting the final hill just after midday, Kyreen reined in the gelding, halting to gaze down at the town. Not even big enough during the height of the mining craze to have been granted a formal name, the village consisted of a dozen buildings clustered along the edge of the wide muddy river snaking south. This side of the river glistened green under the summer sun. On the other side of the river, the Salandingar Desert spread out far and wide, tan and drab, shimmering heat waves distorting a flat terrain of sand and rock peppered with scrawny bushes.

Though she had had five days to speculate, Kyreen, holding no anticipations for her arrival to this village, having never given a thought to anything other than the very next step, did not know what she had expected from this isolated community on the edge of civilization. What she found as she rode her horse into town was a handful of silent observers, standing before their tired, faded buildings, watching her with their tired, faded eyes. Not seeing an inn or a stable, Kyreen dismounted before a squat one-story building. Beneath a faded sign that read 'Mercantile,' three wooden steps led up to a covered walkway connecting the four buildings on this side of the street. As she tied the gelding to the hitching post, the proprietor, his features hidden in the porch's shadows, disappeared into the gloomy depths of his store.

Shouldering her knapsack, heavy with the bulging bag of coinage slipped there by Rhun, money she had not discovered until her first evening after their parting, Kyreen walked up the steps. Upon entering the store, she paused on the sill to allow her eyes to adjust to the dimly lit interior. The store consisted of a shallow front area with a long counter behind which the short, balding store clerk stood. Behind him a chalkboard hung on the wall, advertising the store's products and prices. The entire scene, the man included, had an air of neglect and mustiness. Kyreen reckoned that these days not many people found their way to the little village. For a brief moment her mind wondered on the monotony of life in this village, on what it would be like to wake up to the prospect of the day ahead being exactly the same as every day before. It sounded serene, peaceful, idyllic. Resolutely, before her silence could become drawn out, she pushed those thoughts away.

"Hail," she said, after clearing her throat a couple of times, her voice cracked and hoarse from disuse. When the man nodded a silent greeting, the light from the door flashing on the lens of his round spectacles, she continued, "Is there a place I may secure lodging and food for myself and my horse?"

"Sulwyn has rooms across the way. Wind knocked her sign off a couple years back. No good reason to put it back up," the man answered, his voice surprisingly deep for a man of his slight stature. "She has stalls round back."

"My thanks," Kyreen nodded, turning to go.

"You prospecting?" the merchant asked.

Kyreen looked back at the man. "No."

"You an outlaw?"

Kyreen gave that question a moment's thought before shaking her head. "No."

"We want no trouble here," the man said. "Strangers, in my experience, bring trouble."

Kyreen briefly wondered if the merchant had been elected the town's spokesperson or if he had chosen to take on that role. Her instinct leaned towards the latter.

"I am not looking for trouble," she finally remarked. "Just a place for me and my horse to set a few days. Then we will be on our way."

"On your way? We are not on the way to any..." The man stilled, frowning, his eyes narrowing as realization dawned. He had misspoken. This tiny village was on the way to somewhere. Somewhere the residents here did not think about, nor talk about. Without another word, the man turned, disappearing through a doorway leading to the back of his store.

After a few moments of waiting, when it became apparent the merchant would not be coming back, Kyreen turned, exiting in search of the boarding house. She would need to return at some point to purchase supplies, but that errand could wait. She would be here a few days.

On her third evening in the unnamed town, after watching the sun set over the expansive desert from her west facing window, Kyreen dropped the shades to the room's windows for the first time since she took up residence in the boarding house. While she doubted any of the two-dozen people populating this community would be spying on her, why take the chance? Drawing the opal amulet out from under her tunic, she set the necklace on the wooden washstand beside the porcelain wash bowl full of the water she had requested from Sulwyn earlier that afternoon. Giving the opal a soft farewell pat, Kyreen left the room, closing the door quietly behind her. Then she sat in the hallway, leaning against the wall, and waited. She did not fear being discovered. She was the only boarder and the house mistress had long retired to her own quarters on the first floor. This boarding house, like this town, was quiet and peaceful.

Night had settled proper outside when Kyreen heard a rustling from inside her room. Wearily she stood up and opened the door, slipping inside, just as a mage light flared.

"Turn that thing off," Kyreen hissed, closing the door to the hallway. She moved to the lamp sconce on the wall to raise the flame as Brigit uttered the words to darken the sphere in her hand.

Kyreen turned to greet the mage properly, but her words died on her lips upon spying the other woman. Brigit's face shone in the lamplight with perspiration and shadows lingered under her blue eyes, dark with exhaustion. Kyreen's brow furrowed but she contained her concerns.

"Hail, Kyreen," the mage mumbled, shakily lowering herself to sit on the edge of the bed. She glanced around the tiny room, taking in the worn furniture, the faded floral paper on the walls, the cracked and sooty chimney on the lamp. "Where are we?"

Kyreen cast a silence spell to ward on the room before replying, "Some town on the edge of the desert. I do not know how long it will take to reach the elf lands and who knows how magic works there. This seemed the best place to meet you. Are you alright?"

Brigit had reclined back on the bed, her legs dangling over the edge, an arm thrown across her closed eyes. She casually waved her other hand, dismissing Kyreen's concern.

"Never better," the mage answered, her strained voice contradicting her words. "Transpiring is not all that easy, especially over such a far distance. I have been working on building up my endurance. Evidently, I need more practice. Damned if I know how he did it so effortlessly."

Kyreen did not respond, not needing to inquire about whom Brigit referred. Sten. Just the thought of the man caused her flesh to break out in goosebumps and she repressed a shudder. Kyreen sank down into the rattan seat of the room's lone chair, to wait for Brigit to recover from the spell.

After a few long moments, the older woman pulled herself into a sitting position, and opened her eyes to inspect Kyreen. The younger woman looked fine if you did not take notice of the smudges under her green eyes, or if you did not remember the sparkle that had once glittered in those eyes. Kyreen's clothes hung on her lanky frame, giving testimony to the weight she had lost in the last fortnight. Kyreen's lips lifted into a slight smile, though when she shifted her listless gaze to Brigit no joy or merriment reflected in her eyes.

"I have nothing more to report," Kyreen remarked. "As I said I have not begun the trek across the desert yet. I will cross the river at dusk tomorrow. The locals say traveling by night might be better than in the heat of the day. I will figure it out as I go."

Brigit waited a moment after Kyreen finished before she began speaking. "Resettlement continues moving forward. I will not bore you with the details."

She paused a heartbeat before continuing. "Aren offered the Practitioners, offered me, a seat on the Council." Another short pause. Neither woman feeling the need to verbalize the reason a position had been available on the Council. Kyreen pushed down the memory of Lang, but not before fresh pain blossomed in her heart. Brigit fiddled at the hem of her shirt while Kyreen sat motionless.

"Thank you," the mage murmured. "I know what you did and I am grateful."

"I do not want your gratitude. A mage sitting on the Council was long overdue and Aren should not have told you that I made that request," Kyreen replied, her voice more resigned than cross.

"She did not," responded the mage, only a shadow of her customary teasing in her voice. "You just did. I suspected it when the farmers raised all kinds of hell and Aren stood firm against them. They have lost their majority on the Council and it burns them. I turned Aren down by the way. My temperament is ill-suited for long meetings, let along cooperation and collaboration. Lundy, the Head Practitioner, took the spot. She will do well. She has kept us mages in line for years."

Kyreen listened to the mage's words but she could not care about the politics. Even before.... before Lang's death she had no interest in them. Now? Now only the desire to find her twin kept Kyreen mobilized. Without this task she did not know if anything could have gotten her out of bed in the morning.

"Your friend Synnove has taken your place as the Council's liaison with the Guild Brody Llafur," Brigit continued speaking. "Though I am not sure the wisdom of trusting her after everything her..."

"Synnove has done nothing wrong," Kyreen interrupted, the sharpness in her voice the first flare of emotion Brigit had felt from the younger woman. "She should not be punished for something her brother did."

The women sat in silence again a few moments. Kyreen thought back to her last meeting with her cousin. Aren had not objected to Kyreen's request to look for Quillan, but she had been against Kyreen traveling alone. Kyreen had eventually won by convincing Aren that she needed to be alone, to reset her Connate ability, to be without input from any Calanian. Brigit's visit during the full moon had been the compromise, but Kyreen only had conceded to the mage's visits after Aren had agreed to fulfill three of Kyreen's requests. The first had been the appointment of a practitioner to fill the vacancy left on the Council by Lang's death, and the second being Synnove's appointment as emissary to Rhun's guild. The final of Kyreen's requests had been the guarantee that Kasja, Lang's former mate, would receive his land parcels. Kyreen wanted to ensure Lang's children would not suffer any more than necessary from their father's death.

Brigit pulled open her knapsack to withdraw a small leather-bound journal. Her movements brought Kyreen's thoughts back to the present.

"I copied down a few spells for you to practice while you are…" she paused, searching for the right word. Traveling did not seem appropriate. "…looking for your brother."

The mage stood up to hand the book to Kyreen who opened it, idly paging through the first few pages.

"Thank you," Kyreen said without any inflection or changes in her expression or tone, her eyes already soaking in the new spells.

"I am still sorting through the archives for spells. Most were stored away with the outlawing of magic and a good number are in an archaic language which nobody can read," Brigit remarked. "But the good news is that the Council has decided since we have been targeted by magic, it might be time to ferret out what spells we can, to build up our skills and defenses. So, at last, we are permitted dedicated practitioners, and with what spells we are able to translate, we have a core group learning and perfecting a variety of spells. These spells I put in that journal are specific types to aid you on your journey. In addition to the ones you already know, I added the spell I used to ward your amulet, a couple of healing spells, and, even one I am not certain will work, a messaging spell."

Kyreen nodded, continuing to thumb through the journal. The spells were written in a tidy legible handwriting covering several dozen pages. So much had been written, Kyreen wondered if the mage had begun this journal even before Kyreen had left Calan.

"These look helpful. I have been practicing every day and will add these to that practice. My thanks," she told Brigit. What Kyreen did not add was how she used the practice of magic to exhaust her mind.

"That is good," Brigit responded. "I should probably be heading back."

"Are you rested enough?" Kyreen asked looking sharply at her friend. While Brigit's color had returned, she still looked tired.

"The return trip is easier, takes less energies," Brigit said, slinging the knapsack over her shoulder. "Shall I look for you with the next full moon?"

"You can try," Kyreen remarked. "I might be in the elf lands by then. If the stories are to be believed, your magic may not be viable there."

"I will try every full moon until I find you or until you send me a message," Brigit replied.

Very quickly Kyreen found herself alone once again. She lowered the lamplight to darken the room before raising the window shades to allow the moonlight to splash across the floor. She stripped, seeing no reason to soil the clothes Sulwyn had laundered earlier that day. Naked, Kyreen ran through her meditations, first unarmed then with her sword, until her arms and legs ached. Perspiration ran across her bare body, chilling her skin in the cool night air. Once she had pushed her body as far as she could, Kyreen sunk to sit cross-legged on the rug to practice the handful of spells she already knew. The hour grew late and morning would arrive soon, so tomorrow she would begin studying the spell book that Brigit had brought.

Kyreen practiced her little bit of magic over and over again, until her eyes began to drift shut and her words slurred. The final two spells of the evening were to remove the silence spell on the room and to add a protection ward on the door and windows. Sufficiently tired, Kyreen climbed into bed, sliding between the crisp linen sheets without bothering to put on her underclothes. With one hand under her pillow, wrapped around the hilt of her dagger, she permitted her eyes to close for good and succumbed to deep sleep.

The following morning Kyreen rose at dawn to perform her morning ritual. Afterwards, using the water in the bowl, she bathed, the chilled water raising goosebumps on her skin. Once dressed, hair braided, and weapons strapped on, she went downstairs.

Sulwyn, the boarding house proprietress, upon hearing Kyreen on the stairs laid out a simple breakfast for her lone lodger before disappearing back into the kitchen, leaving Kyreen to dine alone at the large table designed for a dozen or more. It was not that Sulwyn disliked the ebon haired stranger. No, Kyreen had never done anything to generate disfavor. Quite the opposite. Simply put the stranger's quiet manner, the way she could sit motionless and unspeaking, spooked Sulwyn.

Once finished with her meal, her plate clean - though Kyreen could not have said what she had eaten – the Calanian carried her dishes into the kitchen. Her silent entrance startled Sulwyn, who spun around, dropping the pan she had been towel drying. Keeping her dirty dishes balanced in one hand, Kyreen took a large step forward, easily catching the cast iron pan before it hit the floor.

"I will be crossing the river at dusk," Kyreen said, handing the pan back to the astonished woman. "With your permission, I would like to keep my room until then."

"You are paid through the week," Sulwyn replied, turning away to resume her cleanup of the breakfast dishes. "I shall prepare your refund."

"Not necessary," Kyreen responded, shaking her head when Sulwyn opened her mouth to protest, a gesture born more out of societal politeness than a desire to relinquish the coinage. "Where I am going my money will be of no use."

Kyreen knew her boarding fees had been a pleasant infusion of income, but she did not realize the true reason for the intense relief she felt from Sulwyn. The proprietress welcomed Kyreen's coinage as a way to pay her monthly tax. The amount of Kyreen's rent would be enough to gain Sulwyn at least two months reprieve from making payments to the tax collector with the only other asset the woman possessed with which to settle her tax bill. Had Sulwyn cared to share this burden with the stranger in her kitchen, Kyreen would have gladly given the woman the remainder of the pouch's contents, and probably would have delayed her journey for a few more days, just to meet with the tax collector when he arrived, but Sulwyn left her dilemma unspoken.

"I have a few errands this morning," Kyreen said, heading for the back door. "I will return by midday."

Without waiting for a reply, Kyreen exited the kitchen, heading towards the barn behind the house. The gelding whinnied a soft greeting to his mistress when she entered. Even though he was the three-stall barn's only resident and despite the daily runs Kyreen had taken him on during their stay in the village, the gelding did not like being stabled. Born outside in the snows of a Hanorian spring and raised in Kyreen's herd, the gelding preferred to spend his days and nights in the open, grazing in the sunlight and dozing under the stars.

Kyreen gave her horse an affectionate pat on the neck before dumping a generous helping of high energy oats into his bucket. While the gelding munched his tasty breakfast, she gave him an extra thorough grooming, rubbing his sorrel coat until it gleamed in the stable's shadows, running a comb through his mane and tail until they crackled with static. She even rubbed down all four legs with a cloth and lifted each hoof for a thorough inspection. After hoisting the saddle into place for the last time, Kyreen had to pause a moment, blinking rapidly and swallowing the lump in her throat before tightening the cinch. Once the gelding had been tacked, she led him out of the stable into the alleyway where the sunshine glittered off the horse's beautiful red coat.

After giving the cinch a final tug, Kyreen swung up into the saddle and rode out of the village, away from the wide muddy river and the desert beyond. No one gave notice to the stranger taking her horse out for a ride, just as she had done all the days before this, but they did wonder, hours later, when she strode back into town on foot, the saddle slung on her back and the bridle dangling from one arm.

Kyreen dumped the tack in an empty corner of the boarding house's now empty stable. There, in the shadows, she leaned her forehead against a post, her eyes drifting shut. Only then did she succumb to her tears, the hot moisture leaking from between her closed lids. She knew it had to be done, but she had learned that doing the right thing was very rarely the easiest thing to do. Kyreen also had the foresight to realize that, in the larger scheme of things, releasing the gelding into the foothills outside of town had been better than the alternative.

Every morning and every evening, Kyreen had stared at the yawning expanse that was the Salandingar Desert and worried about the crossing. Not for herself did she worry but for her horse. Without knowing how long the trek would be, without knowing if there would be water, she could not guarantee the horse's safety. At her core, Kyreen knew that to take the gelding into the desert would mean the horse's death. Unable to bear the burden of another death on her conscience, Kyreen had chosen instead to release her beloved gelding, her one constant companion on this journey, into the wilds of the foothills. Blissfully unaware of his mistress's conflict, the horse had been content to peacefully graze as she walked away with his tack in her arms, the bright sunlight refracting in her vision as she blinked away unshed tears. Now Kyreen did not need to worry about his safety. This area only had one large predator – man – and that gelding had been wily about being caught ever since he had been a gangly colt.

Swiping the back of her hand across her eyes, Kyreen straightened, let out a shaky breath, and walked back out into the sunshine. She had two more stops to stock up on supplies before midday meal.

Chapter 2

Sunset found Kyreen standing on a wooden flatboat in the middle of the muddy river. A grizzled old man, the features of his dark mahogany face hidden beneath a gray beard that cascaded down to rest on his slightly protruding belly, slowly worked a long pole to push the vessel across the expanse of water which separated the province of Pembroke from the Salandingar Desert. Kyreen watched the lazy current snaking southward where this tributary would meet up with several lesser streams until these waters joined the mighty river which eventually flowed to the city of Myrddin and out into the Great Sea. Idly she wondered how long the voyage would take to the city. Before she allowed her mind to wander any more, especially about her friends in Myrddin, Kyreen turned her gaze upstream. Very dimly, in the setting sun's light, she could make out the shape of the mountain range which surrounded Calan and Galor, isolating those two tiny provinces from the rest of the realm of Nowles, more commonly referred to as the Old Kingdoms. She wondered how her people were faring and what Brigit had left unsaid last night. For Kyreen had the impression that the mage had not been completely forthcoming in her report of the happenings in Calan. Shaking her head to chase away thoughts of her home and her people, refusing to worry about things over which she had no control nor could be of assistance, Kyreen returned her gaze to the desert ahead of her. This had to be her focus, her foremost concern. She could not permit speculations to distract her from the task at hand.

Howell, the old ferry master, kept silent as he poled the boat. His sinewy arms, muscles long and lean from years of hard labor, flexed as he pushed the pole into the water, dark fingers sliding down the full length of the shaft before wrapping and pulling the pole free of the silty riverbed, to begin the procedure anew. With impeccable timing, just as the ferry began its final glide to the riverbank, he pulled the pole out of the water a final time. The drops of the river clinging to the wood glistened in the last of the daylight as the final tiny bit of sun dipped below the far horizon. Setting the pole down on the flat boat bottom, Howell moved to the bow, leaping off as the boat bumped into the bank. Kyreen had not even noticed him picking up the dock line as he moved off the vessel, but the old man had it in his hand when he landed, ready to pull the ferry snug against the shore and tie it off.

Kyreen stepped off as the ferry master tied the line to the post. She pressed her fare into his calloused hand and turned to stride away before he could notice, or protest, she had paid him much more than the agreed upon price, which he had already inflated to account for his return trip in the evening dusk.

Though he had been quiet for the ferry ride, Howell had spoken quite a bit to Kyreen over the previous several days, imparting his knowledge about the desert, tidbits she felt might save her life. Having been raised in the mountains Kyreen knew not the first thing about the desert save for what she had read in books. But most of her reading lay in fictional tales, not facts. So, she appreciated the old man's mention of the nightly dips in temperature; his advice of aiming for any trees she might see as a water source; his caution not to wander too far into a canyon due to flash floods that occasionally flared up from late afternoon thunderstorms in the distant mountain ranges; and his demonstration on how to wrap her head and face in a bolt of linen cloth to protect from the sand and sun. The old man also sketched out a variety of the desert flora and fauna, noting which plants might contain precious liquids and which wildlife might be venomous.

"Do not attempt to ingest any of the creatures," Howell had warned one afternoon as they sat beneath a yew tree on the bank of the muddy river, his hands busily braiding rope together to fashion a line for his ferry. Every afternoon they sat, he worked with the rope. By the third day Kyreen figured out he had been repairing the same rope over and over. She supposed he did not like sitting without a task to keep him occupied. Idle hands attract trouble as Kyreen's foster mother Ildri had been fond of saying.

"Are the wildlife poisonous?" Kyreen had inquired, her gaze fixed on the desert. By now the desert had taken on life, at least to her mind.   The Salandingar Desert was her opponent, standing between her and the elf lands. The desert would attempt to keep her from her destination but Kyreen had every intention of vanquishing this adversary. So, she listened when the old man spoke.

"Not all," he had remarked. "I think the taint of their environment is infused in them. Make you wish they were poisoned enough to kill you. Any excessive loss of fluids in the desert can be deadly. Diarrhea and vomiting are just slower than bleeding."

To a person, everyone Kyreen spoke to about the desert took a sour view of the environ, calling it a plethora of names, the most common evil. Maybe that is why it had become a living foe in Kyreen's thoughts.

All this crossed Kyreen's mind as she took her first steps onto the rocky soil in the fading light of the summer evening. It surprised her how, just across the river from the small unnamed town, the temperature here rose so much higher. Of course, with the absence of sun those temperatures had begun dropping and fast, making Kyreen glad for her cloak which she had not yet packed in anticipation of such an event. The linen she would use as her turban in the daytime now wrapped about her hair and neck to ward off any chill.

"That big blue star, there on the horizon," Howell called out one final reminder to her receding form. "If you orient on that every night, then your course will be true."

Dropping his voice low so she did not hear, he added, "Blessings be upon you and Godspeed."

Howell had liked the quiet stranger, had enjoyed the companionship, had loved having a fresh audience for his tales. Though he did not know the stranger's reason for crossing the desert, the old man did know that of all the people who had entered the desert with the intent of finding the elf lands, none ever returned this way, not even the last strangers to exit this town via the desert, a pair of travelers Howell had ferried across the river many, many years ago, when Howell had still been a young man. Now, as he watched the dark-haired stranger walk away, Howell wondered what ever became of that tall pale elf and the little blond boy.

The moon, one night past full, rose to Kyreen's back. Though it shed some light, Kyreen still illuminated a sphere to assist with the hike, ever mindful of the holes and uneven terrain that could easily twist or worse fracture an ankle. It would not do to end her journey with the lights of the town still visible behind her. She did not yet possess Brigit's powers of spelling the mage light to hover in the air, but it gave Kyreen a goal to work towards. Goddess knew she would have time in the desert to master such skills. For now, she held the light in her hand, regretting the orb did not radiate heat with its illumination as the desert breeze nipped at her bare fingers.

Kyreen walked steadily westward, her eyes fixed on the bright blue star twinkling on the horizon. After several hours, the night sky still velvety black, resplendent with galaxies and stars swirling overhead, she halted. Her body throbbing with exhaustion, she shrugged off her knapsack and engorged water skins. After drawing a circle around her proposed campsite with the heel of her boot, Kyreen cast protection and shield spells on the area. Sitting down on her bedroll, she opened the journal Brigit had given her to begin memorizing the healing spells. If trouble happened, as it most assuredly would, the time wasted pulling out a reference book could very well make all the difference between survival and death. While she read and memorized, Kyreen ate the bread and cheese and meat Sulwyn had packed, leftovers from the midday meal. Though the food most likely tasted good, Kyreen gave no thought to the flavors as her mouth chewed and her eyes drifted over Brigit's handwriting. Kyreen only ate because she knew she needed energy to continue her journey and she chose this meal because the ingredients would not keep very well in the coming days. Once her food had been consumed and her eyes grew heavy, Kyreen extinguished her light and wrapping her cloak tight around her body reclined on her bedroll, allowing sleep to claim her almost as soon as her eyes closed.

Waking with the dawn, as had always been her habit, Kyreen rose, broke down camp, and resumed her walking even as the sun peeked out from the eastern horizon. She continued until the heat of the day prompted her to stop. Hunkered down, entirely cloaked with not even her eyes visible, Kyreen dozed on and off, waiting for the sun to traverse low enough in the western sky to take the heat down a bit. Then she resumed her westward trek until her body aches forced her to stop hours after sundown.

She continued with this routine for nine days, twelve days, fifteen days, until she stopped keeping count. Every day mundane and the same, waking and walking, waiting and walking, then making camp, conserving her water, orienting every night on the big blue star. Until one dawn brought two changes. The first she noticed right away with the sun's first light cascading over the sprawling desert. Far away, shimmering in the distance even though the heat had not yet risen, Kyreen could just barely perceive a shadow of something. Was it mountains or a forest? She did not know. What she did know was that the shadow was something different and, in this case, different was better. The second change Kyreen did not notice until she made ready to stop in the midday heat. A stand of trees tall against the flat land, a dull green against the washed-out tan of the sands and faded blue of the sky, stood northwest of her position. The shimmer of the heat made it difficult to determine the distance but, before pulling the linen cloth over her eyes, Kyreen determined she would veer in that direction once she resumed her trek after the worst of the day's heat had passed.

Though the trees had appeared fairly close, Kyreen did not reach the watering hole until the following afternoon. She had worried during her night walk that she might walk past it or worse get off track and lose sight of the little patch of green altogether. By setting her right shoulder in line with the blue star, however, neither had happened. When she made her final approach, she found herself slightly disappointed and definitely underwhelmed by the oasis. Maybe all those stories she had read made for her unrealistic expectations. The green trees grew scraggly in a clump around a pool of water no wider than Kyreen was tall. She figured she could probably leap across the pond, maybe not flat footed but definitely with a running lead. The trees themselves stood just taller than Kyreen but the brush grew thick on the north and south side of the water. The east and west side contained a collection of sand colored boulders holding the water away from the desert. The middle of the pond rippled and bubbled as though the little watering hole were fed from an underground river.

All of this Kyreen took in as she made her approach to the watering hole, struggling to maintain her walk when all she truly wished to do was run up to the water and dunk her head. Instead she entertained the idea of taking a respite here, camping overnight by the water to give herself a night of rest.

Such thoughts evaporated as soon as she crossed into the clearing. The very bottom edge of the sun, glowing red-orange, had just dipped down to kiss the western horizon and a slight breeze ruffled through the trees. Kyreen paused just inside the perimeter of the watering hole area suddenly overwhelmed by a feeling of great unease. Something cold brushed against her face, pushing away the cloth. Tendrils of cold tugged at the turban, grabbing hold of one dangling end as though to unwind the cloth. More coolness brushed against her arms then her body, lightly at first, then harder, up her back, across her abdomen, against a breast, which made the breeze pause, but only for a heartbeat.

Then Kyreen felt the distinct impression of a hand grasping at her breast, squeezing tentatively then increasing pressure until she hissed in pain through her teeth. Something knocked against her shoulder spinning her around. Now the unseen entity pulled at the cloth wrapped around Kyreen's head, loosening the turban until she stood bareheaded in the dying light, her mane of curls flowing about her face.

Kyreen drew her sword, holding it at the ready, knees bent, eyes wary, as she slowly turned to observe the clearing around her. When she had made a complete circle and once again faced the water, the shape of a man appeared across the little pond, fuzzy in black shadows at first, then the form solidified. A hulking figure of a man stood in the shadows of the tallest palm, his facial features coarse, his skin an unlikely gray, his hair shaggy and as black as the eyes which regarded the woman with malevolence. The clothes upon his bulky form hung in tatters but enough remained to reveal their fashion to be more than a hundred years out of style.

"A woman?" the man asked, speaking with a heavy accent Kyreen could not place, his voice higher pitched than one would expect from a man his size. "I have not felt the skin of a woman for nigh on a century and change. I shall enjoy you immensely, poppet."

Kyreen, realizing this could not be a flesh and blood man, took a step back from the apparition. When it did not react, she took another step and another until the heel of her boot grazed the border between the watering hole and the desert. Only then did the form dissipate. Kyreen found herself being battered by strong gusts of wind forcing her back towards the water, away from the clearing's edge. A hard blast to the side of her face dazed her, almost knocking her to her knees. As soon as she stood well inside the perimeter of the oasis the winds fell away. The cold breezy touches resumed, caressing Kyreen's face, ruffling through her hair, brushing across her body, fondling her breasts, squeezing her buttocks. No matter how Kyreen turned and twisted, shuffling away, she could not escape the cold breeze assaulting her, always it shepherded her away from the camp perimeter, away from safety. As the sun continued to disappear below the far horizon, the touches became firmer, more solid, and the voice began to speak to her.

"Oh, yes, poppet," it whispered, a current brushing across her cheek. "You are so soft, so fresh, so alive."

Unseen arms wrapped around Kyreen's body from behind, large hands grabbing her breasts, pulling her against a firm body, an icy breath against her ear murmuring. "You belong to me now. I shall not be denied. The night makes me strong and I shall take you, my little poppet."

Something icy and wet slid along Kyreen's cheek. Yet when she broke away and turned, sword raised, she faced only the desert in twilight. Swiping the back of her hand at her cheek, she removed the moisture. Warily she turned back towards the water, pulled out one of the empty water skins. When she knelt to fill it, however, the winds rose up again driving her away from the banks of the pond.

The caresses began anew, a flurry of touches all across her body, soft and intimate at first then growing hard and needy. Once again Kyreen found herself embraced from behind. This time the form pressing into her felt firmer, evidence of his desire digging into her lower back. Yet when she looked down at her body, no arms held her, no hands cupped her breasts, even though she could see the indentations of hands.

"You cannot withstand me, poppet," the icy breath whispered in her ear. "I am too strong, too quick, too smart. No one escapes me. I own you."

Kyreen stilled her struggles and allowed the apparition's groping to continue without resistance. The entity was hungry and eager. The voice, no longer speaking coherent words, made impatient mewing sounds. Overhead stars began twinkling as the western sky darkened and night settled over the desert. With her turban removed and clad only her tunic and trousers, Kyreen shivered in the wind, though admittedly more from the icy tendrils molesting her body than from the chill in the air. As the dark deepened, the touching became more corporeal until Kyreen made out shadowy limbs and felt lips moving across her neck. The feel of teeth against her skin triggered unpleasant memories, prompting Kyreen's attack. In a single fluid motion that took less time to complete than it did for her to think it, she took a quick step forward, lifting the sword as she turned, driving the sharp point into the malevolent spirit's midsection before the form could dissipate. With a soft growl, she forced the blade inward, through the soft flesh until it hit bone, presumably the spirit's spine. Then she pulled out the blade, twisting and lifting up as she did. With a quick shift of her grip, she raised the sword to her shoulder and plunged the blade into one of the apparition's eyes, putting all of her strength into the thrust. With a shriek the specter vanished, leaving behind only silence and starry night. Even the wind faded away.

Breathing heavy as though she had been running, Kyreen took a moment to steady her heartrate. Then she picked up the empty water skin that had been torn from her grasp earlier. Kneeling at the edge of the pond, she paused gazing down into the inky darkness, suddenly unsure of the water's safety.

"The water is clean. It will not harm you," a soft voice spoke from across the water. It was a man's voice, young, Kyreen thought, a clear tenor, sounding Myrddin if she had to guess.

Pulling her sword once more, Kyreen rose to her feet. Across the water she could just make out the shape of two men, one tall and lean, the other short and stocky. Reaching into her sack, she pulled out a sphere which almost immediately illuminated the small watering hole. The two figures, much like the earlier apparition, had gray skin, dark shaggy hair and black eyes, though their expressions did not contain the malice of the original spirit. Their clothes, too, hung from their bodies in tatters, though the fashion was not quite as ancient as their counterpart's clothing had been.

"No need for that," the taller of the pair said in his pleasant tenor, raising his hands and gazing at the sword in her hand. "Nasir and I mean you no harm, traveler."

"No harm," the short, stocky one repeated, his words heavily accented.

Kyreen thought about what she might say to them, but nothing came to mind. So, she knelt back down and filled up all her water skins, trying not to dwell on the fact that her water supply had been getting dangerously low and how important it was to ensure she got these skins refilled. The task completed, Kyreen stood, slinging the now heavy water skins and her pack across her shoulders, determined not to spend any more time than necessary at this tiny troublesome watering hole.

With everything situated to her liking, Kyreen glanced over at the spirits which had not moved.

"Is it dead?" she asked, having to clear her throat a few times.

"No," the short stocky one, the one called Nasir, answered. "Just vanquished for tonight. Tomorrow, with the setting of the sun, he will arise again. Only a holy weapon can end him."

"He will be livid," the taller spirit remarked, trancelike, almost as though speaking to himself. "So angry. So cruel. We need you. You would appease his anger, soothe his hunger."

Nasir looked up at his tall companion, then back to Kyreen. "I apologize. For it seems, my friend Sorley forgets that we mean you no harm. Such is the curse of this watering hole. It makes one forget one's humanity, one's honor. Even now my own resolve is withering."

"If Peregrin has you to play with," the tall spirit said, "then he will no longer need to harm us, to torture us, to use us. Someday he may even share you with us."

Even as the spirits had been talking, Kyreen had begun slowly edging her way towards the edge of the oasis. Nasir raised a hand as if to halt her departure.

"Sorley is correct," Nasir said, his accent strangely melodic. "Peregrin is bound to be incensed, angrier even than when that pale creature and his companion slipped through our hands. Peregrin had coveted the little boy's flesh nearly as much as yours. If you stay, Peregrin will no longer hurt us."

Kyreen did not hesitate. With one final backwards step, she scooped up the discarded length of linen and exited the oasis. The instant she entered the desert, the figures across the pond disappeared from her sight. Looking into the watering hole from the outside, nothing looked or felt awry. The mage light in her hand cast illumination over an empty grove of trees and brush surrounding a bubbling spring. Still her ears picked up the faded sound of someone wailing. A second later another voice joined the first forlorn cry, raising goosebumps on her skin.

Taking several large steps to put distance between her and the edge of the grove, Kyreen dug through her pack for her cloak. Once the garment had been fastened around her body and the linen cloth re-wrapped around her head, she resumed her westbound trek without a backwards glance. Kyreen wanted as much distance as possible between her and this oasis before she camped.

Chapter 3

The day following her encounter with the spirits of the watering hole, Kyreen spied another stand of trees to the south. With her water skins full and the memory of her encounter with the malevolent spirits fresh in her mind, she decided to ignore that watering hole and continued due west.

Gradually the terrain began changing and soon Kyreen no longer walked on the hard shale covered in a thin layer of sand and gravel. As rock gave way to pure sand, her boots sank down with every step, requiring extra energy just to walk. No longer did the desert stretch out flat before, behind, and around her. Now she had dunes to climb up and navigate down. While the hills were not tall, they did at times obscure the shadowy mountains in the distance and the blue star on the horizon. Thus, every time Kyreen crested a sand dune, she had to reorient herself to keep her course true. Once in the dunes she did not observe any plant or animal life. The entire time Kyreen walked in the sand, the wind blew steady all day, increasing in strength to batter her fiercely at dawn and again at dusk. Fortunately, she did not experience a true windstorm. Howell, the ferry master from the unnamed town, had indicated these whirlwind events mainly occurred in the early spring. As it was, sand went everywhere, infusing and invading every crack, every orifice, every surface, stealing the moisture from everything. Kyreen's eyes stung with each blink, her clothes chafed against dry and cracking skin, her lips chapped and bled, and her lungs felt gritty. Whenever she stopped to rest, Kyreen emptied her boots, dumping piles of grainy sand to drift away on the breezes.

Shortly after sundown on her fifth or six full day in the sand dunes—she had lost track of the days—Kyreen took a step, almost stumbling when her boot hit hard earth. She had made it thru the sands. No one she spoke with in the unnamed town had possessed a map, but several had spoken, in whispers and only in one-on-one conversations that the desert had four environments…shale, sand, shale, foothills. No one would, or maybe no one could, tell her what awaited beyond the foothills leading up to the mountains. Now that

Kyreen had forged the sands, she calculated her journey had reached midpoint, but she knew enough not to celebrate, not just yet.

While the almost full moon rose behind her, she walked a few more hours as the temperatures dropped. When she stopped for the night, she pulled the opal amulet out from her pack, allowing it to dangle from her fingertips. After staring at the stone a few moments, she drew the leather cord over her head tucking the amulet under her tunic, the stone cool against her skin. Though the protection spells Brigit wove had dissipated, the stone's coolness resurrected a plethora of memories, good and bad, which Kyreen promptly shoved back into the compartment of her mind relegated to them. Breaking off a chunk of her daily rations, alternating chewing with small sips to rehydrate the hard-dried protein, she dutifully ingested the food and worked to keep her mind from focusing on the lightness of both her pack and the water skins. Food and water matters would be resolved or they would not. Until then, she refused to worry.

Once she swallowed her last bit of rationed water, Kyreen began her nightly recitation of spells, leaving the healing spell for last. Before entering the sand dunes, she had discovered, quite by accident, that the healing spells that Brigit had copied down in the journal could manage the aches and pains of her daily walks. Since then Kyreen performed that spell daily to specifically tackle the blisters, the muscle fatigue, and the other little abrasions that could easily turn nasty after the daily abuses of her journey. The journal, now ragged and dogeared, remained inside Kyreen's pack as she had successfully memorized each spell. She hoped her attempt to message Brigit had worked and the mage would bring her a new collection of spells, but only if Brigit were able to find Kyreen with tomorrow's full moon, and if Brigit were able to transpire this distance, and if Brigit's attempt occurred after Kyreen had the water ready. Too many ifs to worry about.

Kyreen extinguished her mage light and reclined back on her bedroll, wrapping her blanket around her body, eyes fixed on the swirling galaxies and twinkling stars scattered across the vast velvet black sky overhead. Quietly reciting her daily meditations, Kyreen forced the memories to stay at bay, gratefully embracing the sleep that eventually fell over her tired body.

The next day, just as Kyreen began to contemplate halting for the midday heat, she spied a cluster of scrub bushes off to her left, growing taller and greener than the other periodic clumps of vegetation. Intrigued, Kyreen altered her path to the small grove. Just as she suspected, a tiny bubble of water trickled up through the hard rock, barely enough to create a puddle. But it was water. Kyreen retrieved the mug from her pack.

After filling her mug, she drank the cool water, downing almost a full cup before her taste buds caught up with the rest of her senses. Something in the water tasted off. She spat her mouthful of water out just as the world began to tilt. Fortunately, she had been kneeling beside the water hole, so when she tipped over she did not have far to fall. Spread eagle on her stomach, rough gravel under her cheek, Kyreen clung to the ground as the world around her spun crazily, waves of dizziness coursing through her. Though she felt as though the momentum tugging at her would pull her up into the sky like a vortex or tornado, her body never left the ground. Behind closed eyelids, Kyreen watched a kaleidoscope of vibrant colors swirl around, keeping time with the pulsing vertigo assaulting her other senses. Her stomach roiled, pre-vomit salvations filling her mouth. Though she was loathed to waste the moisture, Kyreen spat out the liquid without lifting her head. Vomiting would be worse than spitting. Still the world spun on and on, her stomach resisting the ride, until sweet, still darkness claimed Kyreen and she gratefully passed out.

When Kyreen next opened her eyes, the vertigo had passed. So too had the day. The sun sat almost halfway down on the western horizon. Sitting up, Kyreen silently gave thanks that she did not wake in a pile of her own vomit. Her head spun dizzily as she righted herself.

"That was foolish," a voice said from behind her, a man's voice, a voice she thought to never hear again. Cautiously, steeling herself, Kyreen slowly turned her head.

Standing in the long shadows of the late afternoon, the light reflecting in his vibrant green eyes, Lang watched her. His lips curled up in humor as he continued speaking. "You need to be more careful. This is a dangerous place. I cannot keep you safe if you do not take care."

Mutely Kyreen nodded, pressing back the tears, unable to respond for the lump in her throat. She had to get to her feet. She had to get moving. She had to flee, to get away from this place, from whatever that was mimicking Lang.

As she attempted to push herself up, the Lang-thing stepped forward as if to assist her. Kyreen rolled to her knees, drawing her dagger, shaking her head at the Lang-thing, which halted, hands raised.

"I mean you no harm," it said, the voice breaking Kyreen's heart almost as much as its image. She certainly did not wish to feel his touch, its touch. If she did, she feared she would be unable to hold onto her sanity.

Kyreen staggered to her feet, dagger held out in front of her body. Standing, she swayed but remained erect. The tears flowed freely as her voice, hoarse from emotion as well as disuse, cracked. "Who are you? What do you want?"

The Lang-thing lowered its arms, his arms, giving her a puzzled look. The beauty of his face distracted Kyreen so she did not register it had moved closer until it reached out to touch her wet cheek. Kyreen jerked back to avoid the contact, very nearly falling from the vertigo. Fortunately, the thing wearing Lang's likeness did not have Lang's instincts to keep her from falling and did not reach out to assist, as Lang most assuredly would have done. Once she felt steady enough, Kyreen took first one step, then another away from the Lang-thing.

"I do not take this form to harm you," Lang's voice said, softly, soothingly. "I thought it would bring you peace to have a familiar form."

"No," Kyreen shook her head. "Not that one."

Lang's image wavered and faded to be replaced with Ildri, Kyreen's Hanorian foster mother. The short, plump woman smiled warmly, her pale blue eyes filled with love, looking not as Kyreen remembered her from those last years, but as she had been when Kyreen had first arrived in Hanoria. Wiping her hands on her apron, she said, in Ildri's soft matter-of-fact tone, "You need to move, work the demon vine out of your system."

When Ildri reached out to take Kyreen's arm, the Calanian flinched, moving away. Ildri's image then shimmered and faded, only to reappear as a tall, ebony haired woman, a woman Kyreen had not seen in two decades. At Kyreen's gasp, Tyra's head tilted, shrewd green eyes appraising the younger woman.

"Why do these images distress you so?" Tyra's voice rang deep and melodic in the late afternoon air. "Why do you not feel calmer when seeing your loved ones? Are these not those you hold most dear in your heart?"

"You are not them," Kyreen responded. "Why do you not show me your true form? Cease imitating the images of those departed from this world and reveal yourself to me."

Realization dawned in Tyra's eyes and she smiled. "Is that what you believe, child? Is that why you carry such sorrow? Your loved ones have not left you. They travel with you always. How else could I have seen these images to don for you?"

"Please," Kyreen implored quietly.

Tyra sighed. "I cannot manifest my true form, not here, not this far out. It must be something of this realm for you to perceive me. Will this form suffice for now or should I assume one of the others?"

"No," Kyreen responded quickly, then clarified. "Not another. This one will do."

"Very well," Tyra smiled. "Now you should be on your way. This water has been tainted with demon vine growing at its edges. I will take you to another watering hole. The water…"

While she spoke, Tyra had begun walking away. When she realized Kyreen did not follow her, her voice trailed off and she turned to look back. "What bothers you?"

"I cannot sense you," Kyreen replied. "Are you elven?"

"Not exactly," Tyra replied coyly. "I do not mean you harm."

"The last ones to tell me that very nearly turned me over to a raving lunatic spirit intent on raping me," Kyreen remarked.

"You mean the specters of the oasis?" Tyra spat, eyes glittering. "Yes, I was not strong enough there to assist. Now that you are closer, I can better protect you, guide you, keep you on your path."

"Why?" Kyreen asked, her eyes narrowing with suspicion.

Tyra, or rather the thing mimicking Kyreen's long dead mother, tilted her head again, observing the young woman for a long moment before answering her. "I am bored."

"So, helping me alleviates your boredom?"

"No," Tyra shook her head, chuckling. "Making sure you arrive in *Talamh sa bhaile Si'* will alleviate my boredom."

"I do not trust you," Kyreen said.

"Good," Tyra nodded. "Shall we go now?"

Reluctantly Kyreen started after the image of her mother. Her head still reeling from the tainted water, she did not attempt to keep up with the sprit. For a spirit is all that Kyreen could imagine the thing imitating her mother could be. Something from another realm, something she could not sense, something that could either be her rescuer or her demise. Slowly the pair walked as the twilight gave way to night and the moon began its ascent.

When the moon hung proper in the night sky, Kyreen halted. As they had walked, the entity wearing Tyra's image had slowed its pace so as to walk beside Kyreen, still keeping its distance or maybe Kyreen kept hers, the Calanian could not be sure. Setting down her pack and water skins, Kyreen sat down and began making preparations to have her evening meal. She did not prepare camp, for Kyreen planned on continuing her journey after the evening's events.

Tyra looked down at Kyreen, hands on her hips. "Why do you stop? It is still early."

"Full moon," Kyreen commented taking a long drink of water before refilling her mug. Placing the full cup down, she began eating her protein rich rations.

Tyra observed Kyreen, again tilting her head. Kyreen wondered if the mannerism had been Tyra's or if it was the creature's own habit. Finally, the being lowered Tyra's body to the ground, fluidly settling in with legs crossed. "What has the phase of the Lunar Lady to do with your travels?"

Kyreen peered at Tyra, chewing her food. Swallowing she said, "I am expecting a visitor."

"Oh?" Tyra quirked on eyebrow. "So, you do have some tricks. That is promising."

When Kyreen next glanced up, Tyra had disappeared. Taking a sip directly from her water skin, Kyreen thought about her strange new visitor. Before she could arrive to any worthwhile thoughts, however, Kyreen smelled magic in the air and tendrils of smoke began drifting from her mug.

Moments later Brigit stood panting beside the cup. Stooping over, the mage rested her elbows on her knees, breathing noisily. When her breathing slowed, Brigit glanced up at Kyreen sitting in the shadows, as the traveling woman had not bothered to light a fire.

Once Brigit had a mage light illuminated, she frowned at Kyreen. "What in the goddess's name happened to your face? Is that a bruise?"

Kyreen felt at her cheek. She had forgotten about the clubbing she took at the oasis from the spirit called Peregrin. Although the healing spells had taken away the pain and swelling, they evidently had not erased the bruising, which had faded to an unattractive yellow-green stretching down one side of her face.

"Oh, you know," she told Brigit airily, "I have been making friends with the locals."

"Some friendly locals," Brigit muttered, scowling at Kyreen once more before lowering her body to the ground.

"Did you get my message?" Kyreen asked.

"Well, hail and good to see you, too," Brigit quipped. "We received some of the message. It was incomplete, a bit garbled. I told you I did not think it would work."

"What did you receive?" Kyreen inquired, not in the mood to play the mage's games.

"Spells," Brigit replied. "It seemed you wanted spells."

"Then you received the important bit." Kyreen pulled the tattered journal from her pack, tossing it to Brigit. "Here, I have these memorized."

Brigit caught the old journal, then produced a new one from her pack, which she handed to Kyreen. "A little rough on it, were you not?"

"It served its purpose," Kyreen mumbled, already opening the new journal, her eyes greedily scanning the pages. She flipped through a couple of spells, then paused.

"What are these?" Kyreen asked, looking up at Brigit. "These are…"

The mage grinned as the other woman's voice trailed off. "Yes, I know! They are spectacular!"

"Where did you find these?" Kyreen asked returning her gaze to the journal. Flipping a page, she inhaled quietly. "Create water? Truly?"

"Next page," Brigit remarked, motioning with her index finger for Kyreen to turn the page. "Food is there."

A slight tremor in her fingers, Kyreen paged through the rest of the spells, the rustling of paper the only sound in the clearing. Fifteen in total, each more complicated and advanced than the previous.

Kyreen closed the book and looked over at Brigit. "Again, where did you find these?"

"Hidden in your mother's quarters," Brigit responded.

"You searched my mother's apartment?" Kyreen asked.

"Not exactly," Brigit evaded the question and Kyreen's gaze, "and not me."

"Just tell me," Kyreen sighed.

"You know," Brigit remarked, "the desert has done nothing to improve your personality."

"That is not what I am here for," Kyreen snapped. "Now either tell me the tale or leave."

"Fine, no need to bite my head off," Brigit grumbled. "Geir, that greedy goat man, has taken up residence in your mother's apartment. I am not surprised that he would appropriate the nicest rooms for himself. But that is not the worst. He and the other farmers have been pushing their land deals through the Council. They sent some people out to survey the surrounding fields and homesteads but did not share the reports."

"So, you went looking?" Kyreen filled in.

"Not me. Idun," Brigit answered. "That girl stepped up big time. Geir would have bedded me in a heartbeat, without a second thought, but he would not have taken me to his private quarters, nor would he have allowed me to stay while he slept. No way that man would let his guard down around me. Not only is Idun pretty and young, her name is not on the mage registry."

"So Idun found spells instead of surveys?" Kyreen guessed, wanting to move the tale along, her attention already drifting to the book in her hand.

From Brigit's expression, Kyreen's guess had been on target.

"You are not much fun anymore," the mage pouted. "Not that you were much fun to begin with."

Kyreen refrained from snapping at the other woman. The encounter with the spirit had left her edgy, but she knew she should not take it out on Brigit. So Kyreen put aside the journal and focused her gaze on the mage.

"Very well," she said. "Continue with your tale."

"Not much left to say," Brigit responded. "Idun had good fortune finding the hidden shelf in your mother's quarters. We think Geir had no clue about its existence, so Idun brought the entirety of the compartment to me."

"It took her three trips," Brigit continued, leaning back on her elbows, legs stretched out. "Three nights with Geir. That girl deserves some sort of prize."

Kyreen returned Brigit's impish grin with a slight smile, one that almost reached her eyes. Her own encounters with Geir on the Council had never been pleasant. The man had always felt devious to Kyreen and more than once he had gotten under her skin. Lang had always declined to discuss his relationship with Geir, though she had begun to feel Lang's disapproval of his fellow farmer towards the end of the campaign. As soon as the thought appeared, Kyreen clamped down on her memories.

"What was my mother doing with all these spells?" Kyreen asked, swallowing the lump in her throat. "If she practiced magic, she certainly never did it in my presence. I know I was young but she rarely left me the entire time we were on the run."

"I do not believe the scrolls were your mother's," Brigit responded. "I believe they were stored by that elf, her lover."

"Arvis?" Kyreen said, her brow furrowing. "He was not my mother's lover."

"I am not judging," Brigit shrugged. "I am simply repeating what I have heard. Considering these spells were hidden in your mother's quarters, it would seem Tyra and the elf were close."

"Of course, they were close," Kyreen responded with a shake of her head. "Arvis had been my father's best friend. He helped my mother with the Galorians after my father had been killed, then stayed on to be her advisor. He was my guardian uncle, mine and Quillan's."

"You do not need to convince me. I do not care about your mother's bedroom companions," Brigit remarked. "We found other items besides the spells."

"Anything useful?"

"We are not sure," Brigit replied, digging into her pack. She withdrew a cloth bundle which she placed on the ground. Untying the twine holding the cloth, Brigit pulled back the fabric to reveal three objects.

Chapter 4

Kyreen leaned in to inspect the objects more closely. The first item glinted in the mage light, a golden orb about the size of Kyreen's fist, colorful gems adorning the surface. The sphere appeared to have a groove around the middle as if it could be split in half. The second item was a silver ring with an oddly shaped ruby gem about the size of a thumbnail and so dark it appeared black except where the light glinted on the facets. The last item was a black rock, misshapen and rough, just slightly bigger than the golden orb.

"I would guess these are magical items," Kyreen commented, her gaze focused on the collection.

"Yes, the traces of magic are faint from disuse but they are there," Brigit responded. "I have assigned Munin and Eiva to the job of identifying all the items, twelve in total. Those two are so competitive they will not want the other to make a discovery."

Kyreen smiled again, remembering the discussions she had witnessed between the two young mages. Then other memories began to leak out and she once again slammed the lid back down on her thoughts, the smile slipping from her face. "Have they discovered these three objects' purposes?"

"Not definitively," Brigit answered with a shake of her head. "As I said there were a few other items. I picked these two—the ring and rock—for their size and anonymity, and the orb for its possible use."

Kyreen absently picked up the ring, but her gaze rested on the orb, mage light glinting off the gemstones. "Possible use?"

"The orb comes apart," Brigit responded. "We believe it is a communication orb, maybe for scrying."

"Scrying?" Kyreen inquired, her body chilling as a memory flashed unbidden.

Sten sitting on the bedroll, his back to her, his legs crossed, his head bent over an object in his lap. Kyreen, naked, reclining on top of the bedroll, her fingers reaching to stroke his back. Her body aching for his touch, hurt by his indifference. His voice low and urgent, speaking to someone, his words too quiet for her to comprehend...

"Kyreen?" Brigit's voice, her tone alarmed, brought Kyreen out of the memory.

Shuddering, Kyreen inhaled deeply and looked at Brigit with a wan smile. "I am here. You were saying?"

"The orb's pieces are mirrored," Brigit said, returning her own gaze to the orb though her expression remained worried. "I would like to keep one half and have you take the other, so we can test it."

Kyreen set down the ring, moving her hand over to the golden orb. With her index finger she rolled it softly back and forth. "Have you not already tested it?"

Brigit sighed. "To be brutally honest, we have not been able to figure out how to activate the blasted thing nor any of the objects."

"What have you figured out?" Kyreen asked, her tone sharper than she had meant.

"Not much," Brigit snapped back. "It is not like these pieces come with an instruction manual. Despite everything we have found in the tunnels, we are operating in the dark here. Magic is not simply reciting the words. It is much deeper than that, a practice that is meant to be passed down through the practitioners, infused upon the caster. We have no one to do that. We are working with a disadvantage. We do not..."

"Hey!" Kyreen interrupted, holding up a hand. "No need to lecture. I do understand. I am not Aren. Are you getting backlash from her or the Council?"

"Nothing we cannot handle. It is frustrating to have all this..." Brigit shrugged, gesturing at the items before running a hand over her braid.

"Brigit, you have done wonderfully, especially considering all the restrictions placed on mages. I am certain you will figure it out," Kyreen said, her tone and expression softening.

Brigit smiled at Kyreen. Then her eyes moved to a spot behind Kyreen, the smile slipping away.

"Do not be alarmed," the mage remarked cautiously. "But we are not alone."

Kyreen turned with an audible sigh to look over her shoulder. Silently she gave thanks the entity had once again chosen Tyra's image to emulate, not Lang or Ildri.

"Quit lurking," Kyreen said. "Come join us proper or go away."

Brigit gave Kyreen a horrified glance. Then, catching a good look at the figure entering the pool of mage light, scrambled to her feet.

"Troubles?" Kyreen asked, turning back to Brigit, pushing down her discomfort at having the entity behind her. She kept her tone mild as though the appearance of her long dead mother was not cause for concern.

"Tyra?" Brigit asked. "Kyreen, why is you mother here?"

Something in the mage's tone pierced the shield Kyreen had built around her emotions. Though she should have realized it long before now, Brigit was of an age, just a bit older than Aren, that she probably knew Tyra. They may have even been in training together or maybe even friends. Not for the first time Kyreen realized how little she knew of Brigit's past—where exactly she grew up, her Battle story, really nothing except that the scout Olavi was her baby brother.

"If you insist on taking my mother's image, would you at least tell me your name?" Kyreen asked, looking up at Tyra. The spirit had moved to stand beside the still sitting Kyreen.

The spirit gracefully lowered to the ground. "You may call me Lakwen'dil."

The spirit's gaze focused not on the two Calanian women but on the items spread out on the cloth. She breathed in softly but made no move to touch anything.

"This…spirit who wears my mother's likeness is my latest traveling companion," Kyreen explained to Brigit. "Evidently it is bored and escorting me safely to the elf lands will alleviate its boredom."

"She and her," the spirit commented absently without looking away from the magical items. "Unlike your gargoyles, I am female, most definitely and assuredly female."

"What do you know about the gargoyle?" Kyreen asked, exchanging a look with Brigit.

This got the spirit's attention. She lifted Tyra's green eyes to look first at Kyreen, then Brigit, and back to Kyreen before saying, "The gargoyle? Why singular?"

"Because there is just the one," Kyreen replied.

"There was not always," Brigit remarked, her voice uncharacteristically quiet and serious. "There used to be five, but how would you know that, Lakwen'dil?"

"Because I remember you, child," the spirit answered with a serene smile. "I know of you, and, though the years have dulled your memories of me, I still mourn you. Now I rejoice in your return."

"My return?" Brigit looked at Kyreen. "Do you know what she is talking about?"

"I have no clue," Kyreen shrugged, "but that is standard for me since I left Hanoria."

The spirit's attention had returned to the three magical items. Pointing at the ring, she murmured, "Earth mover."

Moving her finger to the rock, she said, "Healing stone."

Before either woman could react, the spirit picked up the golden orb and twisted it into two separate pieces. Mage light reflected off of the mirrored circles inside each half. She held the halves in each hand and looked to the Calanians. "Orb of scrying. These pieces do not belong to you. How do you come to have them?"

"As you said, we have some tricks," Kyreen responded with a shrug.

"Would you help..."

Kyreen held up a hand, stopping Brigit's question. "First two rules of fairies and spirits, do not request favors and do not thank."

"That is just superstition," Brigit responded.

"Like reflected surfaces?" Kyreen shook her head. "Do not trust her just because she looks like Tyra. She is not my mother."

Lakwen'dil reassembled the orb and set it back down next to the other two items. "So distrustful a child for one so young. Where was this caution earlier at the watering hole?"

"As you said, I was foolish," Kyreen said. "Will not happen again."

She lifted the book of spells, adding, "Especially now that I have these."

"The watering hole?" Brigit asked, sitting back down, her voice returning to normal. "Do I want to know?"

Kyreen shook her head. "Just some tainted water. Nothing fatal as you can see."

"I can show you how these work," the spirit offered, gesturing to the items.

"In return for what?" Kyreen asked.

"Nothing."

"No way," Kyreen responded. "There is always something. Nothing is free."

"I told you already, child, I have been bored," the spirit smiled a bright smile, Tyra's green eyes glinting mischievously. "Your arrival will shake them up. Make things a little less boring in *Talamh sa bhaile Si'*."

"You have mentioned that name before," Kyreen remarked.

"It is what the elven call their homeland," Brigit commented.

"So, you are elven," Kyreen said reproachfully.

"I never said I was not," Lakwen'dil answered. "I merely said, 'not exactly' which is true."

Kyreen appeared to be ready to ask another question, but she paused, then shook her head.

"Never mind," she said. "The hour grows late. We will accept your assistance with these three items."

"We will?" Brigit asked, then with her customary enthusiasm returning to her face, she smiled. "We will!"

"As you said, magic is more than reciting the words," Lakwen'dil said, reaching down to pick up the silver ring. "But words are important. You cannot activate the magic of these artifacts because you do not speak First Tongue, the language of magic, the language of *Yeste'Nore,* or elves as you call them."

Slipping the ring on her finger the spirit began speaking in a foreign tongue. The rhythm of the words flowed lyrically with a series of hisses infused into the phrases. As earth began moving into a pile before Lakwen'dil, Kyreen experienced a jolt of adrenaline, her body trembling with the beginnings of a panic attack.

"That is the language Sten used," she whispered.

"I believe you are correct," Brigit remarked, then looked at Kyreen's pale face. "Are you alright?"

Kyreen nodded, not trusting her voice. By the time the pile of earth before the spirit had risen and shaped into a small figurine, Kyreen had regained control of her panic. As Kyreen breathed in and out, steadying her pulse, Lakwen'dil looked over at Kyreen.

"I can help with that as well," the spirit said. "I can fade the memory from your mind."

"No," Kyreen replied, vehemently shaking her head. "Just the artifacts."

"You do not have to live with the pain," the spirit pressed.

"I said, no," Kyreen repeated, her voice firm but not heated. "Stay out of my head."

The spirit shrugged, returning her attention to the earthen idol before her. The sand and rock had molded into a simple figurine of a faceless head atop a rotund torso tapering into legs ending about the knees. Only the two bulging, featureless breasts on the torso gave hint to the statue's gender. As the three watched, the statue's surface began to softly glow as runes appeared, soon covering the entire statue. As the glow receded, leaving a smooth finish inscribed with the runes, Lakwen'dil looked up at Kyreen.

"I cannot do that," she said, then before either woman could react, placed the tip of her index finger to the middle of Kyreen's forehead.

Upon the spirit's contact, Kyreen could not move. No matter how she strained, her muscles refused to respond. She felt the spirit enter her mind. Like a mist swirling through the forest trees, the spirit wandered through Kyreen's memories. Kyreen experienced the flashes of memories from her first awareness, riding a pony, playing with her twin, fleeing with her mother, maiming the Faldorian mercenary, meeting Engla, Jorn's stories, Ildri's love. While her life sped by in flashbacks, Kyreen struggled to free herself from the spirit. Not only did she see the memories but she heard, smelled, tasted, felt everything just as she had experienced originally. As the spirit continued sifting through the memories, Kyreen tugged at the bonds holding her in place. When the flashbacks neared the time of her departure from Hanoria, to her time on the road with Collin, she envisioned ropes holding her down. Then she imagined her sword slicing through the ropes, which held fast as first, but she continued to slice again and again, finally causing a tiny tear in the strands. Repeatedly slashing, the rip expanding with each stroke. At last the rope in her mind severed completely and Kyreen jerked back from Lakwen'dil's touch with a fierce roar, part of her mind still focused on her first encounter with Aren on the road from Myrddin.

"How dare you!" Kyreen hissed, eyes flashing angrily, springing to her feet, the sword she always carried on her back appearing in her hand as she faced the spirit, who rose gracefully to her feet.

Lakwen'dil looked down at the blade with the tri-colored hilt, her expression still gleeful, the sight of the sword only widening her smile. "*Megil tel'kaane*, Sword of Valor, crest of *Tella'Nore*. Welcome home."

She raised her eyes to Kyreen, her index finger lightly pressing down on the tip of the sword. "Your weapon cannot harm me, child. Oh, you can wound this form, but unlike the spirit in the oasis you cannot banish me. I would simply reappear, so sticking me would do no good."

"It would make me feel better," Kyreen muttered.

"Kyreen?" Brigit said quietly, her expression indecipherable. The mage had also risen to her feet.

"What?" Kyreen snapped, her eyes never leaving her mother's face.

"Listen to yourself," the mage responded, her tone cautious.

Kyreen risked a glance at the other woman. "Brigit, what are you talking about?"

"Listen," Brigit urged.

"I do not know…" Kyreen frowned, stopping with the realization she spoke a foreign tongue. She relaxed her fighting stance, standing tall, brows furrowed as she glared at the spirit. "What have you done to me?"

"I have made it possible for you to work the objects," the spirit replied. "As we agreed."

"Meandering through my memories was not part of our agreement," Kyreen remarked, the exotic language flowing off her tongue.

"No, but while I was in there I thought I would look around," the spirit said. "No harm, although I do wonder how you broke free."

"You are not the first to attempt to invade my mind," Kyreen commented derisively.

"Dear child, I was not invading," the spirit declared. "I merely wish to familiarize myself with your life."

"You did not ask me," Kyreen said. "You acted without permission."

"You expect me to ask you for permission?" the spirit said. Tyra's likeness stiffened, the smile slipping from the beautiful face. "Watch yourself, child. I have been understanding and benevolent when I did not have to be. I have offered you assistance when I could have allowed you to continue blundering. I have…"

"I did not ask for your assistance," Kyreen interrupted the spirit, who chuckled quietly.

"You are spirited," Lakwen'dil remarked. "I had forgotten that about you. So lively and so alive. Always challenging, always stimulating, always pushing. It is why you were banished."

The spirit stopped speaking but continued to regard Kyreen. The silence drew on for several moments until Brigit quietly coughed.

"Is everything alright?" she asked. "I could not understand a word you two spoke, but your tones did not sound amicable."

Lakwen'dil took a step towards Brigit, but Kyreen stepped between the spirit and her friend. She held the sword ready, in a defensive position.

"I mean her no harm," the spirit told Kyreen, reverting back to the language of Nowles, or common as most of the Old Kingdom called the language prevalent throughout their land.

Kyreen found that with little difficulty, she too could slip between the two languages. Speaking so Brigit could understand, she said, "Only the language. Do not go wandering."

The spirit tilted Tyra's head at Kyreen, quirking an eyebrow with a bemused smile. "What if I promise to be more subtle? I am out of practice with you. You are so much more emotional, so full of feeling and life, so unlike the others. I can be less intrusive."

Kyreen looked at Brigit. "She will give you the elven language but in exchange wants to 'familiarize' herself with your life."

Brigit thought upon the offer for a long moment, but before she answered, Kyreen looked back over at Lakwen'dil. "You can do this without her feeling, smelling, tasting, hearing?"

"I can do it so she knows not that I have been there," the spirit responded.

"It is not all rainbows and sugar pies in my head," Brigit commented. "But if it gets me access to these items, I have to say yes."

Without speaking Kyreen stepped aside to permit the spirit to pass. Lakwen'dil stepped up to Brigit, pressing an index finger to the mage's forehead. Brigit closed her eyes but did not look or feel distressed. Kyreen cautiously re-sheathed her sword. After a moment Lakwen'dil lowered her hand from Brigit's forehead and looked at Kyreen.

"Now I finish with you," the spirit said in elven.

Reluctantly Kyreen acquiesced, stepping up to the spirit. This time when the spirit touched her forehead Kyreen only felt a slight pressure holding her in place. No flashbacks, no visions, no memories at all.

Afterwards the spirit recited the words to activate the ring for the Calanian women, who found they could both control the earth with it. Then Lakwen'dil demonstrated how to activate the golden orb.

Finally, hefting up the rock, she only said, "This one is not reusable. It is only for the direst of healings. Do not use it lightly."

Kyreen took the rock and handed it to Brigit, saying, "Take it back with you. I do not need the weight. Besides, if I am in need of strong healing, I doubt I would have the time or the energy to activate it."

Brigit nodded. She stowed the rock and her half of the orb in her knapsack. The ring Kyreen wore on the middle finger of her right hand. She glanced at the western sky, dark purple with the promise of dawn. They had been talking all night, yet Kyreen did not feel sleepy or tired. She felt rejuvenated, yearning to be back on her journey.

"Lakwen'dil," she said, turning to face the spirit, inclining her head as she spoke. "Your wisdom this night will be of great assistance to me and my friend."

The spirit smiled. Kyreen realized she had almost become accustomed to her mother's image. Almost.

Looking at Brigit, Lakwen'dil said, "Give me your talisman of travel, child, so I may infuse it with my magic. I cannot travel to your land, but I can assist you with your travels."

Brigit shook her head. "I do not use an artifact for transpiring."

The spirit stilled, tilting her head to gaze upon the mage. Kyreen now recognized this to be the spirit's reaction when faced with something unexpected, though once again she wondered if the affectation had originally been Lakwen'dil's or her mother's.

"You travel this distance using only your magic? No assistance from a talisman? Not speaking First Tongue?" the spirit asked. "You transpired across the desert, from beyond the northern mountains, reciting your spells in the language of the human realm?"

At Brigit's nod, the spirit threw back her head and laughed. The sound had no joy or mirth. It rang out harsh and brittle, raising the hair on Kyreen's neck. When she finished the spirit looked between the two Calanian women, Tyra's green eyes glittering. "Oh, how they underestimated you. This... this shall be glorious."

Kyreen and Brigit exchanged confused looks but before either woman could ask, the spirit leaned down to pick up the earthen idol she had forged. Holding one hand on the statue's head, the other cradling the legs, the spirit quietly murmured and the statue began shrinking. When it had contracted to a size that it rested fully in her palm, the spirit closed her hands together and murmured a few more words. Then Lakwen'dil held it out to Brigit.

"This will make your travels less draining," she said.

"Th...," with a sharp look from Kyreen, Brigit stopped just short of thanking the spirit. Taking the newly crafted artifact, she said, "This shall indeed be greatly appreciated as I travel."

"You will find your spells respond better when recited in First Tongue," the spirit advised, adding, "though you appear to do just fine with the handicap of human language, child. Well done. Well done indeed."

Once the mage had disappeared into vapor, Kyreen picked up the mug, drinking down its contents, unwilling to waste the water, even with the new spell at her fingertips. After stowing the mug and pulling out a piece of jerky, Kyreen resumed her westward trek in the gray shadows of the new day.

Lakwen'dil appeared several times throughout the morning, sometimes walking beside Kyreen, sometimes in front of the woman. Neither of them spoke as the sun traveled across the sky. During her midday rest, Kyreen napped, but her sleep was not restful as images of Lang infiltrated her dreams. When she jerked awake the third time, Kyreen resumed her trek even though the heat of the day had not yet passed. Lakwen'dil stayed away until the sun on Kyreen's face had almost completely set. Kyreen, her eyes focused on the far away mountains, did not acknowledge the spirit's appearance at her side. She concentrated on her goal, memorizing the fuzzy shape of the mountains in the distance.

This time of the day, twilight, when day and night mingled, was the worst for Kyreen. Her mind wandered, allowing memories to seep out from that part of her mind where Kyreen kept them firmly sequestered. Dusk was when the weariness rested most heavily upon her, when she longed to simply lie down and never rise again, when she came closest to giving into despair. Yet, dusk after dusk, she had kept moving, forcing step after step, until the day disappeared, leaving only the dry wind and the night sky overhead bursting with star systems and galaxies reminding one how vast and old the world was.

On the first night after Brigit's visit, Kyreen kept walking. Even after the still swollen moon had risen high into the night sky the Calanian continued. Though her body protested, she did not halt. Some residual melancholy remained, whether from Lakwen'dil's apparitions from the previous day or from her midday dreams, Kyreen did not know. She only knew she could not stop yet. Not until she stumbled, jerking awake after having walked quite some ways with her eyes shut, did she finally relent. Lowering her pack to the ground, Kyreen cast her two protection spells then settled on her bedroll, falling into a deep slumber even as she set down her head. As she slumbered, the bearded, green-eyed man appeared and set to watch over her.

When Kyreen opened her eyes in the predawn grayness, she saw the figure right away. Knowing she did not dream him, she pushed down the myriad of emotions as she slowly sat up. They stared at each other for several long, silent moments. When Kyreen rose to her feet, so too did Lang.

"You may be able to wear his likeness, but you are not him," Kyreen called out, her voice ringing across the sand. She ached to close the distance between them yet feared moving closer. "The expression is wrong. He had a quick smile, one that lit up his entire face. His eyes had a constant twinkle, a merriness, like emerald sunshine. He vibrated with energy. Even when he stood still, restlessness rolled off of him in massive waves. I feel none of that from you, but what is missing most is his love. He loved me so completely, so fully, so deeply. Even before... even before he died, I knew I did not deserve that love, that complete devotion, did not deserve him. Even had we been given more time, I never would have, never could have loved him as completely as he loved me. I can only hope that wherever he is now, he forgives me, and knows that I loved him, still love him, as much as I ever possibly could."

As soon as she finished speaking, Kyreen knelt, hot tears now falling freely to stain the bedroll as she packed. When she stood up, slinging her pack over her shoulder, Lang's likeness had disappeared.

Dutifully she retrieved the last of her dried rations from her pack. Chewing at the food, she oriented her path on the mountains and began walking. When she stopped at midday she would review the spells that Brigit had brought, and tonight she would begin to learn them. Until then, however, Kyreen had a desert to cross

As she continued doggedly westward, the days began to run together with the mountain range never appearing to get any closer. Always it shimmered just on the horizon, a murky purple black haze. Eventually she quit looking, concentrating instead on the next step, and the next, and the next.

The spells Brigit had brought were, as the mage had said, magnificent. After a couple of misstarts with the more complicated spells, Kyreen had quickly mastered creating food and water which made the desert trek much less worrisome. She always began with those two spells, ensuring she had food and water for the following day before moving on to her other chores, such as eating, setting perimeter alarms, daily meditations, and practicing the other spells.

When Kyreen made camp on what she thought was the tenth day following Brigit's visit, noticing the waxing gibbous moon in the sky greatly surprised her, as did the proximity of the mountains. What she had thought to be only a few days had evidently been much longer. No longer did the mountains shimmer in the distance, but their peaks rose into the night sky, creating inky shadows against the carpet of twinkling stars. Kyreen then also realized she had not been visited by Lakwen'dil since the morning she woke up to see Lang watching over her, the morning following the full moon.

Chapter 5

She had become lax during her time in the desert, mistakenly thinking the desert itself and her dreams were the only dangers. Intent on keeping away the dreams, Kyreen had wearied herself into a deep slumber. Thus, she did not hear the approaching footsteps. Fortunately, the protection wards did their job, giving her enough warning that she had awaken and risen to her feet before the first bandit had taken his second step into her encampment. The dagger, which she slept with in one hand, sliced the throat of that first intruder before any of the others could react. Then, like a pack of wild dogs, the men descended upon her. She managed to injure a few of the howling mass, but their numbers were too great. Then she felt the prick of a needle on her neck and her body went numb. As Kyreen crumpled to the ground, her head struck a rock as she landed. The night sky above with its multitudes of stars and galaxies filled her eyes as her vision went fuzzy and she faded into unconsciousness.

When Kyreen woke, she lay on her side facing a campfire with her body still numb. Male voices conversed behind her, but, still groggy from the blow to her head, she had trouble focusing on their words. With some struggle she found she could move her mouth. Licking her parched lips, she attempted to speak, but the dryness in her throat only permitted her to produce soft croak.

"Oh, no, you do not, lovey," a quiet voice hissed in her ear as a foul-tasting cloth was shoved into her mouth. "No magic is going to save you tonight."

Unseen and unfelt hands rolled Kyreen's numb body onto her back so she could look up at the scruffy man kneeling over her. His bearded face shrouded in shadows, he gazed down at the dazed woman. She felt his agitation, his rage, his lust. After so long alone, so long not feeling the emotions of another, Kyreen's stomach roiled and she gagged around the filthy rag. Though she strained and endeavored to move, her body remained motionless. She could not even roll her head away to avoid looking at the man looming over her, leaning in, his putrid breath hot on her face, the stench of stale body odor filling her nostrils.

"My only regret is that you will not feel this," he murmured, reaching down towards her torso.

An instant later the ripping of fabric assaulted her ears as he tore open her tunic, then her undershirt. Though she could not feel his hands upon her body, her imagination filled in the details. Then, as he began to paw at her pants, she registered the voices in the background had stopped speaking.

"Gaspard, what are you doing?" A man's deep bass voice asked. Distractedly Kyreen registered both of the men had been speaking in elven.

She shifted her gaze to the hulking man standing behind the man currently kneeling between her legs. Even from her position on the ground Kyreen could tell he was not just broad, he was tall as well. He carried himself in such a manner that she speculated this big man whose body matched his voice either led these bandits or held an extremely high position in their ranks. The big man reached down a beefy hand to drag her would-be rapist to his feet by his hair, twisting Gaspard around so their faces were mere inches apart.

"Taking my due, Armand," Gaspard answered with a whine. "She killed my brother. I am owed recompense."

"Do you not trust Xarles to give you your due? To ensure your recompense? You swore the oath. You know that, in exchange for his leadership, we take all the spoils to him for disbursement and not one thing before him," Armand remarked, his voice calm and level. Kyreen flicked a glance to the bandits gathered behind Armand, all looking on with great interest.

"Think very carefully on your answer to my next question," Armand continued quietly. "This action you appeared to be taking looks to me as a slight against our leader. Do you challenge Xarles for his position?"

Immediately Gaspard began shaking his head. "No, Armand! No! Never! I forgot myself for a moment from the shock of losing me brother. I meant no foul. Please, no!"

"Too late," murmured Armand. The dagger Kyreen had not seen in the big man's other hand deftly sliced Gaspard's throat. Some of the dying man's blood, hot and sticky, sprayed across Kyreen's face as Armand dropped the body to the ground.

Leaning down to wipe his dagger blade clean on the dead man's shirt, Armand glanced over at Kyreen.

"I would tell you not to fear, my lovely, but you are not a typical woman given to wailing, are you?" he murmured quietly so only she could hear. "You cost us some good men tonight. Xarles will make you pay for them. It will be fun!"

He patted her cheek, streaked with Gaspard's blood. Smearing some of the dead man's blood with his thumb, Armand brought it to his mouth as he stood up. Sucking the blood from his thumb, he kept his gaze on Kyreen. His piercing dark eyes roved across her face and body, assessing her like a farmer buying livestock. With a wink and a smile, the big man turned away, speaking to the men behind him. "Get the corpse out of here, then get the woman stripped and cleaned up for Xarles. Keep her gagged. We do not know what spells she might know."

Kyreen's body was unceremoniously lifted and slung over the shoulder of one of the bandits. Unable to lift or turn her head, she watched the ground move by, light dimming as they moved away from the campfire. After a rustle of canvas, they moved into a more lighted area, her body dumped back down onto the ground. Fortunately, there were no rocks here, only sand beneath her head as she thumped down.

"Get her stripped and cleaned up for Xarles," the bandit growled, succinctly repeating Armand's orders. "Leave the gag and the bindings."

Kyreen was rolled onto her back. Before she could look around, a hand descended down over her eyes, fingers pinching at her nose, then a woman's voice murmured, "Eyes closed. Mouth closed."

Before Kyreen could comply, the woman repeated in heavily accented common, "Eyes closed. Mouth closed. Now."

This time Kyreen obeyed, just as the sting of sand cascaded over her face. Hands began roughly rubbing the granules across her forehead, cheeks, and chin, the tender skin burning. From the way her head kept rolling, Kyreen surmised the same treatment was being given to her still numb body. If she concentrated, Kyreen thought she might be feeling something in her toes and fingertips, though this might have been wishful thinking. Her body was next rolled over a few times onto what felt to be a roughly woven rug under her cheek. She did feel the tugging on her scalp, however, when someone decided to undo her braid and attempt to run a comb through her curls. Exotic scents exploded in her nose as a soothing cream was smeared across her face. Again, she experienced the rocking motion as the hands moved away from her face, and conceivably down her body. Then the hands lightly patted her face with a soft puffy cloth distributing a floral scented powder that went up Kyreen's nose and caused her to sneeze.

"She ready?" the bandit asked from behind Kyreen. Then she was lifted and once again slung over the bandit's shoulder. This time when they exited the tent, Kyreen was certain she could feel the chill of the nighttime desert on her skin, but when she attempted to wriggle her fingers, she felt no response.

"Put her here," Armand commanded and Kyreen's body once more hit the floor. This time, however, she lay upon a soft fluffy surface, some animal skin she deduced. From her angle on the floor, lying on her side, she saw a platform directly in front of her, steps rising up beyond her field of vision.

"The traveler was a woman?" a man's voice asked from the top of the platform.

"Yes," Armand responded. "She came from the east but had a magic ward on her camp. We lost Andre right away. She managed to wound several others before we could get the dart in place. Three of the men need a healer or we will lose them."

"She used magic?" Kyreen sensed more than saw the man stand and begin to move down the steps.

"Not in the fight," Armand answered. "We also found this in her possession. It is elven, Xarles! What is an easterner doing with an elven artifact, a half of a scrying orb?"

Kyreen watched the man from the corner of her eye as he stood on the bottom step, then moved towards her feet, where presumably her belongings lay spread out for him to see. She heard the rustling of items and imagined him inspecting her half of the golden orb. She wondered if the ring had been removed from her hand. She had to believe it had. Then she heard the intake of breath from the man Armand had called Xarles.

"This sword," Xarles said. "Did she wield it?"

"No. She awoke with a dagger in her hand. She never had the chance to pull her sword," Armand replied.

Xarles stood and moved to stand before Kyreen. She gazed at brown bare feet, conscious of him staring down at her. One of the feet moved, pressing against her shoulder, rolling Kyreen to her back. She gazed up at the man, who squatted down to take a closer look. Clad only in trousers, his tawny golden skin glowed in the tent's lamplight. She took note of his bare torso, hard and muscled, an assortment of scars mottling his hairless chest and toned abdomen, then she moved eyes back up to his face. From her awkward angle, she could make out dark hair pulled into a short ponytail framing an angular face with dark intelligent eyes, his expression inquisitive. He stroked thoughtfully at a trim goatee with lean fingers before moving his hand down to gently brush the curls from her face. His eyes assessed her, giving her the impression that he could see straight through her body and into her thoughts.

"This injury?" Xarles asked, stroking the side of Kyreen's face. She definitely could feel his fingers stroking her forehead, then her cheek.

"She hit her head on a rock when the toxin took hold," Armand replied. "I regret the error, my captain."

Xarles moved his fingers to Kyreen's hair, wrapping one of the curls around his finger as his gaze dropped to her body. "She is skin and bones. Nothing but angles. And this scar here, I would wager she has some interesting tales."

"A few weeks in the herd with regular feedings, we can soften her up. She would fetch a good price then," Armand commented. "Though I do not know how soon I would remove the bindings or the gag."

"I agree," Xarles murmured. "She appears much too calm. Usually by now the women are whimpering and cowering, begging for mercy, ready to submit. But not you, darling. You are something else."

He glanced up at the huge man, his second-in-command from what Kyreen could discern, saying, "I think she is one of the Banished."

Kyreen felt Armand's surprise before she heard it in his voice. "I thought they were a myth."

Xarles stood up. "She has the look – ebony curls, green eyes, pale skin, tall for a woman. She proved herself a warrior and, with her wards, a mage. That sword there, with the three metals braided on its hilt and the ancient runes on the blade, is identical to the one in the legends. Plus, she came from the east. The east is where the Banished were sent."

"There is a mark on her back," Armand commented. "I had not given it much thought, though I knew it was not from one of the desert camps."

Kyreen's body was moved so she was face down on the pelt. Though she still could not move, she felt the man's fingers on her shoulders as she rolled. Xarles squatted down, his fingers stroking the tattoo on Kyreen's back.

"There is magic in this mark, Armand," Xarles said. "She is bound to something magical."

"Whatever it is, it was not in her camp," Armand replied. "This is the only talisman we found on her person. I am told it has residual magic but is not currently warded with anything."

"Who told you this?"

"Remy, one of the newly exiled. He was born in the elf lands. This was his first raid. She sliced open his arm, but he will heal," Armand answered.

"Is there anything else I should know before I speak with her?"

"I had to kill Gaspard. He thought he should take his recompense for Andre's death from the woman directly, before she was brought before you," Armand reported, his tone bland as though they discussed the weather.

Xarles pushed Kyreen onto her back once more, his hand gripping tight at her chin. He gazed into her eyes a long moment, then spoke in lightly accented common. "Who are you? Where were you going?"

With his free hand, the bandit pulled the filthy cloth from Kyreen's mouth. She moved her tongue experimentally, trying to work up enough saliva to clear her dry throat. Before she could speak, she felt the sharp tip of a dagger at her throat as Armand squatted down beside her.

"Do not try anything," Xarles said with a quick glance at his second. "Armand does not speak common and he does not trust you. I would hate for him to slice your throat over a misunderstanding."

"I am nobody," Kyreen answered, her voice hoarse. "I am merely traveling across the desert trying to get to the elven lands."

"I find that hard to believe," Xarles chuckled. "But if that is the way you wish it to go."

He shoved the cloth back into Kyreen's mouth, then stood up and walked back up the platform. Switching back to elven, he said, "We will let her stew a while. I believe she can bring us more from the elves than she ever would in the herd, but I need to check out some things. Keep her with you, Armand. I do not want anything happening to this one."

Armand stood as well. "What about the men? She should be theirs tonight, especially after the damage she caused."

"Give them two, no three, from the herd. That should satisfy them for now," Xarles remarked. "Their choice. Tonight and tomorrow night."

"Their choice, my captain?" Armand asked. Kyreen felt the big man's surprise. "Three? For two nights?"

"Yes, Armand. Three of their choosing. Two nights. Have them cast lots," Xarles replied. "After you, of course, take whichever wench you desire, my friend."

Armand scooped up Kyreen, slinging her over his shoulder and turned for the tent entrance. Before they reached it, Xarles' voice stopped them.

"Armand," the bandit leader said.

The big man turned around. "Yes, my captain?"

"Take care of the injured," the bandit leader said, his voice neutral. "I do not want a healer brought in. Not with her here. No word may get out about her presence. No one goes out. No one comes in. Do you understand?"

"Yes, my captain."

"And send Remy to me. His magical knowledge has me intrigued."

When Armand turned back around, Kyreen caught a glimpse of the bandit leader reclining on what looked to be an enormous mattress on top of the platform. Dangling from his fingers, Xarles gazed upon the opal amulet that had been around her neck. For the first time since the magical wards awakened her, Kyreen experienced a jolt of panic. As the flap fell back into place and Armand walked away from the tent, Kyreen desperately tried to remember what phase the moon had been in tonight.

Chapter 6

Armand toted Kyreen around with ease, dispatching his tasks as though her weight was nothing more than a kitten slung across his shoulder. Their first stop Kyreen identified from the aromatic scents as Armand ducked into the tent in which Kyreen had been cleaned up.

"Get the women assembled," Armand said. "Xarles is sending three of them to the men. Tonight and tomorrow. Their choice."

"Three?" a woman's voice asked. Kyreen recognized her as the woman who had spoken to Kyreen in common, ordering her to close her eyes and mouth. "I only have seven in camp right now. The rest are out. And two nights with those beasts? I will not be able to send them out again for a week."

"Get them ready, Genevieve," Armand ordered, his tone firm, a quick flare of anger assaulting Kyreen's senses. "Unless you wish to take your complaints to Xarles?"

"No, Armand," Genevieve responded, her tone now meek, her own emotions flaring with fear and trepidation. "Please, I mean no foul."

"Is Fanchon in camp?"

"Yes, Armand," the woman truckled. "I know you like her so I...."

"Send her to my tent," Armand interrupted. "Have her bring a collar and shackles, wrist and ankle."

"Fanchon is not like that anymore, Armand," Genevieve wheedled. "She is a good girl. She will not be any trouble."

"Genevieve," Armand said, his voice cold and quiet. Though Kyreen could not see his face, she imagined he was not smiling. "You speak too much. Have gotten too familiar. Make sure you are in the lineup for the men tonight. Maybe you still have enough looks left for them to select you, maybe not. In any case, you need to be reminded of your place."

"Yes, Armand." Even had she not been able to feel the woman's terror, Kyreen could hear the tremble in her voice.

"If you do not go with the men tonight, you come to my tent tomorrow," Armand continued. "Yes. Fanchon tonight. You tomorrow. That will work."

The man turned to go, pausing at the tent entrance to glance back. "Do not forget to send the collar and shackles, Genevieve. You do not want me making the extra trip back here tonight."

Before the woman could respond Armand exited. His next stop was the campfire, around which the bandits gathered.

"Is it time for our fun?" one man called out as Armand approached.

"Not with this one, I am afraid," Armand commented, slapping Kyreen's buttocks, an open-handed strike that echoed across the clearing. Though she felt the sting, Kyreen still could not move her head or wriggle her extremities.

"Hold!" Armand commanded as the men began to clamor. Though the big man did not shout, his voice rang out firm, demanding obedience. "To compensate you for tonight Xarles has decreed three from the herd as entertainment, not just for tonight but also tomorrow. Choose wisely, men."

"Three?" a man asked.

"Two nights?" another inquired. Both men's voices had reflected the amazement Kyreen felt from the collective.

"Your choice," Armand added. "Genevieve is lining them up. If you lot can agree upon three, eh?"

Instantly all of the men started speaking at once. Kyreen could not make out any of the conversations but she could feel their excitement as they began walking towards Genevieve's tent.

"Maurice," Armand said quietly, catching one of the bandits by the arm. Kyreen could not make out the man's features but she clearly felt the flare of apprehension from Maurice when Armand stopped him.

"Yes?" the man replied, none of his fear reflected in his voice.

"Make sure Genevieve is in the lineup," Armand instructed quietly. "If she is not, or if she gives you any trouble, let me know."

"Do you want her selected?" Maurice asked.

"That is up to you and the men," Armand shrugged the shoulder holding Kyreen. "Tonight is truly your choice."

"Is she worth that?"

"It is not my place to question," Armand said. Kyreen felt his hand softly stroking her backside, and belatedly realized Maurice had been asking about her, not Genevieve.

As Maurice began walking away, Armand turned back towards the man. "Oh, and send Remy to Xarles."

"Yes, Armand," came the measured response but Kyreen felt the rise in Maurice's nervousness. The men of this camp followed and respected Armand's command, but they also feared the big man.

Armand began walking again, his hand still idly stroking Kyreen's butt cheek. Softly, under his breath, he hummed as he walked. Away from the campfire Kyreen could now feel the cool night breeze on her bare skin.

"Lucien," Armand said, coming to a halt. "The men are picking out entertainment from the herd. Go enjoy your evening."

Kyreen felt doubt radiating from the man who murmured a quiet reply before striding off in the direction Armand and Kyreen had come from. Armand ducked into the darkened tent, then set Kyreen down, the sand rough under her bare ass and the tent wall cool against her back. Kyreen still did not have any control over her muscles, as so soon as Armand released her, her body listed to the side and she toppled over, unable to stop the motion.

"Be a good girl and stay put," Armand chuckled, patting her head before moving over to one of the many cots in the room.

From her spot on the ground, her cheek pressing into the sand, Kyreen could barely make out the big man's shape amongst the shadows as he leaned over the cot, and she could not hear the quiet words he murmured to the injured bandit lying on the cot. She did, however, clearly feel the man's panic when Armand covered his face with one of his beefy hands, cutting off the injured man's air supply. She also felt the injured man's release when he passed out and then felt his essence evaporate as his life slipped away. Armand repeated this with the other two men in the tent. Though she did not know these men, who were probably not very good men considering they had been with these bandits, the void left with their passing tugged at Kyreen.

Tears welled up in her eyes, her breath quickening as she felt a piece of her torn away with each death, reminding her of the castle battle when she had felt every life lost, both Calanian and Galorian. This close to the dying men, had she not already been lying in the sand, Kyreen surely would have collapsed. The edges of her vision grew fuzzy, her head spinning with vertigo. Not for the first time, she cursed her Connate ability and wondered if her brother's presence as an Aegis, her shield, would have tempered her reaction.

When he had dispatched the final injured man, Armand returned to pick up Kyreen. "Alright, my lovely," he said, hoisting her into place on his shoulder. "Almost done. Just one more stop."

The stop Armand made was to the sentry. While Armand spoke with the man, relaying the message from Xarles that no one was to leave or come into camp, Kyreen experimented with moving her head. By slowly rotating her head, she finally located the swollen moon high in the night sky, a faint shadow along its edge. She estimated three, maybe four, days before full moon. She had three days to get back her amulet, to get away, or to get a message to Brigit, or else the mage might transpire directly into Xarles' tent. Kyreen could not, would not allow that to happen.

"Getting fidgety, are you?" Armand's voice, very creepily soothing as he resumed walking, brought her back to the present. Despite her efforts to be subtle, he had felt her movements.

Armand shifted Kyreen's body as easily as if she were a child's doll, dropping her down to cradle her in his arms. With his hands under her back and knees, Kyreen's head lolled against the man's massive shoulder as he drew her close to him. His body heat radiated, warming her chilled skin, creating an intimacy between them that unsettled Kyreen.

Dropping his mouth to her ear, his warm breath and whiskers stirred up memories deep inside Kyreen, but an instant later Armand's words chased away any feelings other than dread.

"Do not attempt anything foolish, my lovely," he whispered. "Xarles wishes you unharmed but he affords me great deal of leniency if you are a trouble maker. I am the expert when it comes to dealing with trouble makers. I like trouble makers."

Even had she not understood the elven he spoke, Kyreen would have easily comprehended the menacing tone in the bandit's voice. When he finished speaking Armand took the top of Kyreen's ear between his teeth, biting down on the sensitive cartilage until she could not help but cry out in pain. Immediately he released her ear and with a moist lick at the throbbing area, he shifted her back up over one shoulder, never missing a step as they traveled across the encampment towards the tents. Kyreen felt, then heard the activities taking place around the campfire. So many emotions assaulted her senses, the fear and pain of the women overriding the sheer delight of the men. She was glad for the shadows surrounding her, glad Armand did not pause. Although the sounds of the men faded, she could still sense the high emotions. Her focus on the activities outside the tent quickly disappeared, however, as an intense wave of terror washed over Kyreen upon their entrance into Armand's tent.

"Fanchon, my pet, you are here. Good. Very good," Armand murmured. Though his voice sounded soothing and kind, Kyreen's stomach turned anew at the malevolence emanating from the man.

He dumped Kyreen onto a rug, leaning her back against the center pole. This time Kyreen managed to remain upright, though her body tilted to one side. Her eyes followed Armand across the dim room as he raised the lights. This tent while not nearly the size of Xarles' tent was still roomy, a testament to Armand's rank in the camp hierarchy. Kyreen, leaned against the center pole, her back to the tent entrance, faced a large bed festooned with startling gold silk coverings and a multitude of pillows in a rainbow of bright colors. At the foot of the bed, her back to Kyreen, knelt a petite woman, a dense waterfall of black hair cascading to the floor hiding her body. Armand fondly patted the woman's head as he bent down to pick up the items resting on the ground before her. Though Kyreen did not see the woman move, she felt the flare of terror under the big man's touch.

Armand squatted before Kyreen, humming quietly as he fastened the thick steel collar around her neck. She tried to pull back when he leaned in to work the clasp at the back of her neck but the pole prevented her any movement. Her attempt earned her an amused look from Armand before he maneuvered his body over hers, his warmth pressing intimately against the cool skin of her naked body, as he nuzzled against her neck, just above the steel collar.

"Your fear smells so tempting," he murmured quietly, rubbing his body suggestively against hers. "I will enjoy breaking you in, my lovely."

Abruptly he pulled back to finish securing the restraints to her wrists and ankles, running the short length of chain through the shackles and her collar before locking it to the center pole. Released from the leather bindings, Kyreen's fingers and toes began tingling as blood rushed back to her extremities. With her arms hidden, pulled back behind the pole, Kyreen felt safe experimentally flexing and wiggling her fingers without Armand noticing. Once he had her positioned and secured to his liking, the big man stood up and moved to the side of the bed where he began pulling off his tunic.

Broad, Kyreen thought. Everything about the man was broad. His broad skull covered with dark bristly hair. His forehead broad with heavy dark eyebrows. His cheeks. His mouth. His face with dark stubble. Even his thick neck. His broad hands pulled the tunic over his broad head to reveal his broad shoulders, chest, and abdomen, all covered in thick dark hair as if he wore an animal's pelt across his pale skin.

After toeing off his boots, Armand moved to a side table where he poured himself a glass of liquid. At first Kyreen thought it to be alcohol but it looked like water. Just the thought made her uncomfortably aware of her parched throat, her mouth dry around the filthy rag. Armand caught her watching him, his eyes crinkling in amusement before she could glance away.

From her periphery vision, she watched him refill the cup then walk to squat in front of her again. Slowly he sipped at the water, regarding her over the rim of his cup. While every instinct inside in her clamored for her to flee, to get away, to retreat, Kyreen met his gaze, forcing her body to remain relaxed and her expression neutral, though she could not prevent her throat from swallowing as he continued drinking. By the time Armand drained his cup, Kyreen gave thanks for the gag. With each of the big man's swigs, her own thirst had deepened. Had she been able to speak, she may have begged for a drink, or worse she would have revealed her knowledge of the elven tongue. Armand licked his thick lips noisily.

"Yes, you will be a challenge," he murmured, ruffling her hair as one would a pet or a small child.

Moving to stand before the kneeling woman he called Fanchon, Armand continued speaking. "Fanchon was a challenge. Were you not, my pet? But she was no match for Armand."

Armand leaned down to grasp one of Fanchon's hands so as to draw the woman to her feet. Standing, the spill of the woman's black hair hung in a brilliant shiny sheet almost to the back of her knees. She was so petite the top of her head did not even reach Armand's chest. Armand petted the inky black hair, then stroked the woman's cheek with the back of his broad, hairy hand as waves of fear slammed into Kyreen. A soft whimper escaped Fanchon and Armand leaned down, angling an ear to her face, as if trying to hear her speak.

"I did not catch that. Were you trying to say something to our new friend?" he murmured, his gaze locking on to Kyreen, a malicious glint in his dark eyes. "Oh yes, I remember. You cannot tell her, can you?"

The man straightened up, his gaze never breaking away from Kyreen. "Unfortunately, Fanchon will not be able to give you any advice since she forced me to cut out her tongue."

With a vicious glint in his eye, Armand extended his tongue pantomiming slicing off it off, so Kyreen would realize what he had done to Fanchon.

"When that did not work to tame her, I had to do something more visible," he continued. Though his tone sounded remorseful, Kyreen felt the glee, the excitement spilling off of the man as he placed a hand on each of the diminutive woman's shoulders to turn her so Fanchon faced Kyreen, revealing the vicious scar running down the side of the woman's face. Ragged and ugly, the red welt stark against her tawny beige skin, the scar started on Fanchon's forehead at the hair line, running down over the blind and milky blue ruined eye, along her cheek, barely missing the edge of her mouth to stop right at the jawline. Armand stepped up so his body pressed against the woman's backside, one arm dropping down to rest on her shoulder, reaching a hand to cup one of the woman's modest breasts, his thumb rubbing across the dark areola, while his other hand continued to softly stroke his handiwork. Though she struggled to control her reaction, Kyreen could not hide the stiffening of her body, earning her a self-satisfied grin from the big man.

"Yes, I know," he crooned, nuzzling against the woman's dark hair, his gaze never leaving Kyreen. "Fanchon may no longer be a beauty, but her body still works. Does it not, my pet?"

Armand leaned down to kiss the ruined cheek. Now in addition to feeling the terror of her emotions Kyreen could see the trembling in the other woman.

In a swift move, Armand scooped the woman up and, spinning around, flung her onto the bed. In other circumstances it might have seemed playful. In this tent, on this night, Kyreen only thought about a predator playing with its prey.

Looming over the bed, his back to Kyreen, Armand pulled off his pants, revealing his broad arse and broad legs the size of tree trunks, all covered in the same thick, dark hair as the rest of his pallid body. When he placed first one knee then the other on the bed, the mattress sunk down from his weight.

Kyreen braced herself for the sound of violence that never came. Instead she listened to the quiet whisper of intimacy, of hands softly stroking skin, of Armand murmuring words Kyreen could not discern. The emotions from the bed continued to assault the Calanian – fear and hatred from the tiny woman, lust and malevolence from the bandit. Then came a moan, quiet at first, slowly growing louder, until the woman's cries rang in the tent, half pleasure, half sob, desperation laced with primal desire as Fanchon's body thrashed beneath Armand's touch. After the first climax, he persisted, continuing until Fanchon cried out again and then again. Kyreen lost count as the sounds and emotions from the tortured woman filled her senses. Kyreen pulled against her shackles, knowing her struggle to be futile, but she could not sit still. The smell of sex permeated the room, making her stomach clench and she retched against the gag in her mouth. Stilling, leaning her head back against the pole, hot tears leaking from her closed eyelids, Kyreen listened as finally Armand began to take his own pleasure from the whimpering woman. As he had been slow in drawing the climaxes from Fanchon so too was he leisurely in finishing his own fun. Even then, after he had rolled to his back on the silks, he once more moved his hands across Fanchon's tired body chuckling when the tiny woman cried out one final time.

"I knew you were not done, my pet," he murmured. "You cannot fool Armand."

For several moments the only sound in the tent was Fanchon's quiet sobbing. Then Armand rolled up to his feet, easily gathering up the diminutive woman and moving to where Kyreen sat. The Calanian kept her eyes on the bandit's face, her eyes glittering with revulsion. Humming quietly, Armand seemed to take no notice of Kyreen as he unlocked the chain, threaded it through the ring in a collar picked up from a side table which he had clasped around the tiny woman's neck. Once Fanchon had been secured, Armand turned his attentions to Kyreen.

"You are feisty. You think you can take on Armand?" he crooned quietly, squatting down to brush a hand across her cheek, pushing the hair from her face. "You are but a scrawny, half-starved waif, weakened from your trek across the desert."

He ran his hand across Kyreen's face, along her neck, brushing her clavicle, her shoulders then down her arm. "So bony. I believe I would cut myself on your angles if I played with you." He laughed at his joke, the humor never reaching the dark eyes watching Kyreen's green ones, glittering up at him with unveiled hostility.

"But I wager your body knows what to do under a man's hand, does it not?" he murmured, lifting his hand to her breast, rubbing a thumb over her nipple which tightened under his touch. He chuckled again, a hollow sound that turned her stomach, especially when coupled with the vile emotions Kyreen felt from the bandit.

He stood up, his naked body looming over Kyreen, his thick flaccid penis dangling in front of her face. She flinched involuntarily, earning her another laugh before he turned to lower the lamps in the tent. She watched the big man pull a dagger from the pile of his discarded clothes and place it under his pillow. Then he climbed into bed and promptly fell asleep, leaving Kyreen and her companion awake in the dark to observe the night's passing.

Kyreen dozed, never completely falling into slumber. She did not know if she would ever be able to sleep fully again. After a while Fanchon, who unlike Kyreen had not had her hands and feet restrained, curled into a tight ball and drifted to sleep. When the tiny woman slept, her emotions released, giving the Calanian's nerves a needed respite. Activity outside Armand's tent seemed to have quieted as well. Kyreen only felt a periodic spike of emotions as the night passed by slowly, so very slowly. She began to wonder if the night would ever end.

Chapter 7

Gray dawn finally began to creep into the tent, softening the dark, eventually chasing it away, casting the tent in shadows. Outside Kyreen felt more than heard the camp awakening. Armand slumbered on, his breathing deep, the sound filling the space. At some point Fanchon woke and sat up. Her distress had faded away to be replaced by fury. Kyreen wished she could comfort the other woman but knew even had she not been gagged she would not be able to speak to Fanchon for fear of revealing her secret. So, Kyreen took comfort in Fanchon's anger. That the abused woman could still feel such an emotion meant Armand had not succeeded in breaking her yet. As Kyreen wondered how much longer it would be before Fanchon's anger was extinguished, she noticed Armand's breathing change.

A moment later the big man sat up. His size startled Kyreen. During the long night, she had thought her mind had exaggerated his bulk in the aftermath of the evening's events, but no, he was a big man, big and broad, menacing even as he woke up. Fortunately, her flinch had been small, though she knew Fanchon must have felt the movement.

Armand rose, moving to a corner of the tent where he relieved himself. The sound of his piss streaming into the chamber pot echoed loudly in the shadowed tent for so long Kyreen began to wonder how one person's bladder could hold that much urine. After shaking his penis dry, Armand turned towards the women and padded over, absently humming. Without speaking he grinned at Kyreen, again ruffling her curls affectionately before turning his attentions to Fanchon.

"Good morning, my pet," he murmured, squatting down to release her collar. Scooping the tiny woman into his arms, he carried her over to the bed where once more he took his time with the woman. Kyreen tried to shut out the sounds and emotions to no avail. When he had drawn Fanchon to multiple climaxes, then leisurely completed his own pleasures, Armand pushed the panting woman off his bed with a loud slap to her ass.

"You go back to the heard tent, my pet," he crooned. "Get some rest for tonight alright, love?"

Without hesitation or a glance towards Kyreen, Fanchon scampered out of the tent. The bright sunshine illuminated Armand reclining on his golden silks briefly before the flap fell back into place.

After a moment, Armand rose, padding over to the side table where he poured himself a cup of water. He carried with him the dagger he had slept with. Kyreen's eyes were drawn to the weapon and not just because of her desire to plunge it into the bandit's chest.

The curved blade of the dagger was unlike any small bladed weapon Kyreen had ever seen, though Rhun had a similar larger curved blade weapon. Almost the size of Kyreen's sword, the guild master kept the curved blade on a wall in his private apartment, a souvenir from his time on the ships sailing the Great Sea. This blade that Armand casually placed on the side table as he drained his cup looked especially deadly. The bandit chuckled when he caught Kyreen looking at his weapon. Setting down his cup he picked up the blade and walked over to squat before Kyreen again, the dagger held loosely in his large hands. He looked at her for several long moments.

"You think you could take out Armand?" he asked. "How about I remove your shackles and we can see how brave you are?"

Never dropping his gaze from hers, Armand set the blade down beside him. Then he pulled her into a kneeling position so he could work the clasps on her shackles. Once her hands and feet were free, the bandit unlocked the steel collar from around Kyreen's neck, shoving the restraints to the side before standing up. Using his foot, his eyes still locked on hers, he moved the blade back center between them and took a step back.

Holding both hands in front of his hairy naked body, Armand gestured at the dagger. Both his motions and his expression inviting her to action, daring her to make a move for the dagger.

Kyreen held Armand's gaze, holding her expression neutral and her body relaxed even though internally she was so, so tempted. But she refused to spring Armand's trap. She doubted he was being overconfident in his abilities. Someone as ruthless as this bandit did not remain alive by being incompetent or foolhardy. Even had she not been so stiff from having sat with her arms behind her all night or weakened from the toxin the bandits had given her, not to mention parched and hungry, Kyreen could not be sure her reflexes would be quick enough to beat the bandit to his blade, let alone strike a killing blow. With someone like Armand, she knew she would have to kill quick. She would not get a second chance. After several long moments, Armand laughed.

"You are cunning like a fox," he remarked.

An instant later the big man lunged for the blade. His movement lightning quick, he grabbed the dagger and sliced through the air in front of Kyreen's face, passing so close she felt the breeze of his movement. To her credit, Kyreen did not move, did not even flinch, only her eyes tracked the man's motions. After two passes, Armand paused, holding the blade directly in front of Kyreen's face. Only then did she move, settling back on her heels, her hands resting on her thighs as she gazed at the weapon in Armand's hand.

The dagger's blade, broad at the hilt and tapering progressively to a needle-like triangular tip, measured almost as long as Kyreen's forearm, the handle being half the length. The steel blade, designed for striking a slanting blow, had a beveled front edge that looked razor sharp and small jagged serrations along the back edge. The ebony stone hilt looked to be inlaid with metal, similar in color to the brass guard, which included a nasty looking hook on one side.

Straightening, Armand turned to pad over to his discarded clothes. Tossing the blade on to the rumpled bed covers he began to dress, keeping his back to Kyreen, though modesty was not the reason. They both knew she would not be foolish enough to attempt to run or attack him, so he felt a measure of safety as he fastened his pants and drew on his tunic. After cinching his belt with a sheath into which he placed the dagger, Armand sat on the edge of the bed to draw on his boots. He moved so smoothly, so deliberately, his motions mesmerizing Kyreen. Though his actions were so mundane, she found herself unable to look away. Drawn in by the grace of his actions, she once more found herself surprised when he stood over her so tall and hulking. It took all of her will power not to outwardly react. She hoped he could not sense her rapid heartbeat, thudding loudly against her ribs, making her feel like a rabbit inside the wolf's den.

Stooping down, Armand expertly and quickly snapped the shackles and collar back on Kyreen. Then, chain in hand, he pulled her to her feet by hooking his fingers under the collar. Standing before him, her head barely to his shoulder, Kyreen felt petite, overshadowed by his bulk.

"You are a tall one," Armand commented. "Too bad you are so skinny. Fanchon probably weighs more than you do. Need to get some meat on your bones, else you will snap like a twig. I would hate to break you before I had the chance to tame you."

Patting her cheek, Armand headed for the tent entrance, chain in hand, forcing Kyreen to shuffle after him or else be in danger of being dragged. Outside in the early morning light he did not pause so she had to keep moving blindly, blinking and squinting against the brightness. Fortunately, Armand did not have far to go. Kyreen's vision cleared as the big man came to a halt, just one tent over from his own, where Xarles stood in the early morning sunshine still clad in only the loose fitting black pants, his torso gleaming in the morning light.

"Hail, Armand," Xarles greeted his second. "I heard Fanchon earlier and figured you would be out shortly. How is our guest this morning?"

Kyreen stood well behind and to the side of Armand, preferring to keep her distance. Xarles let his gaze roam over her naked form before locking his dark eyes onto her green ones. She worked to keep her expression neutral, but her emotions glittered through her eyes.

"She is quiet, Xarles," the tall man replied. "Too damned quiet. She has not cried, or whined, or struggled in any way. It is not natural. I do not trust her."

"Nor should we," Xarles commented, nodding before gesturing to his tent. "Bring her in here while you make your morning rounds."

Armand lifted the flap and tugged Kyreen through the doorway. Xarles entered behind them, moving swiftly to brush past her, passing so close to Kyreen she could feel the heat from his body and smell his exotic scent, a mixture of male and some spice she could not name. He was not a large man, not even as tall as Kyreen, but every visible part of him was toned and muscled, and he had a presence about him. No matter where Xarles went, whether clothed or half-clothed as he was now, this man would garner attention.

Armand tugged at the chain, pulling Kyreen towards the center pole but Xarles shook his head.

"No need to use the shackles in here, Armand," the bandit leader said. "Remove those but leave the collar."

Kyreen felt doubt radiate from Armand, but the big man did not comment. As soon as he finished removing the bindings from Kyreen's wrists and ankles, Armand grabbed the collar, roughly pulling her up onto her tiptoes so their faces were inches apart.

"Do not try anything," Armand growled in a tone that left no question to what he was saying.

"She has no intention of trying anything, Armand. She is too smart for that," Xarles said, his tone merry. "Now go tend to business. Chimere was scheduled for return this morning. I want to see her before anyone else speaks with her."

"Yes, Xarles," Armand replied. Throwing a final dark look towards Kyreen, the big man exited, leaving Kyreen alone with the bandit leader, or so she thought initially.

Xarles regarded Kyreen for a moment before speaking to her in common. "My second does not trust you. He is a cautious fellow while I am more trusting. I hope we can be civilized with no need for violence. If you agree, we can dispense of the gag, maybe even find some food and water. Do you agree to behave?"

At Kyreen's reluctant nod, Xarles beckoned her forward to where he stood atop the sheepskin rug at the foot of the platform. As she walked up, she noticed a human size lump in the bed, under the covers, belatedly sensing the slumbering presence.

"Kneel," Xarles commanded in common, pointing to a spot on the rug. Once she complied, Xarles leaned down and Kyreen felt a prick at the base of her spine. A moment later her hips and legs went numb. Xarles caught her when she tilted to one side.

Bringing her body back to center, he said, "You need to use your core to keep your balance. A warrior such as you should have no trouble staying upright."

Even as Kyreen continued struggling to remain upright, the bandit leader released her and walked up the platform. Sitting on the edge of the bed, Xarles gently shook the lump in the bed, murmuring something so quietly Kyreen only caught the name, Remy.

A figure sat up, drowsily rubbing the sleep from his eyes. He was a beautiful young man, just out of puberty and entering his physical prime. With streaks of sun-bleached blonde, his mop of dark brown curls framed his tanned face, the delicate features bordering on feminine, except for his crooked nose, obviously broken multiple times, adding a bit of handsome ruggedness to his visage. The skin on the young man's face, sculpted torso and toned arms was the same brown as Xarles' skin but, judging from the sapphire blue eyes, Kyreen wondered if most of the young man's coloring came from the sun. Her guess was proved correct when the man stood to pull on his pants, revealing buttocks and legs as pale as Kyreen's skin. When the young man took a step down, looking as though he were leaving, Xarles stopped him with a gentle hand on his arm, just below a bandage stark white against the tanned skin. Turning Remy to him, Xarles slide a hand behind the young man's head, running fingers through the sun-bleached curls and pulled the young man's face to his for a long, sensual kiss. Kyreen did not think Xarles' actions had anything to do with her. He was not putting on a show. The emotions she felt from the bandit leader were of pleasure and affection. Remy's emotions were a mix of bashful excitement and admiration. Smitten, Kyreen thought. The young man was smitten with Xarles. Once the men's lips parted, the young man hurried down from the platform and out of the tent without a glance towards Kyreen.

Xarles sat on the edge of the bed, watching Remy leave, an expression of fondness on the leader's face. Once the tent flap had fallen back into place, Xarles moved his gaze to the kneeling woman, his countenance becoming reflective.

"This scorpion toxin is a marvelous tool," he said in common, "causing temporary paralysis depending where on the spine it is administered. By placing it on the base of your spine, I have immobilized your legs, thus insuring you cannot run away."

He stood up, continuing to speak as he walked down from the platform. "Therefore, when I remove the gag, you will have no reason to work magic on me. For there is no way you can escape."

When he reached the bottom step, Xarles squatted down, his forearms resting on his thighs. "I said I was more trusting than Armand. That does not mean I am a fool. A woman, a solitary woman, does not set out across the Salandingar Desert because she is a nobody."

Xarles pulled the filthy rag from Kyreen's mouth, ripping away a layer of skin where the cloth had dried to the underside of her tongue. Kyreen worked her aching jaw experimentally, moving her tongue and swallowing, though her mouth was too parched to produce much saliva.

Xarles stood, moving to a side table to pour a cup of water. Kyreen watched him as she concentrated on staying upright. When he returned to stand before her, holding the cup to her lips, she tentatively reached for the cup but he lifted it up, out of her grasp.

"You will take your water and your food from my hand," he said, lowering the cup once more, pressing the rim to her lips. "Or you will not take food and water."

Kyreen looked up at him, relenting, allowing the cool liquid to slip over her parched lips and fill her dry mouth. After only a short moment Xarles pulled away the cup. After Kyreen had swallowed that tiny sip, Xarles lowered the cup once more. He repeated this several times, only permitting Kyreen tiny, miniscule sips that did nothing to satisfy her thirst. Kyreen kept her eyes locked on the bandit leader and he nonchalantly returned her gaze. About the tenth time of her sipping, the tent entrance opened.

Without looking away from Kyreen, Xarles said in elven, "Chimere, come kneel beside our new friend. I will be with you shortly."

Kyreen took another of the proffered drinks, feeling more than seeing the woman move up to take her place on the animal skin rug. Xarles went to the side table, this time bringing back a piece of fruit, something soft and juicy and sweet. He began feeding Kyreen small, bite- sized pieces. For a time, a few minutes, an hour, Kyreen had no idea how long, Xarles fed her pieces of fruit and drinks of water, very slowly, all without speaking, their eyes locked the entire time. The whole experience felt unnervingly intimate, not at all sexual, but powerful, provocative, primitive. Kyreen struggled to keep her expression neutral, to control the emotions raging inside of her. She forced down the anger, every fiber of her being yearning to rebel, to strike out, to attack, yet she resisted the urge, knowing her body needed the sustenance. She also knew nothing of this man feeding her, except that he commanded this camp, and he commanded Armand. That fact alone earned Xarles, not her respect, but her caution. At last, Xarles fed a final piece of fruit to Kyreen and stood, wiping his hands on a cloth napkin.

"That is enough for now," he said in common. "We do not want to make you ill."

He turned his attention to the woman kneeling beside Kyreen, switching to elven. "Chimere, my dear, welcome back. I want to know all about your trip. How was the caravan?"

As the woman began to speak Kyreen tried to focus on the words, but her eyes grew heavy and she had a difficult time concentrating. With her thirst quenched and her hunger slaked, fatigue from the previous evening settled over her. Mentally shaking her head, she resolutely forced herself to concentrate, attempting not to tip over. Xarles had sat down on the bottom step of the platform to listen to Chimere's report. Occasionally he would shift his gaze to Kyreen, obviously aware of her dilemma.

Not wishing to appear as though she could understand the conversations, Kyreen kept her gaze diverted from the auburn-haired woman with olive-toned skin kneeling beside her. Nothing Chimere said, however, meant anything meaningful to Kyreen. The woman reported the number of men in the caravan, the cargo being transported, and an incident involving a lone traveler. Nothing to pique Kyreen's interest.

With her eyelids drooping anew, the Calanian clenched her fists, digging her fingernails into her palms, using the pain to wake up. Looking around the room for a distraction, she noticed her sword, laying on a low table. Set beside a tent wall, her knapsack rested on the floor beside the table, looking deflated and empty. On the table with the sword sat the golden orb and the opal amulet, along with her book of fairy tales and the now tattered journal of spells, both blessedly written in common. Before she could stop herself, Kyreen frowned and looked down at her hands resting in her lap, at the naked middle finger of her right hand, wondering about the absent ruby ring. When she looked up, Xarles watched her with his perceptive dark eyes.

Just as Xarles dismissed Chimere, the tent flap lifted and Kyreen felt Armand enter the space. Chimere quickly exited and the flap closed.

Xarles stood up and went back to the dining table where he smeared a thin layer of a pale paste onto a small flat piece of bread. Moving back to Kyreen, he squatted down so as to hold it to her mouth.

"Take a small bite," he ordered in common, his tone much kinder than his words.

Kyreen did as he said. The paste was flavorful with spices she had never tasted before, while the tasteless flatbread was chewy and dense. Her mouth watered and her stomach grumbled for more.

As he fed Kyreen, Xarles spoke in elven to Armand, who gave a report of the camp happenings. As with Chimere's report, most of it Kyreen did not follow, names and events she did not recognize, until Armand mentioned Lucien. That name Kyreen remembered from their trip to the infirmary last night. He had been the guard Armand sent away.

"Lucien," Armand reported without any emotion, "has reported the three men from last night's raid, the ones she injured, died."

"Unfortunate," Xarles murmured. He had kept his gaze on Kyreen during the report and she had returned his gaze as she ate the proffered food, working hard at staying upright and keeping her expression neutral. As she remembered what Armand had done in the infirmary tent, Kyreen's stomach soured, the food she had just eaten threatening to come back up.

When Armand did not continue speaking, Xarles glanced up at his lieutenant. "Is that all?"

"Yes, Xarles," came the reply.

Xarles fed the last bit of food to Kyreen, then rose to his feet, talking as he poured another cup of water. "Good. Sounds like everything is in order. I have an errand I need you to run for me today."

"Yes, my captain."

Xarles returned to squat before Kyreen with the water. "Chimere reported the caravan she worked met up with a lone traveler just last night, an old man with a donkey, selling wares and potions. I think it might be Gautier. I wonder if he would make such a mistake so close to my camp, but maybe he has grown senile over the years."

Xarles took the cloth napkin, dabbing it to Kyreen's lips. "I need you to go investigate. I am meeting someone about this one later today and do not want any of the men out of camp until she is taken care of."

"Yes, my captain."

"The toxin should not wear off until dusk, so you can take her to the herd tent. Have Genevieve clean her up a bit more and brought to me at sunset."

"Yes, my captain."

"Armand, if the peddler is Gautier, I want him alive and able to speak when he gets here."

"Yes, my captain."

"If he is not Gautier, he is not to be harmed." From Xarles' tone and wording Kyreen had the feeling these were not the first such conversations the bandit leader and his second had had.

Xarles stood up, looking down at Kyreen, switching to common, "What is your name?"

Kyreen regarded him a moment, wondering what it would hurt to tell him. She decided it would not, so answered, "Kyreen."

"No, that does not sound right," Xarles remarked, shaking his head. He thought a moment before continuing. "Bijou. I like the sound of that. You will answer to Bijou from now on. Understand?"

Kyreen regarded the bandit leader a couple of heartbeats before shrugging. "You can call me whatever you wish. My name is Kyreen."

An instant later Kyreen found herself dangling from Armand's hand. Even as she had been speaking, the big man had picked her up by her neck. At least she thought she was dangling since she could not feel her feet and legs. Choking she clasped her hands to his thick hairy wrists, so big around that her hands could not get much purchase.

"Do not speak to your master that way," Armand hissed, his hot breath blowing in her face.

"Let her be, Armand," Xarles remarked, unruffled, placing a hand on the man's big arm. "I do not want any bruises on her when I sell her to the elves."

"She should not take that tone with you, Xarles," Armand said, but he dropped Kyreen to the ground where she lay in a puddle between the men, gasping to catch her breath.

Xarles pushed Kyreen onto her back with his barefoot. Still breathing heavily, Kyreen gazed up at him, still extremely conscious of Armand looming on the other side of her body.

"You say she had her camp warded with magic?" Xarles asked in elven.

"Yes," Armand replied.

"How do you cast spells in the language of men, the tongue of the Old Kingdom?" the bandit leader asked Kyreen in common.

"Poorly," Kyreen responded.

It took a moment, then Xarles laughed. He walked over to the low table where Kyreen's belongings rested, picking up the two books. Carrying the books to the platform where he once again sat on the bottom step, Xarles gestured at Kyreen, saying to Armand in elven, "Get her back up."

Chapter 8

Kyreen closed her eyes and gritted her teeth, desperately working to control any other outward reaction to the feel of Armand's hands on her body. Though he quickly had her upright, she felt completely violated by the intimate strokes and touches the big man had been able to minister during the process. When he had her positioned, Armand stood directly behind Kyreen so she could feel the heat of him against her back.

Xarles idly thumbed through the journal's dogeared pages, switching back to speak to Kyreen in common. "Humans back in Nowles, here in the desert, and especially inside *Talamh sa bhaile Si'* are prohibited from dabbling in magic. We are not permitted to cast spells. We may not possess magically enhanced items. Yet, Bijou, these pages appear to hold spells and these items appear to be enhanced."

"They do and they are," Kyreen replied. "Are you telling me that I wasted my time coming to the elf lands to improve my magic skills?"

"Is that why you crossed the desert, Bijou?" Xarles closed the book and gazed at Kyreen. "I had wondered what it was you were running away from or running to."

"Both actually," Kyreen responded truthfully.

"It is a foolish trek to attempt solo, without a guide or caravan," Xarles commented. "Very dangerous indeed, Bijou. Most do not survive."

"I did not consider the journey," Kyreen remarked with a shrug. "I only thought about the destination."

"You joked about your magic skills," Xarles said. "Tell me, Bijou. Do you do more than just protection wards?"

"My skills are limited," Kyreen admitted, "but I have improved since I entered the desert. Why? Do you need a mage?"

"Yes, Bijou," Xarles replied, a slight smile playing about his lips, though his dark eyes regarding her held no merriment. "I could find use for a mage."

Kyreen could not figure out what game Xarles played with her. His constant use of this name he had given her. He must know it irritated her. Why did he continue to goad her? If she had not known elven to learn about his meeting with the elves, she would think he was planning on keeping her, on incorporating her into his herd, on making her a…Kyreen refused to complete the thought. While she felt confident in her ability to endure any physical abuse Xarles or Armand or any man inflicted, the prospect of undergoing the kind of psychological abuse she had witnessed in Armand's tent sickened and terrified her.

Aloud Kyreen said, "What benefits might a mage earn in your camp?"

"Very direct, Bijou. I like that," Xarles chuckled. Setting the journal down beside him, but keeping ahold of the other book, his fingers lightly stroking its cover, he changed the subject. "What is in this book?"

"It is a collection of children's stories. Fairy tales," Kyreen answered, struggling to keep her voice and expression neutral as the painful memories strained to get out, to be free, to assault her.

Xarles placed the fairy tales book on top of the journal. Then, leaning forward to rest his elbows on his thighs, tenting his long slender fingers together, he gazed upon Kyreen for a few moments. "Let us both think about how we could benefit from a collaboration, Bijou. We will discuss it tonight in my tent, over dinner. I have a meeting to get to."

Kyreen allowed her eyes to widen as she said, "You are not leaving me alone with him, are you?"

"Nice try, Bijou," Xarles chuckled once more. "You are not afraid of Armand. You should be, but you are not."

Kyreen relaxed, dropping her guise. "I have been dealing with men like Armand my entire life."

"No, Bijou," Xarles said, his expression and tone suddenly serious. "You have not. The sooner you realize he is different, the better things will go for you, for me, for everyone."

"How is he different?" Kyreen remarked. "Yes, maybe he is stronger and more violent than most, but he does not consider women to be human. The female is just an object to him and men like him. We are simply something to own, to control, to hold power over, then discard when damaged or spent. No different."

"Maybe you have convinced yourself that you believe that, Bijou," Xarles conceded, "but more likely I would wager that somewhere, deep inside of you, you know the truth."

"What truth might that be?" Kyreen asked before she could think better of it.

"That it is not just women that Armand does not consider to be human in the manner in which you meant," Xarles said, his tone quiet and matter of fact. "There are only two people in this world who deserve consideration in Armand's mind. Those two people are him and me. No other lives matter. He has orders to keep you safe, but if he believes you mean me harm, he will snap your neck without hesitation. If he thinks you mean him harm, he will play with you until you beg him to kill you. Armand is not a man who sees gray. His world is black and white. Him and me, together against everyone else."

Xarles stood up, switching to elven. "Take her. I need to get ready."

Once more Kyreen had Armand's hands on her body as he again hoisted her over his shoulder like a bag of grain. When they entered the tent Xarles had called the herd tent, Kyreen could feel the spike in anxiety from the collected women. The air felt heavy as though waiting for something. Kyreen imagined that something was the unpredictability of Armand.

No one spoke as Armand dumped Kyreen onto a rug. When he turned away as though to leave Kyreen felt the first stirrings of hope. If she were left unbound and ungagged, she could get a message to Brigit. Then Armand stooped over and pulled up a set of shackles. Turning back around, Armand caught the transformation of hope to angry frustration in Kyreen's eyes and chuckled.

"Cunning little fox," he murmured as he began fastening the restraints to her wrists and ankles. "Armand would never leave you loose with these little doves."

Once the shackles had been secured, Armand stuffed a gag into Kyreen's mouth and ruffled her hair. Then he stood to speak with one of the women, who had moved forward from the rest of the group. The small woman was naked, as were all the women in the tent. Not as tiny in stature as Fanchon nor as light-skinned, her body was feminine and voluptuous without being fat. She had a slender waist curving out to wide hips, heavy breasts just beginning to droop with age, and glowing dark brown skin that begged to be stroked. The face the woman kept lowered had almond shaped eyes, full lips, and high sharp cheekbones beneath a halo of umber hair, the rows upon rows of tight coils flecked with copper spiraling out like a cloud to frame her face. Though she stood straight, her bowed head and overall carriage projected deference, and Kyreen had the impression her positioning before Armand was an attempt to shield the other women in the tent gathered behind her.

"Xarles wants her more thoroughly cleaned up and taken to his tent at dusk," the big man relayed his leader's instructions succinctly. "Keep her bound and gagged. She has been immobilized. She is to receive no food or water. Her name is Bijou."

"Yes, Armand," the woman responded. Kyreen recognized her voice as Genevieve. While Kyreen could not exactly gauge Genevieve's age, she appeared to be older than most of the women in the tent.

"Where did you spend last night?" Armand asked.

Genevieve hesitated a heartbeat before answering. "With the men."

Humiliation and anger rolled off of Genevieve, assaulting Kyreen's senses, though none of the latter could be seen in either the small woman's voice or countenance. In the instant it took Kyreen to erect her barriers, Kyreen felt a myriad of other emotions from around in the tent. Underneath their fear of Armand, the other women in the tent did not feel charitable towards Genevieve, leaving Kyreen to guess the older woman, who appeared to be their leader, was not well regarded by the rest of the women.

Armand chuckled. "Send Fanchon to my tent at sunset."

Without waiting for a response, Armand then exited the tent. The entire space hung in nervous silence for several heartbeats after the flap fell back into place. Once it was determined the big man was indeed gone, the tent exploded into sound and movement.

Though she only counted nine women including Genevieve, it seemed as if there were twice that many with all their voices and bodies milling around. They reminded Kyreen of a flock of birds – noisy, flitting, colorful birds. Small birds as all of the women were shorter than Kyreen, who had in the last year become accustomed to the tall women of her people. Kyreen had not known there to be so many shades of skin color, from the deep rich darkness of Genevieve to the luminescent milk white skin of a redhead, whose waves of shiny copper hair shone bright amongst all the darker-haired women. Even the textures and styles of the women's hair differed greatly, some like Fanchon with waterfalls of glossy straight hair, others with gentle waves, all in various lengths down their back, then there was the voluminous cloud of springy coils that billowed around Genevieve. One woman's russet hair had been shorn close to her skull, leaving Kyreen to wonder if the style had been a punishment or to better highlight the woman's striking mahogany features and slight, almost boyish figure.

The rest of the day passed with Kyreen being worked over by the women of the herd, sometimes as many as five hovering over her. Eventually, as multiple hands rubbed aromatic tinctures and exfoliants along her tender skin, Kyreen wished the numbness of her lower extremities included the rest of her body. While the women were not especially rough neither were they gentle. They were brisk, efficient, and indifferent. None made eye contact with Kyreen or tried to engage with the Calanian in any way. Under the assumption that their newest addition could not understand their words, they conducted running conversations with each other, chattering about camp happenings, just as casually as the women of Hanoria use to share gossip with Kyreen's foster mother while bartering for Ildri's baked goods on market day.

None of the women wore any clothing and none appeared to care. Kyreen found the women's ease with their nudity particularly unsettling. As they worked on Kyreen, their bare skin brushed against her so casually, each point of contact unnerving the Calanian woman. When one woman reached across Kyreen to scoop up another dollop of cream, her soft tawny breast pressing against Kyreen's jaw, the Calanian quickly turned her face away.

Genevieve, standing nearby to oversee the activities, caught Kyreen's movement and saw the grimace upon the newcomer's face. The dark-skinned woman laughed, low and throaty. "Our new friend here appears to be offended by your lovely tits, Noemi."

All of the women laughed, as did the guard positioned just inside the tent entrance. Kyreen had noticed a few of the women periodically sidling up to the man, their expression coy as they leaned in to speak with him in hushed tones. The man did not pay the women much attention, conversing with them, but paying no heed to their flirtations. Kyreen could feel that the man's indifference was not feigned and had just about determined his preference must run to his own gender when yet another woman approached him. It would be unnecessary to say the woman was beautiful, for all the women in this tent were beautiful, even Fanchon, if not for her ruined face. In the Old Kingdoms, in any province of Nowles, in the city of Myrddin, the woman with the flawless tanned skin who now approached the guard would be heralded as a remarkable beauty with her honey brown hair cascading down her back, artfully framing her pixie face with wide gray eyes, a snub nose, high cheekbones, and luscious pink lips. Here, in this tent, amongst these other women with their exotic coloring and features, however, the woman approaching the guard did not stand out. Still the guard's eyes lit up when he gazed down into this woman's face. Kyreen felt both of their emotions spiking during their brief conversation. The woman radiated a high level of nervousness as well. When she gave a furtive glance over one shoulder, her face reflecting concern, Kyreen realized this was an illicit relationship. She doubted Xarles encouraged, or even permitted, emotional attachments between his men and the herd. Kyreen shuddered to think of what Armand would do to this couple should he discover the relationship.

"Bijou is shy," Genevieve's husky voice drew Kyreen back to her present situation. The dark-skinned woman pushed aside Noemi so as to kneel by Kyreen's head. Then, leaning in, Genevieve took Kyreen's chin in her hand, turning Kyreen's face back towards her. Lying awkwardly on her side, hands secured tightly behind her back, Kyreen had no way to resist. Women knelt on either side of Kyreen, effectively pinning her in place without any extra effort.

Genevieve shifted closer to Kyreen, kneeling with her knees wide apart. Now the Calanian could smell the musky scent of sex and arousal permeating from the other woman. Genevieve's emotions exuded lust and power, as did the other women. The women of the herd were enjoying their dominance over the newest addition to their tent. By the tent entrance, the guard watched with amusement, but did nothing to interfere with the herd dynamics.

Genevieve leaned down, her pendulous breasts hanging close to Kyreen's face. Kyreen clenched her jaw, vainly straining against Genevieve's fingers holding her head in place. Her futile attempts merely earned Kyreen another chuckle from the dark-skinned woman.

"Do we offend you? You think you better than us?" Genevieve asked in broken common. "You are herd now. Get used to it."

Kyreen glared up at the other woman who merely smiled. Without looking away, Genevieve said in elven, "Sequin, roll her over. Hold her shoulders. Rouge, straddle her. Let us warm her up for Xarles. Give her a taste of her new life."

Kyreen felt the shuffle of bodies as she was pressed awkwardly onto her back. She lay uncomfortably, her bound hands driving into the small of her back, their positioning thrusting her hips up suggestively. Struggling to turn her face away from Genevieve, unable to break the vice like grip of the dark woman's hold, Kyreen watched from her peripheral vision as Rouge, the woman with the shorn russet hair and mahogany skin straddled Kyreen's legs, which were still numb from the toxin Xarles had injected into her that morning. When the woman sidled up a fraction, Kyreen could then feel the woman's weight on her pelvis, the dark thighs pressing into her sides. Rouge leaned forward to fondle both of Kyreen's breasts, a thumb running over each taut nipple. Kyreen, unsuccessful in her attempts to hide her distress, squirmed under Rouge's body.

Mortified, her body blushing both from embarrassment and arousal, Kyreen resolutely averted her gaze, avoiding looking at either the woman atop her or Genevieve, who continued to gaze down at Kyreen with amusement. Then Rouge leaned forward, her tiny breasts grazing Kyreen's ribcage as hot breath caressed one of Kyreen's breasts a heartbeat before the nipple was enveloped in a warm, moist mouth. Rouge's tongue flicked Kyreen's nipple before her teeth carefully bit down and Rouge cautiously pulled up her head, playfully tugging.

Involuntarily, Kyreen gasped, unable to stop the shudder in her torso. Genevieve's smile widened and she leaned down once more. Keeping Kyreen's head turned, so that her dark full breasts dangled before the Calanian's eyes, Genevieve placed her mouth close to Kyreen's ear, whispering in common, "Rouge has a talented mouth, eh? She like showing you more later, when you are not numb down there."

Then Genevieve pulled back and stood in one fluid motion, clapping her hands sharply. "Play time is over, girls. Back to work!"

With a collective murmur, the women complied, though Rouge lingered an extra half-dozen heartbeats before reluctantly releasing Kyreen's breasts and standing. A moment later the ministrations of the creams resumed and the women went back to their chattering as though nothing peculiar had just occurred. Kyreen closed her eyes, attempting to block out the sounds and emotions assaulting her senses, her body trembling with rage and humiliation.

A while later, after Kyreen's emotions had calmed down into a cool fury, she was once again rolled onto her back, two women holding down each shoulder and one pressing down on Kyreen's abdomen. Two women knelt by her legs restraining the Calanian that way as well, though the gesture was unnecessary as Kyreen still had no feeling in her legs. Genevieve knelt by Kyreen's head, a hand pressing on Kyreen's forehead. The position would not have been so bad except that her hands, numb and still secured behind her back, prevented Kyreen from lying flat.

"Armand said to keep her gagged," one of the women holding Kyreen's shoulder whispered nervously.

"He also said Xarles wanted her more thoroughly cleaned," Genevieve hissed. "Now do your job, Candide, and keep her still."

Leaning over Kyreen, Genevieve looked down at the restrained woman, and, as she pulled out the gag, said in broken common, "Do not struggle. Do not bite. Or Armand come take care. Understand?"

Kyreen nodded as she could and allowed Genevieve to insert a flat wooden paddle into her mouth. A paste tasting of mint had been applied to the wood and Genevieve now smeared the concoction around the inside of Kyreen's mouth, coating her tongue. The woman was very good, as though she had much experience. The procedure was completed quickly without Genevieve touching too far back in Kyreen's mouth, but everywhere else so that when a fresh cloth, this one silk and fragranced, was put in place Kyreen's mouth felt tingly and clean.

Genevieve backed away but directed Rouge to continue restraining Kyreen's head. The russet haired woman took Genevieve's place, cradling Kyreen's head between her mahogany hands, her pink tongue flicking out to lick her dark lips as her amber eyes gazed down at Kyreen with amusement. Genevieve moved around to kneel between Kyreen's legs which Genevieve had instructed the women to spread. Kyreen strained in Rouge's grasp but could not lift her head.

"Hand me the bottle," Genevieve ordered absently.

Kyreen could not feel anything and, with Rouge firmly holding her head down, could not see anything. So, she tried listening but the women had continued their chatter. None seemed to be paying attention to whatever Genevieve was doing. Belatedly Kyreen realized the conversation revolved around her.

"Five men dead."

"I will miss Andre. He was sweet."

"Gaspard not so much."

"How could they be brothers?"

"How could she kill five men?"

"She looks like she would fly away in the breeze."

"No, she is strong. Look at her muscles."

"She is scrawny."

"Why would Xarles want her?"

At the mention of the bandit leader's name, Genevieve snapped at the women to shut up. A moment later, she stood up. Now Kyreen could watch the woman gaze down on her prone form. Genevieve slowly dried her hands on a cloth.

"Noemi. Cerise," Genevieve said. "You two work on her hair. It is a mess. Comb it out and get some cream in it."

Genevieve looked towards the tent entrance. "Orane, can you get the new girl moved? She is taking up too much space here in the middle of the room."

A moment later, Kyreen found herself hoisted around once more. The guard, Orane, easily picked up Kyreen and moved to deposit her where Genevieve indicated, but he did so with an air of indifference. The man did not roam his hands across her body like Armand had done when he carried her. Kyreen found herself reclining on a much softer surface, a silk covered pad lying on the ground. Orane placed Kyreen on her side so he could affix her wrists behind her to a post. Kyreen did not really care as, being on her side, the blood began circulating in her hands. Cautiously, she began flexing her fingers as the feeling returned to the digits.

As the two women worked on Kyreen's hair and prattled, Kyreen found herself dozing on and off, unable to fully relax but also unable to keep her eyes from drifting shut. Eventually the two women finished working on Kyreen's hair and moved over to another pad where they lounged and continued talking.

As the day wore on the interior of the tent warmed. The women, their work on Kyreen complete, lazed about in groups of two or three, reclining on cushions and pads strewn throughout the area. Some groomed each other, but mostly they dozed or chatted in quiet conversation, lounging on and beside each other, their bodies entwined in a cacophony of colors.

The only woman who remained alone, aside from Genevieve who relaxed on the tent's lone piece of furniture, a bed raised up from the floor, was the tiny black-haired woman called Fanchon. She had not participated in Kyreen's grooming, but instead had remained supine with her face to the tent wall, removed from the group in a deserted area far from the tent entrance. With her hair pooling on the green silk pad, Fanchon's back was visible to Kyreen for the first time, exposing a myriad of thin white scars marring the woman's tan skin. Kyreen could only guess the scars to be a result of a very thin whip or from a knife blade, maybe a combination of both.

Chapter 9

As the light in the tent began to soften, the women stirred and began moving around. Genevieve rose and walked over to gaze down at Kyreen. Her dark eyes narrowed as she scanned the prone woman's face and body. Kyreen fought to remain unmoving under the woman's scrutiny, though her stomach roiled with angst and anger. Genevieve gestured to the two women who had been working on Kyreen's hair earlier.

"She is too pale. She needs color," Genevieve said. "Put some kohl around her eyes and rouge up her cheeks. Nothing can be done about her lips with that gag. Get her upright and try to do something with that hair. Those curls are still out of control."

As the women pulled and tugged, getting Kyreen upright into a kneeling position, Genevieve looked sternly into Kyreen's eyes, speaking in common. "You be still. No move. No mess face."

Kyreen had never had makeup on her before. She found the experience of the two women applying it, leaning in so close, examining her features with their analyzing gazes, strangely intimate and unnerving. By the time the two stood back nodding in satisfaction, Kyreen wanted to slap them both and scrub her face clean. Her intent must have shown in her expression for the women exchanged alarmed glances then went back to their abandoned pad. Genevieve moved in front of Kyreen to inspect her again.

"Better," she murmured in elven. Kyreen narrowed her eyes at the woman, who clucked her tongue and switched to her broken common. "Do not be mad at me. I follow orders. You be good to follow orders too. Less pain."

Shortly the tent flap opened to admit a man carrying a large covered tray which he placed on the mattress Genevieve had been resting on earlier.

The bandit joked around with Genevieve for a few moments before heading out. As he ducked under the flap his eyes met Kyreen's and she felt his emotion – guilt – before the entrance closed behind him. As she pondered this interaction, Kyreen watched the women move to kneel around the foot of the bed as Genevieve took the lid off the platter to reveal several small bowls. The smell of the aromatic food wafting through the tent made Kyreen's stomach growl and her mouth water.

Genevieve handed out bowls of the food to the women. She gave an extra bowl to a small dark-haired woman who bore a strong resemblance to Fanchon. Kyreen watched as the woman attempted to rouse Fanchon, murmuring quietly, obviously urging the prostrate woman to eat. Finally, Fanchon rolled over and sat up to grab the bowl. Angrily she scooped the food into her mouth with her fingers. From where Kyreen sat the food looked like a grain with chunks of vegetables and maybe cubed meat. Once everyone had finished eating, Genevieve moistened a cloth with a small bit of water. The cloth was then passed around for the women to cleanse their hands.

Orane, began taking the women out of the tent in small groups, returning with them a few minutes later to take another group. Once the women returned from wherever Orane took them, they began grooming themselves – powder, lotion, makeup, hair. Sometime during this Kyreen regained feeling in her toes. She watched the proceedings while experimentally wiggling her toes. With interest Kyreen noted when Orane exited with a single woman, the only one he escorted alone, the gray eyed beauty who piqued his interest, a woman Kyreen now knew to be called Sequin. Returning after an especially lengthy absence with Sequin, Orane began lighting the lamps around the tent. A few moments later, when Genevieve exited without an escort, no one appeared to pay attention. Kyreen had a feeling this was a typical day in the herd tent. Just one day here and Kyreen was fed up. She could never stay here. She had to find a way out.

As Kyreen watched the women, she thought about her priorities. Number one she had to get a message to Brigit. Kyreen could not let the mage get caught in this camp. Number two she needed to get away from the bandits and get into the elf lands. Neither one of these tasks seemed especially attainable at the moment. She wondered what Xarles had done this afternoon with his meeting with the elves. Maybe he had sold her and she would be done with the bandits. If not, she had another issue to address, one she had avoided thinking about, but as she watched Fanchon being readied by the woman who looked like her sister, Kyreen thought about Armand.

Xarles had been correct when he said Kyreen was not afraid of Armand. She was not, but the big man made her angry, irrationally so. He reminded her of the bullies she had encountered in Hanoria, men with power who abused those in their care. The biggest difference between Armand and those other men was Armand's ruthlessness, his complete lack of concern towards things like murder. This did not scare Kyreen but it did concern her. She could not predict the bandit's reactions and she had a difficult time holding her own rage towards Armand in check. Based on the past day, he found Kyreen's anger amusing and harmless. Maybe she could use this at some point. She just had to survive long enough for these bandits to let down their guard.

"Bijou," Genevieve's voice broke through Kyreen's musings roughly shaking her shoulder. From the woman's tone this had not been the first time Genevieve had said the name.

Kyreen frowned at the woman, who dabbed some flowery perfume behind each of Kyreen's ears and along her breast bone. Kyreen wrinkled her nose at the scent which tickled the back of her throat, making her want to sneeze. Instead Kyreen shook her head and exhaled sharply trying to clear out the scent. All she managed to do was get her nose running. Genevieve looked exasperated as she took a cloth to Kyreen's nose.

"Trouble," the woman muttered in common. "He take care of you. Then no more trouble."

The bandit who had brought the food stood behind Genevieve. Once Kyreen's nose had stopped running, Genevieve stood back so the man could unlock Kyreen's chain.

"You stand?" Genevieve asked Kyreen.

Kyreen experimentally wiggled her toes and feet. She had feeling up past her ankles but nothing in her knees, thighs or hips. She shook her head at Genevieve, who looked over her shoulder at the bandit.

"Pierre, she will need to be carried," Genevieve said in elven.

The bandit picked Kyreen up, slinging her easily over his shoulder, saying, "Get the others ready. That way I only need to make one trip."

Kyreen recognized the man's voice as the one who had brought her to this tent last night for cleaning. Why did he seem so nervous now? She continued to wonder as Genevieve, two of the women, and Fanchon lined up by the tent entrance. From her position hanging upside down with her head falling somewhere around the bandit's stomach, her view was limited.

Outside the sun had dipped behind the western mountains, dropping the temperature to just slightly hot and washing the desert in bright twilight. Though none of the women had appeared nervous as they filed out of the tent, their anxiety rolled over Kyreen as they walked across the compound.

Kyreen had felt Armand's approach so was not surprised to hear his voice but the bandit holding her did not. He startled physically when the beefy hand dropped on his shoulder and Armand said, "Pierre."

"Yes, Armand?" Kyreen had to admire this bandit's calm exterior. Though she had felt his spike of nerves, he revealed nothing in his voice.

"This one is not safe," Armand was saying. "You need to take care how you carry her."

"My apologies, Armand," Pierre replied. "She is immobile, shackled, and gagged. I thought her harmless."

"Not this one," the big man remarked. Armand's rough hands lifted Kyreen's body, turning her around so that her head now hung down Pierre's back. Once he had her in place on the other man's shoulder, Armand slapped Kyreen's ass. She still had no feeling there but she sensed her body moving as the sound echoed across the clearing.

"That is better," Armand remarked. "Go on, Pierre. No need to restrain Fanchon, but make sure this one is secure. Double check even."

"Yes, Armand," Pierre replied, his relief so palpable to Kyreen she wondered how no one else felt it.

Once Genevieve and the other women had been dropped off at the center fire area, Pierre escorted Fanchon to Armand's tent, leaving Kyreen for last. The lamps in Xarles' tent had been lit already when they entered. Pierre lowered Kyreen to the ground by the center pole, not looking at her while he fastened the chain to the post. Kyreen kept her gaze locked on the bandit but he never met her eyes. She watched him stand, run a nervous hand across his head and glance over at the table where her belongings rested. Only then did he exit.

Alone and waiting, Kyreen concentrated on blocking out the emotions filtering in to her from outside the tent. She had enjoyed her solitude in the desert and had been lax with her energy practices. As the feeling slowly returned to the lower part of her body, she experimented moving her legs so that she sat upright with her hands behind her back around the pole. Then she slowly began to attempt to stand using the pole at her back.

"I am glad you found something to keep you busy while you waited, Bijou," Xarles commented from behind Kyreen as she finally managed to stand, though she still leaned heavily on the pole.

She had, of course, sensed his approach but chose not to reveal that talent just yet. She thought it might be helpful at some point not right now though.

"I hope your day was pleasant, Bijou," Xarles remarked in common, moving to stand in front of her. "It looks like the herd was busy on you."

He stepped closer, wrapping one of her curls around a finger, and leaned in to inhale deeply.

"You look and smell delightful," he commented quietly before stepping back, "but that expression in your eyes destroys the vision."

The tent flap opened as someone entered. From the nervous energies Kyreen guessed the person to be Pierre. She turned her head to look at him over her shoulder. The bandit carried a covered tray, looking calm and nonchalant. Without a glance towards Kyreen, Pierre carried the tray to the table where he set it down before heading towards the entrance. Kyreen watched Pierre the entire time trying to figure out what could have the man so concerned. When the tent flap fell back into place, she straightened around to find Xarles watching her closely. For a few moments the two stared at each other. Then Xarles pulled the gag from Kyreen's mouth and released the shackles from her wrists. He pulled the chain through the restraints, dropping it to pool on the floor by the wrist manacles, leaving Kyreen with the ankle shackles and collar in place.

Xarles moved over to the table to take a seat. He gestured for Kyreen to approach, pointing to the floor beside his chair. "Kneel here, Bijou."

Kyreen took a few tentative steps, immediately halting to keep from tipping over. She experimentally wriggled her toes and flexed her feet. The chain between her ankles clanked with her movements. When she was certain she could walk without losing her balance, she finished crossing the space, reluctantly dropping to kneel at the indicated spot.

Xarles had lifted the lid of the platter while Kyreen had been struggling to move. Now, as he dished out a plate, the enticing aromas made Kyreen's mouth water. Silent, she observed him. He did not speak as he ate. Eventually he began offering food to her, glancing down to hold her gaze as she took the proffered bits staring back at him. The food tasted divine. Kyreen could not discern if it was from the exotic seasonings or because she was famished.

After a while, Xarles pushed away the empty plate and wiped his mouth with a cloth napkin. Then he pulled a small bowl towards him, plucking out a plump berry. When Kyreen saw it, she reflexively inhaled before she could stop herself and involuntarily her eyes watered. Xarles glanced at her, noting her body recoiling.

Kyreen had successfully not thought about Lang for almost an entire day. But that was how it seemed to go with her mind lately. She could be in control then a sight, a sound, a smell would trigger a memory, create just a crack in the seal she set on her memories. Just one little crack and all the feelings and emotions came tumbling to the front of her mind. These times were almost as bad as the panic attacks. In some ways they were worse. At least the panic attacks did not leave her feeling as though her heart had been torn out of her chest, like the sight of that plump dark berry in Xarles' hand did to her right now.

This was not where she was supposed to be, not kneeling in this sand, in this tent, in this desert. Anger roared through Kyreen, dousing the pain. She should be in her homeland, working with Brigit on a way to communicate with Vaktare the gargoyle or deciphering spells while Lang sat through boring Council meetings and helped lead the recovery of their people. She should be delivering foals, going on picnics with Lang and his children, something, anything mundane and ordinary. She should be with Lang in Calan, not alone in this wretched desert. Before the recollections of their brief time together could engulf her, Kyreen gritted her teeth, forcing all of those 'should be's' and 'what if's' back, willing the dreams and memories away until she could once again breathe.

"Now that was interesting," Xarles remarked quietly, popping the berry into his mouth. Keeping his gaze locked on Kyreen, he plucked another berry from the bowl, holding it to Kyreen's lips. "Do not like berries do you, Bijou?"

Kyreen closed her eyes, unable to stop the leak of hot tears spilling down her cheeks. It took all of her will power to not pull away, the sweet smell of the ripe fruit filling her senses. This reaction was stupid, she silently chided herself. She needed to get control. She took a deep breath to center herself only to have the aromatic smell of berry threaten to release a fresh batch of memories. So, she bit down on the inside of her cheek using the pain to ground her.

After a moment Xarles pulled back the berry and popped in into his mouth. He sat back in his chair, his eyes never leaving Kyreen's face.

"I have intimidated many people over the years," he said wryly. "Driven them to tears. Both men and women. But I do believe this is the first time I have caused tears with a berry."

Kyreen kept her gaze down. She hated that Xarles saw her in this vulnerable state. She needed to get control, she thought again.

She refused to become a victim. She would not be at this man's mercy, not for any longer than absolutely necessary.

A cloth applied gently to her face surprised Kyreen, drawing her attention back to the bandit leader. She glanced up. Xarles had wetted his napkin and was softly rubbing her skin.

"You smeared the makeup with your tears," he remarked. Kyreen felt horrified at the amount of black and red paint the cloth removed. She could not imagine how horrendous she had looked. Something in her expression must have reflected her thoughts for Xarles chuckled.

"No, you do not strike me as the type for painting your face," he said, leaning back. "Genevieve does good work though. She knows how to accent the good and camouflage the bad. Not that you have much that needs camouflaging, Bijou."

He grabbed another berry and watched her as he savored the fruit. For the first time Kyreen felt a tiny tickle of fear, just a little prickle in the back of her mind. She had been wary of Armand and still would be, but this man here, sitting in the chair, looking down on her naked, kneeling form, he was the one she truly needed to watch. That Xarles controlled Armand made him that much more dangerous. She realized with a start that she had underestimated Xarles, just as he had probably intended. Before Kyreen could wallow too deep into her self-flagellation about her error, Xarles stood up, placing the soiled napkin on the table.

"Come," he said, "I feel like taking a walk."

Kyreen rose to her feet, grateful to be moving. The chains about her ankles rattled noisily. Xarles looked down with a frown, then cocked his head at her.

"You know you cannot escape," he stated.

"Yes," Kyreen replied, her voice hoarse.

"After hearing about your performance during the raid, I do not doubt your skills," he commented. "But I do not like the sound of chains. I wish to stroll in the evening without that noise and maybe have a conversation with you. I so rarely have the chance to speak the language of the Old Kingdoms."

The thought of following Xarles through camp without clothing did not bother Kyreen as much as it would have just the previous day. She thought this would be a good opportunity to see the camp layout in an upright position instead of from some man's shoulder.

"I know that even should I be able to slip from your grasp, I have nowhere to go," she said. "I do not know where I am. Without supplies or transportation, I would not get very far before your men would find me."

"True," Xarles remarked. "So, do we have an accord for the evening? I will remove the restraints and you will not run."

"Yes," Kyreen agreed.

"Or fight," Xarles added, his eyes moving to the small table where her sword lay.

Kyreen followed his gaze. In her mind she imagined drawing the blade and striking Xarles down, or better yet, killing Armand. She turned back to look into his dark eyes.

"I came into the desert because I was despondent and running away from my memories," she remarked. "But I was never, and have never, been suicidal. I will not provoke an attack."

Outside of the tent, reds, golds, and purples erupted across the sky overhead. The soft breeze still held the warmth of the day and Kyreen relished the feel of it on her face, across her bare skin, and through her curls. A short distance away, where the fire had been stoked for the evening, the sounds of merriment could be heard. The feelings hitting Kyreen were not as intense as they had been the previous evening.

'Of course,' she thought, 'last night the men's emotions had been elevated even before the herd's arrival as their entertainment, most likely from the raid on my camp.'

She closed her eyes and inhaled deeply. The air smelled of wood smoke, barbecued meat, and the impending night. Exhaling she centered so when she opened her eyes, Kyreen felt more grounded than she had since awakening to her camp ward alarms and killing Andre. She saw Xarles watching her.

"Walk behind me to my left," Xarles instructed her. "Do not lag too far back."

They walked in silence past Armand's tent and the herd tent. When they reached the kitchen area, Xarles instructed Kyreen to stand outside the area while he spoke with the cook. She took the opportunity to glance around but outside this area all she could see was desert foothills in the fading evening light.

"Plotting your escape?" Xarles asked, walking up and grinning as he saw her gazing into the darkening desert landscape.

"Would you expect anything less from me?" Kyreen quipped, flashing the bandit leader a smile which sparkled in her eyes, but did not reveal her true feelings. In Xarles' absence, she had decided that quiet and sulky would not be most beneficial to her cause. Maybe humor and charm could work though. It seemed to work for both Brigit and Synnove.

If her answer surprised Xarles, he did not show it. He did, however, chuckle quietly as they began walking back the way they had come. Enjoying the respite from being cooped up inside, Kyreen felt a measure of relief when they continued walking past Xarles' tent. They did not pause at the center fire where Kyreen could hear and feel the emotions of the men and women there. She did not look. Kyreen could not worry about these women, the herd as Xarles called them. She had enough concerns without worrying about a group of women whose existence she had not been aware of the previous day.

Then the tangy aroma of horse piqued Kyreen's attention. She must have made some outward indication of her interest because Xarles gave her a glance.

"You like horses then?" he asked.

"Better than most people," Kyreen responded truthfully.

"In that you and I agree," Xarles replied, stopping before a pale tent set up outside a grouping of corrals in which dark shadows of the horses could be seen. Lifting the tent flap, he gestured for Kyreen to precede him inside.

Chapter 10

The tent interior was dimly lit with two lanterns. Across half of the tent a thick layer of straw had been strewn and standing in the middle was a small gray mare, her abdomen painfully distended with pregnancy. Allowing the entrance to close behind him, Xarles walked up to the horse, who whinnied a soft greeting. The mare's coat was a silver gray with white dappling. Her mane and tail, the most luxuriously flowing that Kyreen had ever seen, were inky black as were her four legs. The mare's confirmation could not be truly observed due to her pregnancy but her hindquarters appeared heavily muscled and the line of her neck bowed gracefully. The black muzzle, now nuzzling at Xarles for treats, tapered daintily. The eyes which gazed at Kyreen when the woman approached were large and liquid brown and full of intelligence. Much like Xarles, the creature did not stand very tall but had a commanding presence. After a glance to Xarles who nodded, Kyreen placed a hand on the mare's neck, softly stroking down and over her withers.

"Hey there girl," Kyreen murmured, allowing her hand to skim across the mare's belly. "You are running a little late, are you not? Looks like it is past time for you to have this little fellow. He is more than ready to come out."

"Yes, she is due any time now," Xarles remarked rubbing the white spot between the mare's eyes, almost hidden beneath the thick black forelock. "That is why I had the tent erected and moved her in here."

"She does not feel quite ready," Kyreen said, sliding her hand down the mare's back to softly pat her hind quarters, "but he does. He is anxious to get out and see the world."

Impulsively, Kyreen rested her cheek against the mare's swollen belly. The life within radiated strong and healthy. She imagined a wobbly kneed gray colt with a black mane and tail. When she opened her eyes, she caught Xarles looking at her, his expression inscrutable. Self-conscious, she straightened, taking a step back away from the mare.

"My apologies," she murmured, suddenly very aware of her nakedness, though her feeling of vulnerability came more from her actions than her lack of clothing.

"No," Xarles said. "You did nothing which calls for an apology."

He pulled a piece of fruit from his clothes and fed it to the mare. For several moments, the only sound in the tent was the mare's teeth chewing the fruit.

"I have not met many women who are familiar with horses," Xarles commented, scratching behind the mare's ears.

"My people are..." Kyreen paused. How to describe her people? "Both women and men alike are trained in all things. For example, in a fair contest of skills—horsemanship, archery, hand-to-hand combat, swordplay—I would put myself as the winner against any of your men."

"Even Armand?" Xarles asked, his eyebrow arching.

"I said a fair contest," Kyreen replied. "Both contestants would have to follow the rules. And yes, I believe I would best Armand in the arena, but I do not trust him to play by the rules."

Xarles laughed. "I would enjoy seeing that but you are correct about Armand."

He looked back at the mare, now nosing about his clothes, hoping for more tasty treats. "You sound like you have experience with mares and delivering foals."

"I do," Kyreen responded.

"You referred to her foal as he. Is that just your way of talking or is it magic?"

Kyreen shrugged. "I do not believe it to be magic. It is just something I know. I have done it my whole life knowing the gender of the unborn."

"So, you have some ability. Do all your people?" Xarles continued to pet the mare as he talked, his dark eyes apprising Kyreen.

"Yes, to some extent," Kyreen responded. Maybe if she could pique his interest she could avoid being taken back to the herd tent or at least stop having her body numbed. She enjoyed having feeling in her toes. "We are empathic and each person has a special ability such as predicting weather, hunting, or...discerning truths. Mine is being especially empathic and knowing the gender of unborn babies, animals and human."

"Fascinating," Xarles remarked, giving the mare a final pat. "Follow me."

They exited the tent into the night. While they had been inside, the sky overhead had darkened and the stars had come out. Out over the desert the moon had begun to rise, reminding Kyreen once more that she needed to get a message to Brigit. Xarles led her away from the horse area towards a darkened area. In the dim light Kyreen made out the shape of a tent. As they drew closer she began to feel the emotions of someone from inside the structure—fear, panic, and pain. At some point, unconsciously, Kyreen stopped walking. When Xarles paused before the tent's entrance, he turned to look at her in the dark.

"Tell me what you feel," he said.

"Terror. Apprehension. Agony," she replied quietly. She did not want to go in the tent, but she knew she would and she would not let whatever she saw in there keep her from her current aim. She had to charm Xarles enough to get out of this camp and to keep her out of Armand's path. So, she pushed away her revulsion and closed the distance between them, standing close enough to feel the heat from Xarles' body and smell his exotic scent. Keeping her voice neutral, she remarked, "The man in there is in agony, on the edge of hysteria."

"Good," Xarles murmured, lifting the flap and entering the tent. Kyreen followed.

Tied to the center pole in the middle of the tent sat a man, his wrists shackled above his head. Neither of his legs appeared to be capable of supporting his body as both limbs bent out at unnatural angles. Though the man wore no clothes, he did not look naked as every visible inch of his body was smeared in blood, some spots fresh, slick and bright crimson, other patches dried to a dark, almost black, red. The rank smell of soured sweat and fear made Kyreen want to cover her nose but she refrained from visibly reacting. Like when he kissed Remy this morning, Kyreen did not think Xarles was putting on this display for her. She simply happened to be present.

From Xarles, Kyreen felt a profound sorrow, a heartache so deep it almost eclipsed another piercing emotion, that of hatred. Almost as soon as she had identified the two emotions in Xarles, the sadness dissipated so that only hatred remained. Surreptitiously she took a step away from Xarles. The loathing spilling off of the bandit leader washed over her, filling the space so that she no longer felt any of the beaten man's emotions, or anything else. Thus, she missed Armand's entrance into the tent, flinching visibly when the big man grabbed her arm.

"She should be shackled," Armand complained.

Xarles glanced over at the two. Much to Kyreen's surprise, Xarles did not look angry. He did not even appear overly emotional. For a split second, their eyes met and she knew he knew that she could feel his emotions. Then his eyes dropped to Armand's hand squeezing Kyreen's upper arm.

"Mind your grip," he said offhandedly in elven to his second in command. "Skin like hers bruises easy. She cannot look abused when the elves get her."

"If she were in restraints, I would not have to hold her," Armand responded, but his grip on her relaxed.

"She and I have an agreement for this evening," Xarles explained then moved his gaze back to the battered man who had not moved or made a sound since they had entered the tent, except for his ragged breathing which echoed against the tent walls after Xarles' voice faded. "She has promised not to run or fight so I took off the shackles."

"And you trust her?" Armand scoffed. "Like any other woman, she will lie as easily as she breathes if it suits her, if it gets her what she wants."

"That is just it, Armand. I do not believe she lied," Xarles remarked, keeping his gaze on the bleeding man. "I have not figured out her game. She is a puzzle, an exquisite, complicated mystery."

"I do not know about mysteries, Xarles, but I do know she is dangerous and not normal. She is crafty," Armand responded. "You be careful."

"I always am."

Xarles prodded the man with his toe. Kyreen did not think the man had passed out. His emotions still radiated too strongly. Slowly the man lifted his head opening his eyes to stare at Xarles. The whites of his eyes looked so bright against the blood staining his surrounding skin. Kyreen thought the man's long hair and bushy beard might naturally be light brown or gray but right now they were caked with blood, giving the man a crazed look as he gazed up at Xarles, who peered back down at the beaten man.

"You are certain this is Gautier," Xarles said, more of a statement, less of a question.

"Yes, Xarles," Armand replied. "Check his hand."

Xarles produced a cloth from somewhere. Reaching down he began wiping the blood from the other man's right hand. Kyreen involuntarily flinched from the fresh panic the restrained man Armand called Gautier sent forth. The battered man did not feel confused or perplexed. Based on the man's collection of emotions, Kyreen felt fairly certain Gautier did know Xarles and knew exactly why he had been brought to this tent and the prospect terrified him deeply.

"Squeamish, are you?" Armand chuckled in Kyreen's ear.

Xarles glanced over at them, saying, "No, she is not."

Switching to common he continued, "What do you feel?"

"More of the same," she replied. "I am not a…Truth Seer. My talent is not that refined."

"But…"

"I believe he knows you, knows why he is here," she responded. "I feel he recognized the name."

"Did he?" Xarles returned his gaze to the bloodied man's hand, which looked odd, startlingly pale with the blood cleared away.

"There it is," he murmured in elven.

From her position Kyreen could not clearly see what Xarles looked upon. Whatever it was served to convince the bandit leader of this man's identity.

"Take her back to my tent," Xarles commented, taking a step back to look Gautier in the face. "She could probably use a stop at the trench."

"Yes, Xarles," Armand responded, tugging Kyreen's arm.

Speaking common to Kyreen, Xarles said, "Go with him. He will take you to relieve your bladder then leave you in my tent. I ask that you not ruin the evening by doing anything foolish."

"I will not," Kyreen replied, her tone reflecting her thought that she would not be the problem.

As they reached the tent entrance Xarles spoke again in elven. "Armand?"

"Yes, Xarles?"

"Thank you. I have dreamt of this moment for so very long."

Armand did not respond, but Kyreen felt the big man's intense pleasure at Xarles' words. When they had exited the tent, Armand scooped Kyreen up onto his shoulder. As she struggled to remain perfectly still despite his hand roaming across her bare skin, she realized Armand exuded no feelings of lust or desire. His emotions did not match his actions. This was simply the big man's attempt at intimidating her. So, she forced her body limp, resigned to ride on his broad shoulder.

Even before Armand tipped Kyreen onto her feet, her nose told her clearly where they were. She glanced down through the shadows to see a gaping hole between her feet which rested on smooth wooden planks. Armand pushed down on her shoulders forcing Kyreen into a squatting position. Only her natural abilities and sheer stubbornness of not wanting to touch the bandit kept her upright without grabbing his legs for support.

Armand grabbed a handful of Kyreen's hair, positioning his body so near her face she could not help but inhale his scent, a mix of stale sweat and musky sex. She bit back the bile rising in the back of her throat, refusing to pull away, to give him the satisfaction of a reaction.

Continuing her pragmatic attitude, Kyreen quickly did her business. Though Xarles did seem interested in keeping Kyreen healthy, who knew when she would next be offered the opportunity, she reasoned. She also wondered how long before the elves took her, or if they even would. She thought back to Xarles' comment from just the night before – which seemed so long ago. He referred to Kyreen as one of the Banished.

Lakwen'dil had used that term as well. Lakwen'dil! Even as her mind shouted the name, Kyreen murmured it aloud.

"What is that you said?" Armand growled, jerking her to her feet by her hair, returning Kyreen's thoughts to the present. She kept her gaze lowered, attempting to give the impression of submission, refusing to look up at him. For if Armand saw her true feelings reflected in her eyes, her fury and her loathing, he might forget Xarles wanted her unharmed. The big man glowered at Kyreen for several silent heartbeats before once again slinging the woman back over his shoulder, his hands once again crawling across her body as the pair made their way back to the main camp. At the campfire Armand paused.

Kyreen felt the spike in nervousness as the men fell silent.

"Where is Genevieve?" Armand asked.

For a long moment no one spoke. Kyreen felt a presence approach, and when he spoke she recognized the voice of Maurice from the previous evening.

"She was here, but left," Maurice said. "She sent Chimere over in her place."

"Chimere just returned this morning," Armand commented. "Xarles would not want her back out so soon."

Kyreen reflected at the calm tone Armand used. He did not sound or feel angry. He sounded almost bored but his emotions told her different. He exuded joyfulness. Though the big man's voice reflected detachment, Armand looked forward to whatever he planned to do.

"Maurice, take Chimere back to the herd tent," Armand ordered. "Without saying anything, gather up Genevieve and bring back here. Do not rush or make a fuss, but do not dally. Ensure

Genevieve knows that I requested her presence, but only after you arc on your way back. Do not tell her before you leave the herd tent. Do you understand?"

"Yes, Armand," Maurice replied. Kyreen felt the man's relief in full force as he moved away.

It did not take long for Maurice to return. He carried Genevieve over his shoulder much like Armand carried Kyreen. When he stood before Armand, Maurice stood Genevieve up and Armand moved Kyreen off his shoulder, keeping a grip on her upper arm as he gazed down at the dark woman. Though she gave no outward appearance of it, Kyreen felt the anxiety rolling off of Genevieve.

"Armand, I ..." the woman started to say, her words cut short by a backhand across her face. The force of Armand's blow rocked Genevieve down to her knees where she cowered. Just witnessing the strike made Kyreen's teeth hurt.

"Shut up unless spoken to," Armand snapped. Then he looked at Kyreen. "Genevieve, tell this one she better stay put and behave while I discipline you."

Kyreen looked down at the woman and waited for the message to be delivered in Genevieve's broken common. Once it had Kyreen replied, "I have an agreement with Xarles. Besides, I am not stupid enough to wander into the desert without clothes."

In hind sight Kyreen had to admire Genevieve's quick thinking especially under the stress of knowing Armand would be punishing her. In the moment, as the words rolled out of the small woman's mouth, however, a stunned Kyreen could only listen in horror.

"What did she say about Xarles?" Armand demanded.

"That he is a foolish man to think she would honor their agreement," Genevieve responded, her dark eyes focused on Kyreen's face glinting malevolently.

Even as Kyreen's mind wrapped around what Genevieve had said, around how Genevieve had shifted Armand's focus away from herself and onto this strange new woman, Kyreen also registered Armand's fury slamming into her. Though the big man's swing was swift and powerful, months of training guided Kyreen's dodge. She pulled back, breaking away from his grasp, twisting and ducking so that she landed crouched on the ground, out of Armand's reach. Dimly, in the far reaches of her mind, she acknowledged that this reaction would only make Armand angrier but her survival instinct had kicked in without conscious thought.

Shock ran through the gathered onlookers and Kyreen braced herself for Armand's lunge. From behind her, however, Xarles spoke quietly in elven, "Armand, hold!"

Armand glared at the crouching woman, but he did not move. "You heard what she said, Xarles?"

The bandit leader stepped up to stand behind Kyreen, who remained motionless, worried that if she stood she may draw Armand's attentions back fully onto her. Xarles rested his hand on top of Kyreen's head, his fingers gently pressing into her curls.

"Yes, I did hear her," Xarles remarked, "and Genevieve lied. Bijou did not insult me. In fact, she affirmed that she would honor the agreement she had with me."

Armand's big hands clenched into fists as his gaze shifted to the brown skinned woman cowering at his feet. He looked back up to Xarles. "What would you have me do, my captain?"

"Disperse punishments however you wish. It seems Genevieve has multiple transgressions for which she must pay," Xarles replied. "In the morning, I will deal with Genevieve's future in the herd. Therefore, safeguard that she can still speak when you are finished."

"Yes, my captain."

"I will take this one with me so she will not be a distraction," Xarles commented, pulling Kyreen back up to her feet. "When your business here is complete, Armand, come to my tent."

"Yes, my captain," Armand answered but Kyreen saw the big man's attention already focused on Genevieve.

"Come with me, Bijou," Xarles murmured in common.

Kyreen gladly complied. She had felt this morning that Armand's actions with Fanchon were simply a matter of routine. She really did not care to witness or feel up close the brutalities he had in mind for Genevieve, considering the woman had disobeyed his orders then lied to him in front of his men. Gritting her teeth as she walked behind Xarles, Kyreen steeled her own emotions, attempting raise a shield against the emotions flying around the camp fire. Her fingers itched to cast a protection ward, thus her attentions were not on Xarles and his emotions as they entered the tent.

Chapter 11

The instant the tent flap fell into place, Xarles turned to Kyreen, striking without warning an openhanded blow across her face. Despite her distractedness, Kyreen could have avoided him. Instead she refrained from moving and from striking him back.

"That is for lying to me," he commented in elven, moving towards a side table upon which a bowl of water and towels had been placed. His back to her, Xarles removed his soiled tunic and began to clean the blood from his hands.

Kyreen regarded the bandit leader thoughtfully for a few long moments. The strike from Xarles had been an open-handed slap. Her cheek would sting and be red for a while, but there would be no bruise as Armand's blow would have left had he connected with Kyreen's face.

"Do not further insult me by continuing the charade," Xarles remarked over his shoulder, drying his hands on a towel before pouring himself a cup of water.

"Very well," Kyreen conceded reluctantly in elven. "What gave me away, if I may ask?"

Xarles turned to regard Kyreen, his eyes widening with surprise. "How?"

"I am confused," Kyreen shook her head. "How what?"

"You are speaking the First Tongue perfectly, with no accent," Xarles said. He moved back over to stand in front of Kyreen, absently rolling the cup between his hands. "Tell me, Bijou. How an Easterner, one of the Banished, can speak the elven tongue perfectly, without hesitation or accent?"

"My name is not Bijou," Kyreen stated, stalling to give herself a moment to explain. She did not want to reveal Lakwen'dil's existence to this man if at all avoidable. Her thoughts raced, one scenario rejected after another, until she thought of Arvis. "My father's best friend was an elf. After my father died, he helped my mother raise me and..."

Kyreen managed to stop herself just before saying 'my brother'. Xarles did not need to know everything about her.

"And?"

"And he preferred speaking his native tongue," Kyreen answered. "That is how I learned to speak elven so well."

"Is it now?" Xarles murmured, reverting to common, taking a sip of his water. "I suppose your story about coming here to improve your magic skills was also a lie?"

"I did not want to tell you I looked for an elf," Kyreen shrugged. "I do not know the relationship the humans have with the elves. He left my home many years ago."

"What is this elf's name? Maybe I know him," Xarles said.

"Maybe you sold me to him?" Kyreen shot back, a challenge in both her voice and her face.

Her comment caught the bandit leader off guard and Xarles looked sincerely sheepish. He flashed Kyreen a lopsided grin, the expression making him look younger and enhancing his boyish good looks. His dark eyes twinkled as he chuckled, nodding his head.

"Well played," he remarked, taking another sip of water. His eyes apprised Kyreen over the cup's rim and she felt a change in his emotions towards her, a respect that had not been there before. "When Genevieve lied to Armand, I saw the look you gave her before Armand reacted. That is when I knew for sure, though I had harbored suspicions before that moment."

"If I may," Kyreen remarked, "I never said I could not speak elven. Everyone assumed I did not."

"And when I asked you about casting in common?" Xarles inquired, continuing to looked amused, clearly enjoying Kyreen's attempt to defend her deception.

"You asked how I cast magic in common and I answered truthfully," she countered. "I do not cast well in the language of the Old Kingdoms. I am no mage."

"Very well," Xarles remarked, draining his cup. "Armand is correct. You are wily like a fox. Twisting words, answering in half-truths and omitting information. Now I know and will not be so easy to fool."

"Easy to fool?" Kyreen scoffed. "Less than a full day and you figured out my ruse. Do not be modest. I would wager you are more crafty and wily on your worst day than I could ever dream of being."

While she kept her tone light and her expression relaxed, Kyreen struggled playing at this game of words, though she found a small part of herself enjoying her conversation with Xarles. Except for her brief time in the river town, most of Kyreen's interactions of late had involved Kyreen shielding herself from the other person's concern about Kyreen's wellbeing, but this man did not feel pity for Kyreen. Where the townspeople had been suspicious and guarded, Xarles' emotions were open, without judgement, cascading over Kyreen in exhilarating waves, radiating his admiration and amusement. In addition to the burgeoning respect, she sensed a growing interest in her coming from the man. If she did not dwell upon the previous evening's abduction, Kyreen could find his attitude towards her refreshing.

"Bijou, I want to see you cast," Xarles announced.

"Anything in particular?" Kyreen asked after a slight hesitation. She wondered what she could cast for him, looking forward to the opportunity, hoping she would have something worthwhile. Aside from practice sessions with Brigit she had never cast in front of anyone. What types of spells could she produce easily that would be visible? This was her opportunity to engage the bandit leader, to distract him, to figure out her escape. The elven lands were near. They had to be. If only she could slip from this camp and continue her search for her brother.

As the silence stretched on and Kyreen realized Xarles had not answered her question, she returned her thoughts to the present and glanced over at him. He had moved to set down his cup and now stood with his back to the side table, leaning lightly against it, looking the picture of casualness, another of his unfathomable smiles playing about his lips.

"Your mind," he said. "It wanders quite frequently."

Kyreen had thought she would be beyond embarrassment after the day's events but evidently not, for Xarles' words brought a blush to her cheeks. She dropped her gaze, murmuring, "Yes, it does."

He walked back over to her, placing an index finger under her chin to tip her face up. She did not resist the motion and reluctantly raised her eyes to his. The expression on the bandit leader's face—musing and inquisitive—caused the color in her cheeks to deepen.

"I would be very interested in discovering where it goes," he mused thoughtfully. "I am sure the journey would be fascinating."

For a long moment, they gazed at each other. This close Xarles' emotions enveloped Kyreen—respect, admiration, desire. For that brief moment she forgot where she was, how she came to be here, who she was, who he was. For one fleeting instant, she felt complete, not broken, undamaged. Then she came back to herself and remembered.

Mentally shaking her head, she made to step back, but Xarles' hand tightened on Kyreen's chin, his other raising up to clamp on her upper arm, and their amicable connection vanished. Her enmity and frustration flaring anew inside, she allowed the emotions to glitter in her eyes.

"Do not ever pull away, Bijou," Xarles cautioned quietly, unperturbed by her anger. "What you did out there, dodging Armand like that, in front of the others? That type of behavior is not tolerated in the herd. Only Genevieve's multiple transgressions gained you respite from retaliation, and only for a moment. Do not fool yourself into thinking you got away with something, Bijou. Armand will remember and he will make you pay."

"I am not herd," Kyreen spat between gritted teeth. They remained motionless, staring at each other, then she relaxed, flashing an insolent grin. "I suppose I should hope your meeting today was a success and I will not be long in your camp."

Xarles moved his hand from her chin to softly rest upon her cheek, gently caressing her skin, still red from the slap. His amused emotions confused her momentarily as he chuckled. "Oh, my dear Bijou. Clearly you do not know the elves. Nothing moves quickly with those people. I should not expect to hear anything from them for quite a while, not until the next full moon and only if they are very interested. It will be several months if you are of little concern to them."

Though Kyreen attempted to conceal her surprise, Xarles still saw the widening of her eyes and most likely felt the quickening of her pulse.

"You act like your time here in this camp, in the herd, with me is fleeting and temporary," Xarles continued, his low smooth voice amused, matching the gaze that still held her eyes. "It may be temporary, Bijou, but I doubt your sojourn with us will be fleeting. And do not waste energies planning an escape. That does not happen in this camp. I am a man who keeps a hold of that which he deems valuable."

With his warning complete, Xarles stepped back, placing both hands on Kyreen's shoulders to squeeze softly. Then he flashed her a broad smile. "Now, about your casting. What is your best spell?"

The abruptness of the change in topic and tone took Kyreen by surprise. She suspected this was Xarles' way for him to keep her off balance.

"Do you mean best as in the spell I cast most easily?" Kyreen asked. "Or best as in the one I use the most?"

"Both," Xarles replied, walking up the steps of the platform. He sat down on the top step, leaning back against the mattress. "We have time to explore all your spells, Bijou."

"In the desert, I concentrated on just a handful of spells, ones I found most helpful," Kyreen said. "Create water meant I could avoid watering holes. Create food meant I did not need to burden my pack with the extra weight of food. Although I will confess my created food is rather tasteless, much like when I attempt to bake. I do not know if it is the spell's fault or the caster's."

"Cast food for me," Xarles commanded.

Kyreen closed her eyes, pressing back her anxiety. Murmuring quietly, she moved her hands, mimicking the gestures she had learned from the diagrams in the journal. After a long moment she felt the pull of energies and the smell of magic wafted softly around her. Just as she had hoped, after all her practicing in the desert, the smell of magic no longer triggered the panic or fear inside her. When she opened her eyes, she looked down on the square brown block resting in her open palm. Unlike her first attempts at casting food, this piece was perfectly shaped, the surface smooth, the edges straight. Kyreen felt relief at having performed the spell for Xarles, but she felt more than that. She felt powerful and accomplished. A flash of exhilaration shot through her. She enjoyed showing off her skills. She did not attempt to quell the grin on her face as she looked up at Xarles.

"Very nice," he said. "Bring it to me. I want to taste it."

Kyreen stepped forward, making to climb the platform but Xarles raised a hand, commanding quietly, "Stop. Do not walk up here, Bijou. Get on your knees and present it to me."

Kyreen halted but did not kneel. She stood there, glaring at him, holding the cube lightly in her hand, trying to control the emotions coursing through her veins.

Xarles sighed. "Bijou, I am trying to instruct you on the law of the herd. It is better for all that you comply. Soon you will not be given so much leeway for noncompliance. You are an intelligent woman. Do not permit your stubborn pride to be your downfall."

Clenching her jaw, Kyreen dropped to her knees at the bottom of the platform. Staring up at Xarles, she extended her arms, lifting the cube in both hands.

"You look so fierce," Xarles chuckled, leaning down to take the food from her. He sat back and took a small bite. After chewing thoughtfully, he placed the brick of food to the side with a nod. "You are correct. It is bland. You can create that every day?"

"Yes," Kyreen replied, settling back in the kneel, her hands resting lightly in her lap. "I do have limits on how much I can cast every day. If I deplete my energies too much I start having issues getting the spells to work."

"What else can you show me?"

Kyreen thought a moment. "Most of the spells I have perfected were for my trek and would not be visible. I had protection wards on my camp. I made food and water. I also did light healing spells nightly."

"I had wondered," Xarles remarked. "You are in much better shape than anyone else I have ever known to come out of the desert. Most choosing the east passage do not survive."

Kyreen looked over to the low table where her knapsack listed against a table leg. "If I could retrieve something from my bag, I could do an illumination spell."

"I will get it. You stay there," Xarles said, rising to go to the knapsack. "What am I looking for?"

"A sphere about this big around," Kyreen replied, motioning with her hands.

Xarles opened the bag, peering in before reaching in. He pulled out a sphere, holding it up. With Kyreen's nod, he walked it over to place in her hands.

"Thank you," Kyreen said.

"At least you are polite," Xarles remarked taking his seat at the top of the platform steps.

At her questioning look he said, "Fanchon had a rebellious streak a little like you, except she was rude and vain and vocal about it. When she first arrived at the camp, she felt she was too good to be with the rest of the herd. She also proclaimed Armand to be a filthy animal who repulsed her. When the beatings had no affect and he tired of her verbal barbs, Armand took her tongue. Still she preened and acted out, so he disfigured her. Now that I cannot send her out to the caravans, she remains here to be available for the men in camp. But, since it is well known Fanchon is Armand's favored plaything, the men will never pick her, and their rejection of her humiliates her. Then there is what Armand does to her, making her body respond, getting her to cry out in passion after she compared him to a goat."

Kyreen listened, rolling the ball between her hands, her stomach churning. She could not be sure if her unease came from Xarles' story of Fanchon or from the increased turmoil she felt from outside this tent.

"Bijou, if you are going to continue to challenge Armand, you need to know what you are dealing with," Xarles continued quietly, his perceptive dark eyes focused on her face. "He is brutal. He is also creative and clever. My decree to keep you from looking abused will only go so far. He is up to any challenge thrown his way and does not back down."

Xarles looked toward the tent entrance. "Can you feel what is happening out there?"

"Some," Kyreen answered.

"Armand will have stirred the men up by now," Xarles commented. "He will have meted out a punishment for Genevieve that will include using her in every way imaginable with beatings in between, then Armand will have the men pass her around. The other women in the herd will be there, but only as witnesses to Genevieve's punishments. They will not be touched again tonight."

With a visual image to accompany the feelings she had been receiving, Kyreen feel truly ill. She swallowed the bile rising in her throat and focused her gaze on the sphere in her hand.

"Bijou, look at me," Xarles said quietly. When Kyreen lifted her gaze to him he continued, "What is happening out there is punishment, not abuse. Genevieve disobeyed and lied. She knew the consequences of her actions. Armand punishes Genevieve in such a manner because it causes her the greatest distress. That woman has a very high opinion of herself, thinking that her status as the head of the herd grants her protections and exemptions that it does not. Having her girls witness her punishment shames her that much more."

"Why tell me this?" Kyreen asked, her voice tight.

"Because you are so different than anyone else I have ever met," Xarles replied, his voice and expression sincere. "Because after the miracle I just observed I would truly mourn if you did not survive your stay here. Because, in order for you to survive your stay here, you need to understand what kind of man Armand is."

Kyreen lowered her gaze to the sphere once more. Under her breath she murmured the spell and maneuvered the ball until it began to glow softly. Continuing to speak softly she commanded the sphere to raise up slowly until it hovered in between them. Kyreen held the sphere for several moments before she could not continue and had to release the spell. As the sphere dropped down, she reflexively reached out, plucking it out of the air before it had a chance to drop to the floor.

"My apologies," she murmured, cradling the sphere in both hands, a soft sheen of perspiration glowed on her upper lip. "I am still trying to perfect that one."

"It is an impressive feat. You, Bijou, are impressive," Xarles remarked. "Aside from the elves, I have never seen anyone cast magic. Over the years, I have met many men who professed the talent of magic, but whenever I pressed these men, all they possessed were simple tricks, sleights of hand, elaborate illusions, nothing as wonderful as what you just showed me."

Kyreen felt a flash of pride hearing Xarles' praise. She knew his opinion should not matter. She knew she should not want to please him, just as she knew that given the chance, she would not hesitate to harm or even kill him if it meant her escape. Still she preened at the admiration radiating from this man. Xarles did not consider her a misfit, or a freak, or a blunderer. In his eyes, she was not aberrant or incompetent or broken. The look he gave her right now filled Kyreen with such potent energies and satisfaction and smugness. She felt powerful. Powerful and beautiful.

The instant those words crossed her mind, the memories began to leak out. Resolutely she slammed them back to the far recesses of the most shadowed corners of her mind. This internal struggle took but the blink of an eye and she managed to avoid any external responses. So, when Kyreen smiled up at Xarles, her eyes glittered, not with unshed tears but with newfound awareness of her abilities, of her potential, of her power.

Chapter 12

Setting aside the sphere, her gaze locked on Xarles, Kyreen began moving her hands once again. Quietly, she murmured the words memorized from the journal, a spell she had not had the confidence to attempt before now. The energies that responded to her gestures and her chants filled her senses. Her head swam with the sensation, exhilarating her to the point of inebriation. Deep inside she felt something move, something click, something change, and a fresh torrent of energy flowed through her, potent and alive.

When the flames burst out on her palms, Kyreen looked down at them and laughed, an almost giddy sound. So focused on the casting, so mesmerized by the fire flowing across her hands, Kyreen did not notice Armand enter the tent, but Xarles did. He held up a hand to halt the big man's progress with a shake of his head. Judging from the look in Kyreen's eyes, Xarles figured neither of the men in the room mattered or even existed to the woman wielding the magical fire in her hands. Knowing how she had responded to the raid upon her camp, Xarles did not wish to see what Kyreen could do with the flames if she were startled out of her trance.

"Bijou," Xarles said quietly, then once more he repeated the name. After the third time, he said, just as quietly, "Kyreen."

Slowly the woman lifted her gaze from the flames. When her eyes focused on him, Kyreen blinked and Xarles saw the recognition slip into place. Glancing down at her hands, she extinguished the flames and Xarles exhaled the breath he had not realized he had been holding.

"That was quite captivating," Xarles remarked to Kyreen in elven, before shifting his gaze to Armand. "She speaks elven."

Kyreen felt the surge of outrage from Armand. With his proximity, the force of his fury blocked out the rest of the emotions that had begun filtering in after the high of her casting. She did not move or turn to look at the big man, but she did tense up, her eyes narrowing, jaw tightening.

Kyreen had always felt competent when forced to defend herself. At this moment, however, coming down from the emotions of the spell, she felt so much more than competent. She felt confident, invincible even. Her hands, resting on her thighs as she knelt at the bottom of the platform, fisted in her lap.

"Bijou, look at me," Xarles said in a soft even tone, speaking in common. With reluctance Kyreen raised her gaze to his. Xarles was glad Armand could not see this woman's face at this moment. For his lieutenant would not have tolerated the naked boldness glittering in those green eyes.

"You and I have an agreement," Xarles reminded Kyreen in common. "We are being civilized this evening."

"You call this civilized?" Kyreen responded in common, her voice eerily calm, reflecting none of the emotions that shone in her eyes. "Me abducted from my camp, stripped of my belongings, kneeling naked at your feet? Tell me, how is that civilized?"

Armand shifted restlessly in the doorway. Though he did not understand what was being said, he was an intelligent man and he recognized the tension in Xarles. The dark-haired woman did not look tense from where he stood but he did not trust that one. His hand moved to the dagger on his belt. Xarles saw the motion and once again shook his head at the big man.

"I will strike him down if he so much as takes a step towards me," Kyreen promised Xarles, still speaking in common, and he believed her.

"I do not doubt you would," Xarles said, also continuing to speak in common, thinking that this conversation would go better if it remained just between him and her. "I also believe you are a smart woman. You cannot possibly eliminate both of us. If you go for him, I will, as much as it would pain me, kill you while your back was turned. If you go for me, then he will take you. He will not be as quick as I, but in either scenario, you will, eventually, be just as dead."

Seeing some of the tension in her body relax, Xarles leaned back before continuing, "You are my captive, yes. Yet you are unrestrained, ungagged, and unmolested. You have been fed and cared for. In this area, that is civilized treatment for a woman."

"And if I were a man?" Kyreen asked.

"If you were a man, Bijou, you would already be dead," Xarles admitted. "I have no need to keep any man around who is not my own brigand, especially one who is responsible for so many deaths."

"Yet you discard your own men without thought," Kyreen countered, remembering the three men Armand had killed last night. Had it been just last night? By the goddess, this had been an interminably long day and evening.

"The leader of these men cannot afford to be sentimental or become attached to anything or anyone," Xarles responded. Kyreen felt his remorse as he continued speaking. "The men know this. They know if they are careless enough to get injured or captured that their lives are forfeit. I cannot afford for word of your presence here to leak, especially if you are who I believe you to be."

Xarles stood up and walked down the steps to stand before Kyreen. She held still not pulling back as she desired, her eyes staring straight ahead for she refused to crane her head to look up at him, but she also refused to look down.

"Better," Xarles murmured in elven. He squatted so as to look into her eyes. "The hour grows late. As I said we have time, so we will continue the magic and the conversation tomorrow. Regarding tonight, I am sure you have thought about where you would prefer to stay."

Kyreen regarded Xarles silently. He had just reaffirmed she was his captive. Now he seemed to be asking her what she wanted. She bit her tongue, refusing to answer when all she wanted to do was blurt out 'anywhere but Armand's tent.'

Something must have shown in her face for Xarles nodded. He then gently took both of her hands in his and stood, drawing Kyreen up to her feet as well. Standing they stared at each other. Though Xarles stood slightly shorter than Kyreen, he still filled her senses, his presence such that he seemed much larger than he actually was. She inhaled deeply, relishing his intoxicating, exotic scent. Xarles released her hands and reached up with both his hands to push her curls away from her face, then almost tenderly held her face in his hands.

"I am not a man who enjoys taking his pleasure by force or by violence," Xarles told her, speaking again in common. "Those who share my bed do so willingly, without coercion, even eagerly. So, when I ask if you wish to stay with me, know that you have a choice, but remember so do I."

He paused to let his words settle in before continuing to speak. "You have used your mouth to speak your defense and your opinions very well tonight, Bijou. Now it is time to use your mouth to convince me that you desire to spend the night with me instead of Armand."

Again Xarles paused. When he felt sure Kyreen comprehended his words, he released her face and stepped back a half step.

"Kiss me, Bijou," he said quietly in elven. "Make me believe you wish to remain here."

As she moved to close the short distance between them, Xarles held up a hand. "Your mouth only. No hands. No body."

Kyreen stared at him for several heartbeats. Then she leaned in, angling her head slightly, to press her lips to the bandit leader's lips. Softly at first, she continued the kiss, tasting him, inhaling his exotic scent. Slowly she deepened the kiss as Xarles responded, though he never took control of the kiss. For several long moments Kyreen kissed Xarles, her mind spinning with a myriad of emotions while her body awakened to memories of kisses from another. Then the memories of Lang surged forward eagerly, finally released to swirl unchecked through her mind, memories of Lang's hands upon her body, Lang's warm breath tickling her skin, Lang's strong heartbeat under her ear. When Kyreen finally pulled away, her breath ragged, heart racing, a flush across her pale skin, she opened her eyes to gaze at Xarles with brazen desire, but the bandit leader saw beyond all that. Somehow, he saw and he knew her thoughts were not of him, but of someone else, and he shook his head.

"Armand, she stays with you," Xarles said in elven.

Armand moved quickly and quietly, coming to stand beside Kyreen even before Xarles finished speaking. Through her own disappointment, Kyreen felt the big man's jubilation as he clamped a beefy hand around her upper arm.

Xarles' gaze moved to Armand's hand, then he lifted his own hand to softly move across Kyreen's cheek, stroking gently at the skin no longer tinted pink from his earlier blow.

"Remember to take care and not bruise her," Xarles quietly remarked. "As long as her hands are restrained there is no need for the gag unless she gets cheeky."

"Yes, my captain," Armand said, tugging Kyreen away from Xarles, out of the tent and into the night.

Armand did not say anything as he pulled Kyreen through the night towards his tent, but she felt the two conflicting emotions inside the big man. He radiated joy, but the rage still simmered, waiting to explode.

The first thing Kyreen saw upon entering was Fanchon kneeling before the huge bed, just as she had the previous night. The expanse of golden silk glowed in the lamplight. Seeing the small woman and now knowing her story caused Kyreen a pang of sorrow.

"Look, Bijou," Armand remarked, tugging Kyreen towards the center pole. "Fanchon waits so patiently for us."

He chuckled as he snapped the steel collar around Kyreen's neck before fastening the shackles around her wrists and attaching them above her head to the pole. Leaving Kyreen standing with her hands well secured, her body stretched tall and lean, her back against the pole, he walked over to pour himself a cup of water which he drained while staring at the Calanian woman.

Kyreen tried to quell her discomfit as the big man's eyes roved her naked body, his emotions full of lust and power crashing over her, even as her Hanorian foster mother's words rang through her mind.

Ildri's voice, full of censure, enumerated one of the many lessons from the Ten Lords of Hayrik, "Nudity is a sin against the Lords. One must always shield one's body from others. Even in the bonds of matrimony one must be diligent. Our bodies are not our own. They belong to the Lords. Modesty in dress, modesty in thought, modesty in behavior...these are the principles to keep our body and soul sanctified, consecrated, a sacred place within ourselves, in which the Lords may reside, to watch over us, to protect us, to guide us."

When Armand finished his water, he walked towards Kyreen, pausing to squat in front of Fanchon, softly stroking the petite woman's ruined cheek, to croon quietly, "Poor little Fanchon, waiting here all alone while everyone else was having fun. I am afraid I may have spent all of my energies entertaining Genevieve and have nothing left for you, my pet."

Patting the top of Fanchon's head, Armand stood and moved over to Kyreen. "Besides I still have to deal with this one."

Kyreen had been distracted by Fanchon, feeling the woman's great relief at Armand's words. Even then she would not have, could not have anticipated Armand's next move. Grabbing Kyreen by the collar, Armand kicked Kyreen's knees out from under her, causing the Calanian to drop, the motion aided by his strong downward jerk. Though the steel of the collar dug into Kyreen's flesh, the pain was quickly overridden by a sharp pain in her shoulders. Her body dropped towards the floor, but her wrists, affixed firmly over her head to the pole behind her head did not budge. Despite the weight she had lost since entering the desert, Kyreen's shoulders were not designed to bear the full impact of her weight when her body jerked downward. With an audible pop, her right shoulder dislocated, quickly followed by another pop as the other shoulder followed. Blinding white hot pain caught Kyreen unaware and she let out a piercing howl. Dizzy and lightheaded, she writhed against her shackles, struggling to regain her footing, but Armand slipped a booted foot against her shins, pulling her lower legs up so it appeared Kyreen knelt on thin air. After a few heartbeats which felt like an eternity, Kyreen ceased her struggles. Panting heavily, she concentrated on slowing her breath, on finding her center, on working on a way to shut out the pain. Tears streamed down her face and the entire room swam before her. Even had she been permitted to stand, she doubted her legs could have held her as the tent tipped and whirled.

Her head lolled and Armand had to lower his own broad head to gaze up into her half-closed eyes, his hand on her collar pulling the steel tight against her windpipe.

"That," he hissed, "is for your deceit and your actions at the campfire. You are herd. You do as you are instructed. You do not lie and you do not pull away. Ever."

He released his hold on her and turned away. By the time he reached the other woman, Kyreen had dropped her feet to the ground, and stood shakily, grateful to relieve the weight on her shoulders. She gulped air, her windpipe burning. The initial pain had receded but her shoulder joints still throbbed and ached. The tears streaming down Kyreen's face dripped off her chin to land and trail along her quivering naked body.

Armand grabbed a handful of Fanchon's luxurious black hair at the nape of her neck in order to lift the small woman to her feet. Humming quietly, he brought her over to the center pole. Pointedly ignoring Kyreen, Armand began running the chain through Fanchon's collar, clicking the lock and patting her cheek affectionately. Then he ruffled Kyreen's hair and went back to the side table for another cup of water. As he drank, his dark eyes watched the two women over the rim of his cup.

When he put down the cup, Kyreen felt the change in his emotions. With the pain clouding her thoughts she did not have energy to wonder why the bandit suddenly exuded exhilaration as he watched them a few more moments.

Then Armand threw back his head and laughed. The booming noise reverberated off the canvas walls, the sound incongruous with the malice Kyreen felt from the big man.

"Oh, alright, my pet!" he chortled. "Do not look so despondent. I will not deprive you of your fun!"

Fanchon's fear hit Kyreen with a force so strong the Calanian gasped aloud. Both women, each mired in her own private terrors, watched as Armand stalked back to the center pole. Deep down inside, way down in a place where she did not have to acknowledge the feeling, sweet unadulterated relief flooded Kyreen with the realization that Armand's hands unfastened Fanchon's restraints, not hers. Later Kyreen would feel ashamed of the thought but right now, in this moment, the Calanian struggled not to sob with her overwhelming relief at this reprieve from the big man's attentions.

Fanchon made no sound as Armand picked her up and threw her onto the bed. Kyreen felt the small woman's strong resolve as Armand repeated the scene from the previous evening and this morning. Kyreen also felt when Fanchon's fierce determination dissipated a few minutes later and the humiliation seeped in. As the diminutive woman's moans filled the tent, Kyreen closed her eyes tightly, fighting to block out the noises coming from Armand's bed, the pain coursing through her body, and all of the emotions—inside and outside this tent—assaulting her senses.

Kyreen had no idea how long Armand kept at Fanchon. Exhaustion overtook the Calanian long before the bandit finally brought the other woman back to be fastened to the center pole. Armand tipped Kyreen's face towards him, chuckling at the pain-glazed eyes peering up at him.

"Get your rest, Bijou," he murmured, running the back of one broad hairy hand across her clavicle. "Tomorrow is another full day with many more adventures. It is time to have you branded, burn Xarles' mark upon his newest acquisition."

Then, abruptly, Armand kissed Kyreen. His big hand wrapped behind her head, fisted in her curls, yanking her so roughly that the pain erupted anew in her shoulders and Kyreen gasped her surprise. His broad tongue thrust into her mouth, taking her so viciously she felt just as violated had he assaulted her the way he just had Fanchon. Given time to think about it, Kyreen would have expected Armand's mouth to be as vile and unappetizing as his personality, a hovel of garlic and onions, but surprisingly Armand tasted only of the water he had just drank, his mouth warm and slightly moist. It was his anger and lust washing over her that nauseated Kyreen so tremendously that it took all of the Calanian's will power to not gag or pull away, to not provoke the big man any further, to not bring more punishment down upon herself. Even through her hatred and pain, Kyreen anguished at her cowardice as Armand's assault upon her lips continued. When he pulled back, the big man squeezed one of her shoulders, reigniting the piercing pain. Involuntarily, she inhaled sharply with the agony.

Armand remained standing close to the Calanian, his penis, broad and flaccid, nestling against her hip, while the rest of his naked body barely brushed against hers. He leaned back in to whisper in her ear, "Xarles said as long as your hands were restrained I could leave you ungagged. Do not make me get up to gag you. Do you understand, Bijou?"

Mutely, Kyreen nodded.

Armand grabbed a handful of hair, tugging her head to the side, reigniting the pain in her shoulders with the motion. "I asked a question, Bijou. Herd answer when asked a question."

"Yes," Kyreen gasped between gritted teeth.

"Good girl," Armand chuckled softly, releasing her with a final ruffle of her hair and padding back to his bed.

In moments the tent fell silent save for Armand's deep steady breaths of sleep. Though Fanchon made no sound, Kyreen could feel her emotions, could sense the tears being shed by the small woman curled in a tight ball beside her.

Chapter 13

Kyreen did not know how long she stood in the dark, fading in and out of consciousness, unable to fully relax, but darkness still shrouded the tent when she became aware of the change in atmosphere. Armand's breathing quieted. Everything else faded away as well. The little nighttime noises that are always present but unnoticed in the background silenced. All of the emotions Kyreen had been sensing throughout the evening disappeared. The only thing that remained constant was her pain, both physical and emotional.

Suddenly Kyreen realized a body stood in front of her. For one short panicky instant she thought Armand had awakened without her notice and had come to inflict another punishment. Instinctively, she jerked back, releasing a fresh wave of pain.

"Shh, child," Kyreen's dead mother's voice comforted in the dark, a gentle hand smoothing Kyreen's sweaty brow. With the touch, Kyreen's pain receded and she could once again breathe freely.

"Lakwen'dil," Kyreen whispered hoarsely, more a prayer than a greeting.

"Yes." The restraints holding Kyreen's wrists to the pole released and her arms fell useless to her sides. Leaning heavily against the pole to her back, Kyreen slowly collapsed to a sitting position. Hot, salty tears of relief and shame seeped from Kyreen's closed eyes, leaving fresh, wet trails down her face. When the woman opened her eyes, the spirit had raised the lighting in the tent so Kyreen could gaze upon her mother's form. For once the Calanian felt only gratitude at seeing her dead mother's image.

Tyra's form squatted down to gaze upon the injured woman. "I leave you alone for just a moment and you disappear from your path."

Kyreen shook her head slowly, unable to follow the spirit's words clearly. "You were gone...days."

"Your time is different." Lakwen'dil waved a hand dismissively and stood.

She moved to stand over Fanchon. The small dark woman lay in a tight ball, her black hair pooling about her in an inky puddle. Lakwen'dil squatted once again, softly stroking the woman's hair. Kyreen lolled her head to watch the spirit, who lifted Tyra's face to gaze back at the Calanian.

"You have wandered into interesting territory," the spirit commented.

Kyreen barked a hoarse laugh, her mouth so parched it took her multiple tries to speak. "I did not wander. I was brought forcibly and without consent."

"Whatever the case, I wonder at your treatment of each other," Lakwen'dil's gaze dropped to the unnatural jutting of Kyreen's shoulders. "How do you gain pleasure from inflicting pain, from witnessing another's agony? Sometimes I believe I shall never understand you."

Kyreen glanced to the bed where she could see Armand's big form moving as he breathed. A part of her grieved that the spirit had not killed the bandit while another part felt relieved that Kyreen would still be able to be the one to kill that particular man. She smiled tiredly, an expression that looked more like a grimace. "Some people earn their pain."

Lakwen'dil followed Kyreen's gaze. Then she stood up to move over to the bed where Tyra's eyes looked down on the slumbering man. "Yes, I suppose you do," the spirit remarked quietly.

Kyreen allowed her eyes to drift shut, basking in the blissful reprieve from pain. She might have drifted away, dozed a few minutes. For the next time she opened her eyes, Lakwen'dil had returned to squat before the Calanian. Kyreen thought she must be feeling better because the completely neutral scrutiny of her mother's gaze now made Kyreen decidedly uncomfortable.

"I could only find you because you called me to you," the spirit commented. "Just as I can only help you if you ask me to help."

"No," Kyreen whispered, slowly moving her head back and forth, a lazy shaking of the negative. "I am not so far gone as to ask a favor from the likes of you."

"Really?" the spirit crooned, softly brushing a finger along Kyreen's cheek.

With a vengeance the pain exploded fresh in Kyreen's body. Caught by surprise, the woman gasped loudly, unable to stay a fresh volley of tears from springing to her eyes. In a heartbeat, the pain disappeared. For several moments the only sound in the tent came from Kyreen's struggle to catch her ragged breath.

When she could speak again, Kyreen said, "That…was not a nice thing to do."

Lakwen'dil rocked back on her heels, chuckling. "Nice? What do I know of nice?"

"Still," Kyreen responded, pausing to clear her throat. "Either take the pain or leave it. Quit toying with me. I am not a plaything."

Lakwen'dil glanced over to the bed then back at Kyreen. "You may be wrong about that, but I am gracious. The pain will stay away."

"Th…that is most gracious," Kyreen responded. With the fatigue of the evening clouding her mind she very nearly thanked the spirit.

"Do you still affirm you do not need my assistance?" the spirit asked, gently caressing Kyreen's tear stained cheek.

Kyreen allowed her eyes to close once more. The spirit's touch frightened the woman almost as much as Armand's. Neither one's attentions were safe she knew, but, also, she had something that needed to be done. It might be time, she thought, to take a chance.

"I can make sure that one never hurts you again," Lakwen'dil suggested, her hand lightly skimming across Kyreen's shoulders. "I could take you away from here. I could heal your wounds. This close to *Talamh sa bhaile Si'*, my powers are much stronger."

Kyreen's mind raced, remembering her priorities. She focused on the first priority, getting a message to Brigit, but she had to make very sure that her request of the spirit did not fail, did not make matters worse, as so often happened in the tales of fairy favors. Once she felt she had examined her limited pool of possibilities, Kyreen opened her eyes to gaze into her mother's face.

"Lakwen'dil," Kyreen croaked hoarsely. "If it pleases you, may I request your favor in exchange for my agreement to acquiesce a return favor of your choosing?"

Tyra's green eyes gazed at Kyreen for several long moments. Then the spirit grinned a slow self-satisfied smile of triumph. "You have made a generous offer, my child."

"Yes," Kyreen whispered.

"If I grant you this favor, you will be in my debt."

"Yes," Kyreen's throat felt so very dry she could barely speak. Her eyes would have watered anew had her body any moisture to spare.

"I may request anything of you," the spirit remarked, more of a statement than a question.

Still Kyreen answered, "Yes."

"Your life would be forfeit. Your future mine."

"Until which time you redeem your favor," Kyreen reminded the spirit. "Yes."

Lakwen'dil stood up to walk about the room. Her strides were not quick or long enough to be a pace, but more of a thoughtful, leisurely stroll.

"An even trade then?" the spirit asked. "One favor for one favor?"

"Yes," Kyreen replied.

The spirit paused to look down at Kyreen. "I cannot bring you back. That is beyond my power. Once you have departed these realms to enter the fifth hall and drink from the Chalice of the Hereafter you are beyond my reach."

Kyreen realized the spirit referred to her dead loved ones and slowly shook her head. "Good to know, but that is not my request."

"Very well," Lakwen'dil remarked, squatting down before Kyreen once more. "We have an accord. What do you desire? Is it death to those who hurt you? Escape from this wretched cesspool? Power to wreak your revenge yourself?"

"A message," Kyreen responded, her voice quiet in the silent tent. "I need to send a message to my friend, to Brigit, to the mage."

The spirit blinked in surprise. Clearly this had not been something she expected. Then she frowned. "A message? You are certain?"

"Yes," Kyreen replied.

"But this is something you can do. You can be assured, I will not squander my request of you in such a manner," the spirit commented.

Kyreen looked down at her numb arms then at the spirit. "At the moment I do not have the means to cast, let alone send a message. Will you do it or not?"

"No need to get testy with me, child," Lakwen'dil cautioned. "Of course, I will do it. Are you ready?"

"Ready for what?"

Lakwen'dil stood up. "To deliver your message. The mage has my talisman."

Without any outward motion, the spirit opened a circle in the middle of the tent, a window through which Kyreen could see a room with rough, stone walls. Her heart caught in her throat as Kyreen remembered another stone-walled room, one much smaller, vacant of any furniture. Then she reined in her thoughts and focused her gaze upon the bed, where, beneath heavy blankets to ward out the cold, lay two forms, one of which sat upright when Lakwen'dil's portal illuminated the room.

"Brigit?" Kyreen cried out hoarsely then looked with horror at Armand's bed where the big man slumbered on.

"He and the broken child are spelled," Lakwen'dil said. "As is the child in the mage's bed."

"Munin is not a child," Brigit retorted, peering into the portal. "Princess? As flattered as I am to see you unclothed, may I say, you look horrible. What happened to you?"

Kyreen chuckled, then coughed. "I thought this might be the best way to get your full attention."

Brigit slipped from the bed, not bothering to cover her own naked body, and approached the portal. Without touching anything, the mage leaned in as close as possible, inspecting the portion of the tent visible from the Calanian side.

"Are you making friends again, Princess?" she asked, unable to keep the worry from her eyes.

"You might say that," Kyreen replied. "I need you...need you to stay there. Stay in Calan. Until I send another message."

"But I can..."

"No!" Kyreen interrupted. "Please Brigit, I do not know how long the portal will remain open. I cannot explain everything now. I will as soon as I can. For now, please simply listen. The amulet and scrying orb are not in my possession. I can take care of myself but not it I am worried for your safety."

Kyreen paused to catch her breath and Brigit took the opportunity to say, "You sound, and look, like you need help, Princess."

"I have the situation in hand," Kyreen took a deep breath to quell her frustration then stared at the mage, adding quietly, "I am asking you to trust me. Do not come here until you hear from me."

Something in Kyreen's voice or her eyes finally registered with the mage. The humor slipped fully out of the Brigit's eyes and her voice became eerily calm. "I do trust you, Kyreen."

"Good. I traded favors with Lakwen'dil to get you this message so do not make it for naught by getting impatient."

"How long shall I wait?" Brigit asked.

Kyreen gave a moment's thought. Harvest season loomed too close. If the elves moved as slow as Xarles said she may not be free by then. Aloud she said, "If you do not hear from me by the winter solstice, then assume I was unable to locate Quillan or Arvis. Do not transpire to the amulet. The man who holds it is not one to be trifled with. He is ruthless and intelligent."

"Why do I have the impression that you are trifling with him?" Brigit interjected with a quirk of an eyebrow.

"I am working on a plan to escape this trap, which I cannot do while worrying about you," Kyreen retorted, her anxiety and exhaustion making her short tempered.

"Princess, I did not know you cared," Brigit joked, falling back into her habit of injecting humor when she felt sentimental.

For a few moments the two women stared at each other. Neither feeling comfortable enough to break the silence until Lakwen'dil spoke from where she knelt beside Fanchon, softly stroking the sleeping woman's hair.

"Is the message delivered?" the spirit asked, pulling Kyreen back to the present.

"One more thing," Kyreen said, her voice grim. "Brigit, if I make any reference to Olavi when we talk, then it has become too dangerous. Sever the connection and make sure no one can reach you from here. Do not attempt to contact me. Take cautions against anyone reaching Calan. I do not trust these men, especially their leader. If he figures out that I can communicate with you, that you can transpire here, that you are such a talented mage, I believe he would stop at nothing to add you to his herd."

"Not very nice people you seem to be meeting on this little trek, Princess."

"No, they are not, which is why I need you to stay away. To stay safe," Kyreen repeated. She prayed to the goddess that Brigit would listen. Maybe she would for a few days, a fortnight perhaps, but long before Winter Solstice arrived, the mage would surely grow impatient and attempt to locate Kyreen. At least this message would have bought Kyreen a little more time. She did have the beginning of a plan but she needed time.

Bringing her thoughts back to the present, Kyreen smiled through the portal. "Take care, my friend. I do wish I were there with you now. With you and Munin."

She gave Brigit a wink then looked at Lakwen'dil. "It is complete."

The portal collapsed even as Kyreen finished speaking and before Brigit could recover enough to react to Kyreen's impromptu flirtation.

Lakwen'dil stood up, stretching like a feline before grinning down at Kyreen. "That seemed too simple. I almost feel bad asking for my favor in exchange."

"You do not have to take a favor if you do not want to," Kyreen remarked.

The spirit laughed. "Almost, child, almost. No, you will give me my favor and it shall be wondrous."

Kyreen wearily leaned her head back on the pole. "I hope you do not expect that favor tonight."

"No," replied the spirit reaching out a finger to lightly touch the center of Kyreen's forehead. "Not tonight, my child. Tonight, you sleep."

And Kyreen slept.

Chapter 14

When Kyreen opened her eyes she immediately became aware of a hand on her thigh, softly shaking her awake. Pressing back her initial flare of panic, Kyreen gazed through the semi-dark to Fanchon. Once the diminutive woman saw Kyreen was awake, she began to pantomime wildly gesturing towards Kyreen's unbound hands.

Adrenaline flowed anew when Kyreen discerned what had Fanchon so agitated. Lakwen'dil had released the shackles on Kyreen's wrists. Armand would be furious if he awoke to see Kyreen unfettered. Kyreen doubted the bandit would believe a spirit had released her so he would think either that Kyreen had done so magically or, more likely, think Fanchon had released her.

After a failed attempt to gather her feet under her and rise up, Kyreen quietly said, "I cannot stand up on my own."

Fanchon gestured to Kyreen's shoulders emphatically shaking her head, making soft, urgent grunts from the back of her throat.

"Yes, it will hurt!" Kyreen whispered. "But you have to help me."

Awkwardly the smaller woman assisted the taller one to a standing position. As painful as that act had been it did not compare to the sheer agony when Fanchon pulled Kyreen's hands over her head, straining to reach up and click the shackles back into place on the Calanian's wrists. Kyreen managed not to cry out or moan, but just barely. As Fanchon returned to her curled-up position on the floor, Kyreen concentrated on centering, on slowing her heartbeat, on quieting her breathing. None of which she completely accomplished before Armand sat up just a few short moments later. Thankfully the big man woke up distracted and did not notice Kyreen's struggles.

Having been so focused on her dilemma inside this tent Kyreen had not spared any thoughts to what her senses had been getting from outside. Armand, however, heard the commotion as soon as he awoke. Kyreen reckoned the unusual activity outside had been what had awakened the man. He swiftly pulled on his trousers and boots, striding out into the early morning grayness without acknowledging either woman, except for a quick glance to assure both still waited for him.

When the tent flap fell back down behind Armand's exit, Kyreen looked over to Fanchon. The other woman had lain back down, avoiding eye contact with Kyreen so the Calanian resolved herself to thinking of her escape plans while waiting for Armand's return.

She had no idea where this camp lay in relation to the elf lands. From what little she had seen yesterday, they were still in the desert. She needed to find the mountains, get herself oriented. She would need transportation. The bandits had horses. She would need clothes, preferably her own, along with her other belongings. That meant being able to access Xarles' tent.

While Kyreen was still pondering the details of her half-concocted escape plan, Armand walked back in followed by another man. The Calanian did not glance up, did not want to give the impression she was curious, but most of all did not want to let Armand know how well she felt this morning. The pain of standing and having her wrists reshackled aside, Kyreen felt better than she had in a very long time. Whatever spell Lakwen'dil had cast upon Kyreen had done a wonderful job of restoring the Calanian's health.

Armand released Fanchon first, giving the woman a slap on the ass, saying, "Go directly back to the herd tent."

The big man's voice held no mirth, no teasing, only a harsh command. While the bandit was cruel and unpredictable in the best of circumstances, Kyreen felt a new type of anger from Armand. This fury echoed in his voice, leaving no room for anything else. As Fanchon scurried from the tent, Kyreen wondered what had happened outside the tent, out in the camp. Then Armand turned his gaze on Kyreen. She steeled herself, barely succeeding in not visibly reacting.

Kyreen began sensing the other man standing behind her just out of her line of sight. His nervousness washed over her, a familiar emotion. Once again Kyreen wondered what had Pierre so nervous.

All of the bandits exuded a slight nervousness around Armand but this man's anxiety level far exceeded that of even Fanchon, whose emotions were more pure terror than nervousness.

Before she could give much more thought to the issue, Armand moved to stand directly behind Kyreen, and began unshackling her wrists, making her own nervousness spike.

"Pierre, stand in front of Bijou," the big man commanded. "Press up against her, pin her to the pole."

Even as Pierre complied, his clothing rough against her skin, and Kyreen wondered what Armand had planned, the big man grasped the elbow of her right arm. Lifting up and out and twisting with a firmness that told Kyreen this was not Armand's first time doing such a maneuver, the bandit slipped Kyreen's shoulder back into place with a loud pop. The initial pain of the movement made her draw in a sharp breath but the relief after was divine. Deftly and quickly Armand set the other shoulder.

Pierre's anxiety broke through Kyreen's own emotions. This close, with his warmth pressing against hers, she finally recognized an underlaying of terror to the man's nervousness. Then she caught scent of a familiar smell—magic. Without thinking Kyreen grabbed Pierre's arms, holding him against her even as he attempted to step back. She gazed into the man's eyes, looking for answers she did not have the skills or talent to intuit.

"Bijou likes you, huh, Pierre?" Armand chuckled, tugging the collar around her neck to pull her away from the man she clung to. "I will remember that when we initiate her into the herd. Give you an early turn at her. You would like that, eh?"

Pierre nodded, a charming smile sliding across his face, none of his internal struggle visible. "Oh, yes, Armand. Very much."

The two men laughed as Armand fastened Kyreen's wrists behind her back and released the ankle shackles. Armand handed Pierre the chain.

"Take her to the smith. Have Fabrice stoke the fires, but do not begin without me."

Armand grabbed Kyreen's collar, pulling her up onto her tiptoes, shoving his face close to hers. "Do not cause trouble."

"Would never dream of it," Kyreen retorted before she could think through his possible reactions.

Armand twisted the collar tighter, lowering his voice. "You just wait, little fox. You think you are clever? You think the elves will save you? No one is coming for you. When Xarles finally realizes you have no value to the faerie folk, I will be there to welcome you to your place in the herd. It might be next moon or several after that. No matter. I am a patient hunter. Your body will be mine."

With his warning delivered, Armand released the collar and, producing a rag from his pocket, stuffed the cloth in her mouth.

"Do not release her hands and keep her gagged," Armand instructed, motioning for Pierre to take Kyreen, even as he reached for his discarded tunic. "I shall be there shortly."

As soon as Pierre tugged Kyreen outside the tent, he slung her up over his shoulder. This time the bandit ensured Kyreen's head hung down his back, although with her arms secured behind her back and her shoulders still throbbing, Kyreen was in no position to attempt overpowering her escort. Hanging with her head close to the man's shirt she caught a whiff of magic once more.

Filing this fact away for later use, Kyreen swiveled her head, taking in the camp sights. She caught a glimpse of the mountains, verifying the camp sat along the border between the desert and the foothills of the tall mountains. The sun had just begun to clear the vast desert horizon to the east but already the air hung heavy with the promise of the impending heat, the sun's rays slowly chasing away the night, infusing the cool air with warmth. In the blue shadows of the dawn Kyreen took note of the tents they passed, then the center fire which served as the men's evening gathering spot – the area now empty, the fire extinguished until dusk. By the time Pierre stopped walking Kyreen had a fairly good idea of the camp's layout and orientation to the mountains where the elf lands lay.

The bandit tipped Kyreen onto her feet in front of a tent where a man worked at rolling up a canvas wall. Two of the walls had already been raised to expose the accoutrements of a blacksmith

– a forge waiting to be stoked, a bellows, a huge anvil, and an assortment of tools hanging from the ceiling.

"This her, then?" the man asked over his shoulder. Though he stood about Kyreen's height, his work had made him almost twice as wide as the Calanian and not one bit of his bulk was fat. With arms bigger than most men's thighs, he finished rolling up the last canvas wall before turning to take a good look at Kyreen. The blacksmith's gaze held no emotion except the expert appraisal of a tradesman.

The man ran a hand across his dark stubbled chin. "I had heard she was a fair one. She will mark easy enough but the scar will be light. Most likely it will never raise up, never be prominent like with the darker girls."

"You can tell him yourself when he gets here," Pierre responded with a shrug. "Armand said to wait for him."

"Very well then. I best get this old thing heating." The blacksmith walked into the tent to stoke the forge.

Pierre moved Kyreen over to the side where they stood watching the activity of the camp, or rather Pierre watched the activity. Kyreen noted the number of tents and the location of the horse pens, all without moving her head. She also noticed the lone tent off to the side, where she presumed Gautier, the man who ignited hatred in Xarles, was being held. From this distance she could not sense any emotions. Kyreen did not know how long they waited, but, by the time Armand strolled up, the forge fires had heated up the area so that both Kyreen and Pierre had a layer of perspiration on their face.

The man holding Kyreen's arm had been fairly relaxed as they waited. His anxiety soared, however, with the arrival of Armand. While Armand went up to the blacksmith, calling him Fabrice, Kyreen turned her head to gaze fully upon Pierre. The man stood at an average height, neither tall nor short, with an average build, neither heavy nor thin, his nondescript brown hair shaggily cut, neither long nor short, and several days' growth of brown beard upon his average face. Even the eyes he now turned on Kyreen were an average brown.

"What is your problem, woman?" Pierre hissed at Kyreen. "Quit looking at me."

Kyreen smirked as well as she could with the gag in place. Her single raised eyebrow daring him to do something to make her avert her gaze. Armand picked that moment to call out for Pierre to bring Kyreen into the tent.

Fabrice grabbed Kyreen's hair, pulling it back into a band, then began swabbing the left side of her chest just under her clavicle, right above the rise of her breast. The liquid he applied felt cool and dried quickly. A sterilizer Kyreen presumed.

Ever since Armand had made his off-handed comment about having Kyreen branded, she had kept pushing the thought away, having other more important matters to focus upon such as messaging Brigit and dislocated shoulders. Now, confronted with the inevitable prospect of this blacksmith picking up one of the tools currently resting within the fires to press a mark into her skin, Kyreen suppressed the flare of panic. She knew that in her current state—restrained and weakened—she could never fight off these three men. Though she had never seen branding, as it was no longer practiced in the Old Kingdoms, she had read about it. Kyreen fully expected it would be an excruciatingly painful experience, which would explain Armand's jubilance, though his happy mood continued to be marred by an underlying tension.

"The wrists need to be released to get the area to lay right," the blacksmith commented, bringing Kyreen's thoughts back to the present.

Armand moved behind her to unlock the restraints. He then instructed Pierre on how to hold Kyreen from behind, leaning her body fully against the anxious man.

"You like that, Bijou?" Armand asked, moving to stand in front of her, taking her face in his hand to squeeze tightly as he pulled the gag out with the other hand. "I see you looking at Pierre. Does he remind you of the east? Do you crave his cock inside you?"

"Hold her other shoulder," Fabrice instructed Armand, who shook his head.

"No, Fabrice. You hold her," the big man replied. "This wench is mine to mark. She will scream loudly, knowing it was me who inflicted her pain. Then, once she is fully incorporated into the herd, writhing beneath my hand and crying out in passion, I will gaze upon her mark and remember this moment with great pleasure."

Kyreen closed her eyes and began silently reciting her morning ritual. These words, handed down through the generations, had served to center and focus Kyreen since before her first memories, but Armand's words right now had focused her in a different way. The big man, completely unaware of his part, had shown Kyreen her goal, her firm determination that she would never give him the satisfaction of her screams. As always, once she had her goal, Kyreen could find her path. Pushing away the external chatter of the men's emotions, Kyreen channeled her energies, visualizing the waterfall, centering just as Lang had taught her, silently reciting her mantra. Calmness descended upon Kyreen more quickly than it ever had. Whether it was the result of her first full night of restful sleep since Lang's death or last night's connection with Brigit, seeing Calan, speaking with her friend, not worrying about the mage's safety, Kyreen did not have time to wonder why.

An instant after Kyreen centered, Armand lifted a thin metal rod from the fire and pressed it to her skin. Instead of bracing, instead of anticipating, instead of resisting, Kyreen relaxed against the man behind her, allowing her energies to expand, to meld with Pierre's. She reached out, diverting the flow of energies around Armand, guiding them to flow through the blacksmith and then through his fire. When the red-hot metal strips shaped into the mirrored image of two crescent moons touched her skin, Kyreen let the energy of the brand flow into her. The pain registered far away, in the back reaches of her mind, and she did not even flinch.

Fabrice's angry bark at Armand to pull off the brand brought Kyreen back to herself, back to the present. Though her chest felt as though it were on fire, she knew the worst of the pain had passed. Fabrice snatched the rod from Armand's hand, tossing it on a table before turning to inspect Kyreen's burnt flesh.

"Dammit, Armand," the blacksmith muttered. "You may have gone too deep."

When she opened her eyes to gaze back at the big man staring at her, his eyes full of rage, a realization jolted through Kyreen. Armand was no threat to her. Not really. There was nothing that this brute could do to her that could surpass all she had already endured. Kyreen had borne the separation from her twin, the hostilities of the Hanorian people, the disdain of her own people upon her return, Sten's enthrallment, Lang's death. Any physical damage Armand could inflict upon her could never surpass any of those previous trials. Whatever he did, he would do, and she would survive. No, she would do more than survive, she would live. To her surprise, Kyreen realized that she did want to live. Yes, she would always mourn Lang, but to give up? To continue to wallow in the aftermath of his death? This would be an insult to Lang, to the vibrant person he had been, to their love.

Kyreen glanced down at the angry looking wound in her chest. The sight made her want to flinch but she remained outwardly calm. The smell of burning flesh, her burning flesh, filled her nose, making her empty stomach churn. Still, she kept her body relaxed, shifting against the man holding her from behind. Even without her empathic abilities, the hard bulge digging into her backside gave testament to the fact Pierre had enjoyed Kyreen's branding. Her pain and the anticipation of her pain had excited him, both physically and emotionally. Kyreen suppressed a growl as she calmly gazed at Armand.

"Are we done here?" she asked, calmly, evenly, tilting her head and arching an eyebrow.

Kyreen saw the blow when it first bloomed in Armand's fury filled eyes. She had time. She had space. Pierre had released the hold around her waist. With her hands unshackled and her mouth ungagged, she could have dodged. She could have parried her own counter strike. She could have even cast a defensive spell. Instead she allowed the big man's big hand swing towards her head without moving, without flinching, without looking away from Armand's gaze.

The blacksmith also saw the blow. He also had time. Fabrice reacted with lightning fast reflexes honed from years of working with red hot steel that sometimes sputtered or spilled. The blacksmith wrapped his hand around the hammer fist Armand swung, making the move look effortless.

"Not in my tent," Fabrice remarked stepping between the bandit and Kyreen. "Out there you do as you wish. In here, such antics cause accidents. The wrong people get hurt."

Armand looked like he could just as easily turn his rage onto the blacksmith but he paused, looking down at the shorter though just as broad man for a long moment. Then he barked a laugh.

"This is your palace, Fabrice," he said. "I will abide by your decree. Damn lucky you make the best weapons this side of the Salandingar."

"Any side of the Salandingar, Armand," Fabrice countered with his own laugh and Kyreen felt the tension between the men dissipate. "I put my work up against anything here or across the sands."

Armand nodded, then shifted his gaze to Pierre. "Take her to Xarles' tent. I have a few more rounds."

Then Armand walked out of the tent, completely ignoring Kyreen, who could not stop a soft exhalation of relief at his exit. Her knees felt shaky and the tent swam before her vision as she looked at the blacksmith. She could not say if her reaction stemmed from her face-off with the big man, her empty stomach, or the intense pain pulsing from her chest, perhaps a combination of all three.

Fabrice produced a small jar, a floral scent wafting out when he uncapped it. With two fingers, the blacksmith scooped up a small dab of salve, which he smoothed across Kyreen's burnt skin. When she tried to look down to watch, her body swayed and Pierre had to steady her. She gazed down at Pierre's hand gripping her upper arm a moment before turning her eyes to the blacksmith.

"I like you," she proclaimed. "You, dear blacksmith, may be the only man in this camp that I do not feel compelled to kill."

Fabrice chuckled putting the lid back on the salve before handing it to Pierre.

"Xarles will want this," he said, wiping his hands on a rag. "Now get her out of my tent. I have real work to do."

Chapter 15

Pierre tugged Kyreen into the morning sunlight. She squinted against the brightness. After the forge's intense heat in the tent, the desert heat did not feel so terribly warm, an illusion that quickly melted away.

As Pierre moved to pick up Kyreen, she took a step back, shaking her head. "Not so fast."

Pierre shot her a dark look and she briefly wondered if she should have added some term of endearment like 'handsome' or 'darling.' For her plan to work, Kyreen would need to give some thought to her bantering skills. She never thought she would miss Brigit's sass. She smiled thinking of her friend and pressed forward.

"I am simply looking out for you, my dear," Kyreen said, bringing her wrists together and wriggling her fingers, "Someone would be in big trouble if I were to overpower him because I was not properly restrained."

Pierre mumbled an obscenity under his breath, dragging Kyreen back under the blacksmith tent to retrieve the shackles. A few moments later Kyreen rested up on Pierre's shoulder riding back towards Xarles' tent. In his haste the bandit had not only fastened Kyreen's hands in front of her, he had completely overlooked gagging her. As she jostled thru camp, Kyreen mentally reviewed the many ways – both magical and physical – that she could escape Pierre's grasp. Her real problem, she silently acknowledged to herself, was not getting free, it was staying that way. Without the proper planning and resources, she would not get very far before these bandits would catch up and recapture her. While Kyreen did not fear Armand, her recently renewed desire to remain living tempered her actions. No reason to push the big man into a murderous rage when it could be avoided with a little forethought.

When the pair entered his tent, they found Xarles sitting at his dining table. The bandit leader glanced at Kyreen's hands shackled to the front to her body, then looked up at her face. His concern washed over her, giving her a boost of confidence. Waving her fingers at Xarles, Kyreen shrugged awkwardly from atop Pierre's shoulder, then flashed a grin she hoped looked like the impish ones Brigit always donned. Pierre approached the table at which Xarles sat, intending to place the jar of salve on the table, but Xarles grabbed the other man's wrist, staying the motion, his eyes never leaving Kyreen's face.

"Go easy on the poor boy," Kyreen purred to Xarles in common. "He is so very stressed being in here with you."

Xarles glanced quickly at Pierre then back at Kyreen. The bandit leader stood up, releasing his grasp on the other man's wrist, commanding, "Set her down."

After Pierre had complied, Xarles moved over to Kyreen. Even as he reached out for her wrists, the bandit leader's eyes dropped down to the fresh brand upon her chest. Xarles' burst of anger washed over Kyreen though he did not exude any change in emotion or tone as he said in elven, "You cannot be lax around this one, Pierre."

"My apologies, Xarles," Pierre responded. Both of these men's outward composure amazed Kyreen, who felt Pierre's anxiety cresting as he watched Xarles, still seething anger, efficiently fasten Kyreen's shackles behind her back.

The bandit leader still wore only the loose fitting black pants, his tan torso and feet bare. Standing so close behind her Xarles' body heat radiated, warming her bare skin. Inhaling, she tried once more to identify the exotic smells that he exuded. The heady aromas awakened a part of her that wanted to snuggle against him, to bathe in his scent, but the rest of her sent out alarm bells, concerned at being so close to such a dangerous predator.

While Kyreen toyed with the idea of flirting with Xarles as he stood behind her, something cautioned her to take care. This man saw too much and revealed very little. If he perceived her flirtations to be a charade as he had her feigned unfamiliarity of the elven language, he would only be that much more cautious. So, Kyreen kept her mouth shut, but she did lean back against his warm body, exhaling a soft murmur from the back of her throat.

Xarles stepped away, but chuckling, some of his anger giving way to amusement. He moved over to the platform where a small lump lay under the covers in the middle of the bed. Just as he had the previous morning Xarles gently shook the sleeping form in his bed. Only this morning the person he roused was not Remy. It was a woman from the herd, Cerise, one of the two women who had worked on Kyreen's hair. The woman sat up, her flaming red hair tousled, rubbing at sleepy blue eyes. Xarles murmured something quietly which made the woman's freckled face blush and Kyreen felt the woman's burst of enjoyment when Xarles kissed her. Unlike yesterday, however, Kyreen had the distinct impression Xarles did this specifically for Kyreen's benefit, to remind her of her failed kiss, to hint at her missed opportunity. The emotions the bandit leader exuded right now were detached, indifferent, passionless. Xarles did not feel affection towards this woman, not like he did for yesterday's companion.

Xarles glanced at Pierre over his shoulder. "Take Cerise to the herd tent. Then seek out Maurice. He is scheduled to deliver my breakfast. Tell him I asked you to bring it this morning."

"Yes, Xarles," Pierre nodded once.

"I had fun," Kyreen quipped, flashing a smile at Pierre. "Hurry back, handsome."

Pierre gave Kyreen a dark look as Cerise slipped from the bed. As Kyreen's gaze followed the red head, she reflected, not for the first time, on how petite this woman was, how all the women of the herd were. Kyreen had spent so much time with Calanians this past year, where she was not considered exceptionally tall that she had forgotten how short most women were. Still she kept her eyes on the woman as Pierre placed a hand on Cerise's elbow to lead her from the tent. Without turning her body, Kyreen's gaze followed the pair's path, twisting her head as they exited. When the tent flap fell into place, Kyreen turned back around, gazing up at Xarles still sitting on the edge of his bed. The bandit leader had watched Kyreen's actions with an amused expression on his face.

"Good morning!" Kyreen said cheerily, returning Xarles' smile.

"It is morning," Xarles responded. He stood up to begin walking back down off the platform and stand before Kyreen. His eyes dropped down to the fresh brand on her chest. His expression never wavered, but Kyreen felt the fresh surge of anger from Xarles, and the eyes he lifted to Kyreen's showed no emotion. Neither did his voice. "I would not call it good, yet you seem to be in an especially chipper mood this morning."

"It is amazing what a good night's sleep will do for a person's attitude," Kyreen responded.

"You had a good night then, Bijou?' Xarles' eyes explored her face, then dropped to inspect her naked body. "I heard your scream, but to look at you, it appears Armand did not get too rough."

"As you commanded, he left no marks. I confess he was a tad angry with me about the elven thing and his actions caught me by surprise," Kyreen remarked. "It will not happen again."

"The screaming, the catching you by surprise or him being angry?"

"The first two, of course," Kyreen chuckled. "Armand will always be angry with me. At least that is my plan."

"Be careful how you poke the dragon, Bijou," Xarles cautioned.

Kyreen allowed her smile to slip and a fraction of her anger to shine in her eyes before answering. "What if I am the dragon? Mayhap you should caution your friend to watch his step."

Xarles nodded, unmoved by her threat. He moved towards the chair at the table he had been sitting in when she and Pierre had arrived, gesturing for Kyreen to follow him. "I could but he would never listen. Come kneel by my chair while we wait for breakfast."

Once Kyreen had moved, her reluctance clear in her expression as she dropped to her knees, Xarles picked up the jar of salve with a thoughtful expression. Then he leaned over to take a closer look at the brand. "This looks…"

"Deep?' Kyreen finished for him when Xarles' voice trailed off. "The blacksmith was upset with Armand. I guess your man held the brand too long. Truth be told I was not paying attention."

"Armand did the brand?" Kyreen felt another flare of annoyance as Xarles leaned in to gaze at the wound on her chest. "He is not trained."

Kyreen nodded, murmuring an affirmative sound, then leaned in to sniff at Xarles' neck, whispering, "You smell wonderful. So very appetizing."

Xarles chuckled, sitting upright to glance over at the entrance as Pierre entered with the breakfast tray. The two had been conversing in common and the bandit leader now switched to elven, instructing Pierre to place the tray on the table.

"Once I have finished eating, Bijou will be accompanying me on an errand. Armand is busy with other matters so you will accompany us," Xarles told Pierre before he gestured Pierre to exit. "Go eat, then report back here."

Kyreen, who had fixed her gaze on Pierre from the moment he entered the tent, allowed her smile to widen. She murmured a soft noise of excitement and anticipation, earning her a frown from Pierre as he made his way out of the tent.

Once Pierre exited, Kyreen returned her gaze to Xarles, who regarded her placidly over the rim of his coffee cup. Without comment, he turned to his breakfast and began eating. Shortly, just as with the previous meals, he began feeding Kyreen small bites of food, making sure to hold her gaze as he did so. Occasionally he held a cup of water to her lips. Kyreen's mind flew, thinking of things she might say but again something warned her not to press too hard, too quickly. So, she kept her silence, until Xarles wiped his mouth and stood up. He picked up the jar of salve again, once more examining it thoughtfully.

"Fabrice has never sent salve to me with one he has branded," Xarles remarked.

"I did tell him I was inclined not to kill him," Kyreen responded. "Maybe he is grateful."

"Did you now?" Xarles glanced at the angry red wound on her chest. "Maybe he is worried this will not heal properly. Fabrice is proud of his work."

"You have your theory," Kyreen shrugged. "I prefer mine."

"Bijou, you have to realize there is no escape," Xarles explained. He did not sound or feel emotional. He simply stated the situation as he knew it. "You should release this fantasy. Life will be much easier once you do."

"Maybe, but where is the fun in that?" Kyreen responded, surprising herself that she meant the words.

When Kyreen had entered the desert, she had done so without anything but the goal of finding her brother and escaping the pain of Lang's death. Now she had rediscovered...what? Her purpose, her desire to live, herself? Kyreen may have traded her life to Lakwen'dil last night, but, until the spirit claimed that owed favor, Kyreen refused to surrender herself to whatever these men had planned. The abduction from her camp aside, Kyreen now felt more in control of her destiny than ever before in her life. These thoughts made her smile, giving Xarles pause, his reply lying unspoken on his lips as the tent entrance opened behind her.

When Xarles glanced over at Pierre standing in the rectangle of bright sunlight, Kyreen rose to her feet, drawing his attention back to her. She thrilled at the slight flare of anxiety Xarles experienced at her movement, so she took the half-step necessary to close the space between their bodies, leaning in so that the warm skin of his torso barely brushed her cool skin. Closing her eyes, Kyreen inhaled deeply.

Her voice quiet, she whispered in common. "Whatever your friend Armand has planned for me, whatever he or you or any of your men do to me, whatever happens, none of it will ever be enough, not even my death will break me, for I am certain would be avenged. It is you, Xarles, who needs to release your fantasy...of my compliance...of my obedience...of my submission."

She opened her eyes, straightening so that she and Xarles could stare at each other for several long moments. Kyreen felt Pierre's anxiety increase with every heartbeat which served to stoke her internal emotions. Xarles, on the other hand, did not react to Kyreen's words. She did not anger him or frighten him. She felt no extreme emotions. Her words had intrigued him but nothing more than that.

After a few heartbeats, Kyreen took a step back, immediately missing the loss of warmth from his body against her. Still speaking in common she murmured, "We should be going before your man behind me has a heart attack from the stress."

Xarles glanced over at Pierre, who from all appearances looked to be calmly awaiting his instructions. Kyreen turned so that she and Xarles stood shoulder to shoulder. With a tilt of her head and a bright smile she spoke cheerily in elven. "Welcome back, sweetie. I missed you."

Xarles headed out of the tent, saying to Pierre, "Take her to the trench, then meet me at the holding tent. Ensure her hands stay restrained. No need to fuss with a gag."

When Pierre set Kyreen down on the planks, she leaned against him to steady herself as she completed her business. After, as she stood, Kyreen allowed the right side of her body to press against the length of Pierre's body carefully avoiding rubbing the wound on her chest, while giving the impression he was the only reason she did not fall over.

"Thank you," she murmured against his ear. "It is nice that we help each other."

Pierre, in the process of pulling away from Kyreen, stilled. She suppressed a grin at his nervousness.

"What do you mean?" he asked, his eyes scanning the area behind her.

"I know what you are. You know what I am. Like helping like. That is how it should be," she replied quietly, allowing her body to continue to press firmly against his.

"I do not know what you are talking about," Pierre growled, grabbing Kyreen by her upper arms.

Undeterred Kyreen pressed her face against Pierre's neck and forced herself to inhale deeply. The experience was not nearly as pleasant as breathing in Xarles' intoxicating scent, but there, under the sour sweat, the fresh fear, and the stale scent of tobacco, Kyreen could still make out the faintest aroma of magic.

"Sure, you do, magic user," Kyreen whispered, breathing into his ear. "You are the one who took my ring, are you not?"

Pressed as she was against him, Kyreen felt his body stiffen and heard his quiet intake of breath. So, even had the surge of emotions not washed over her, she would have been certain her hunch about this bandit had been correct. After a couple of heartbeats, Kyreen pulled away to gaze at the man standing before her, still grasping her upper arms.

"Oh, Pierre, now you have waited too long to answer me," she chided playfully. "No denying it now."

"I suppose we should be getting a move on," she continued, squinting into the bright sunlight to gaze around the deserted area. "We do not want Xarles to get suspicious, do we, lovey?"

Pierre growled an obscenity then tipped Kyreen up onto his shoulder, muttering, "I have nothing to hide."

"Too late," Kyreen quipped in a sing-song tone as they began moving.

The sun had cleared the vast horizon, bringing with it the day's heat. Kyreen watched the ground go by as Pierre walked. The coarse desert sands would be scalding in just a few minutes. Yet another reason she needed to be clothed and shod before her escape.

When Pierre set Kyreen down inside the holding tent, they both hid their surprise at seeing Armand standing beside Xarles. The two men stood shoulder to shoulder, gazing down at Gautier, still sitting fastened to the center pole. Kyreen could only assume the bloodied man was the same man she had seen the previous evening. Somehow, she did not know how, Gautier looked even worse than he had before. Then she realized not only did his legs still jut out at unnatural angles, so too did his arms. Judging from the lack of emotion emanating from the injured man, he must be unconscious. Kyreen forced her gaze away from Gautier to look at the two men standing in front of him, her eyes pausing on an empty tub sitting to the side. It reminded her of the metal washtub Glain kept in her kitchen in Myrddin for bathing, only not so big. That tub, that kitchen, that city, all seemed so far away and so long ago.

"Pierre, bring Bijou over here," Xarles commanded in elven. Then he looked at Kyreen. "I said we would have more magic today."

"You did," Kyreen responded in common warily, now looking at the tub that Armand was dragging closer to Gautier. When the big man moved behind her to begin releasing her shackles, she successfully suppressed any flinch at his touch.

Once the manacles had been set aside, Armand pulled Kyreen's arms behind her back, the pressure making her shoulders ache anew. Leaning close to her ear, he hissed, "Speak elven, woman."

Kyreen turned her gaze to Xarles, making her expression as neutral as possible. As Armand continued to pull back, she began concentrating on her breathing, resolved that nothing short of a broken bone would get a reaction from her. Xarles wanted her to demonstrate magic? That would be difficult if Armand snapped her bones.

After a few heartbeats of staring at each other, Xarles moved his gaze to his lieutenant.

"Armand," Xarles said quietly. "She will need both arms untethered and operational to cast her magic."

Armand hesitated just a moment and Kyreen wondered if the big man had determined to disobey his leader, but then he released her. Even as she pulled her arms forward to stretch them in front of her, rotating her wrists, Kyreen heard the dagger being pulled from its sheath. Armand pressed the dagger's tip against her rib cage, just above the ugly pink scar she had received the previous summer from her fight with another bully, Falk, the Faldorian mercenary, the one who had destroyed her people's lives for a generation and who had killed her mother.

"Can you fill the tub?" Xarles asked her in elven.

"It will take me at least two spells," she responded in common, nodding. "Do you think you can keep this one from gutting me while I cast?"

As she spoke Armand's anger had been increasing. So too had the pressure he exerted on the dagger. Without looking down Kyreen felt the warm trickle of blood running down her side.

Xarles kept speaking in elven. "Armand, give her space to cast."

The big man did not loosen his grip of her collar but he pulled the tip of the dagger back.

"Xarles," Armand said, "I do not like this. She needs to be taught a lesson in manners."

Kyreen looked down at the washtub and began to mutter the chant she knew so well now, her hands moving the familiar patterns, gesturing towards the empty washtub. As she uttered the last words, thrusting her hands forward, she felt the surge of energies surrounding her swell then pour into the washtub, the water appearing in the blink of an eye. The whole process took less than two heartbeats.

Straightening, Kyreen returned her gaze to Xarles, reveling in his wonder as well as the surprise from the other two conscious men in the tent. She had rushed the spell for effect, but none of them needed to know how it had pulled at her, how it had drained her.

"You may have marked me," Kyreen told Xarles in common. "You may have taken my clothes. You may have even thought you were breaking me, but you were not, are not, will not. I am not like these soft, helpless women you treat as chattel. Your man here is the one who needs to learn some manners before I lose my patience with him and decide I would rather kill him now instead of later."

"I have something you desire," she continued. "If you wish more from me, you must understand this. My magic is not something this man can compel me to do. If and when I cast, it is only because I chose to do so. It will not be done out of fear, or under duress, or because he threatens me with violence."

As she finished speaking, Kyreen felt Armand shift his weight. While she considered her options, on whether to evade or take the hit, Xarles moved with a speed and a grace unlike any Kyreen had ever witnessed, even from her own people. The bandit leader interceded, easily deflecting and spinning Armand's body away from Kyreen. The way in which Xarles moved and maneuvered the much larger man gave Kyreen the impression this had not been the first time Xarles had been called upon to step in and intercede.

"Armand," Xarles said evenly as he escorted his second to the tent entrance, "I need her fully awake and mobile to work her magic. You still have some interrogating to conduct elsewhere, do you not?"

"Yes, my captain," Armand replied, giving Kyreen a glare over his shoulder as he exited.

Chapter 16

Kyreen refrained from saying anything but she did allow a grin to spread across her face as she turned to watch Armand leave. Once the flap fell down behind the two men, she shifted her gaze to Pierre, whose nervousness had spiked. Kyreen pressed a single finger to her lips to signal silence, then she turned back to the tub to cast another water spell. When the spell finished, water lapped at the tub's edge.

"Now heal him," Xarles commanded from the tent entrance. With Armand gone, the bandit leader had switched to speaking common. Eagerness rolled off of Xarles in heavy, dense waves, the first truly sincere emotion Kyreen had ever felt from him.

She looked down at the unconscious man. "This much damage will take more than one spell."

Xarles moved over to the tub of water. He produced from somewhere a small, white square cloth, which he wetted before walking back to Kyreen. Xarles kept his gaze on the tiny wound that Armand's blade had created as he gently wiped away the blood. Once the blood was gone, Xarles used another corner of the cloth to dry Kyreen's skin. Though his actions were overly intimate, they did not feel at all sexual.

His task completed, Xarles raised his brown eyes to gaze at her, his voice quiet. "What do you desire in exchange for healing this man?"

At her hesitation, he smiled. The expression transformed Xarles' face, made him look so young, more like a youth who should be apprenticing with his father, not commander of this band of ruthless men, not a man intent on further torturing this unconscious man sitting in front of Kyreen.

"You were correct," Xarles said. "You have something I desire. Additionally, I am a businessman. What can I offer you in exchange for your magic?"

Kyreen's mind raced. Xarles kept changing the game, keeping her off balance. To buy herself time to think, Kyreen said, "I presume my freedom is not available?"

"I can grant you your freedom," Xarles shrugged, "but where can you go? It would be a matter of hours before you were recaptured. If not by me, then by one of the other camps. Believe me when I say you are better off here."

"You are saying I should consider myself fortunate to have been captured by your men?" Kyreen asked, arching a single eyebrow.

"One could make that argument," Xarles commented. He turned so that they stood shoulder to shoulder gazing down at Gautier. "What do you say? Shall we enter into negotiations?"

Kyreen regarded the unconscious man. Though his wounds appeared extensive, she had confidence in the healing spells Brigit had given her. During her time in the desert, Kyreen had only used the lowest level of healing spell. This would give her the chance to increase her range, try out the higher-level spells. She presumed Xarles wanted Gautier healed so that he could inflict more torture upon his prisoner, and she knew she should feel more remorse at the task Xarles requested of her, should feel some sympathy for this battered man, but she already knew she would agree to heal Gautier if it meant manipulating her escape. Briefly Kyreen contemplated the morality of healing Gautier just so he could experience more pain, but then, resolutely, she decided she could not worry about this man. Maybe he was an innocent, maybe he was not. She owed him nothing. She needed to be concerned with her own predicament. Her mind set, she turned away from Gautier, gazing fully into Xarles' face.

"What can you offer me?" she asked.

Xarles' gaze dropped to the fresh wound on Kyreen's chest and she once again felt his flare of annoyance. It seemed Armand had chosen to have Kyreen branded without Xarles' approval or knowledge. This man standing before Kyreen, the leader of these bandits, Xarles, kept his feelings and reactions very carefully guarded for none of his emotions showed on his face.

"There is nothing I can do about the brand," Xarles remarked, lifting his gaze to Kyreen's face, "but I can discipline Armand for the action. Although, admittedly I am at fault for not being more specific in my instructions. I told him not to leave any evidence of abuse. Branding is not abuse. It is something routinely done to the herd."

"I do not need you to discipline Armand," Kyreen replied. "I will take care of him myself."

"Very well then," Xarles raised a speculative eyebrow. "What do you suggest?"

"Can we agree that I am not herd? Despite this mark here?" Kyreen countered.

"You and I can agree on that," Xarles responded. "Convincing Armand and others may be a challenge."

"I believe your convincing everyone in your camp could be worth one healing spell," Kyreen commented, returning her gaze to Gautier.

"Three, minimum," Xarles countered, also looking down at the unconscious man.

"How healed do you want him?" Kyreen asked. "How many times?"

She felt the spike in emotions from Xarles and suppressed her grin. Xarles wanted her healing spells very much. He wanted to extend Gautier's suffering. He would give her a great deal in exchange for her skills.

"I will make sure everyone understands you are not herd," he said finally.

"Shall we start with returning my clothes?" Kyreen remarked, looking down at the tub. "And I would appreciate borrowing this for a bit, after you are done with it, of course."

"Three spells?" Xarles inquired, the eagerness slipping into his voice.

"Three healing spells," Kyreen clarified with a nod.

To seal the pact, Kyreen worked her most advanced healing spell. Though his arms and legs did not mend, Gautier did awaken. When the man opened his eyes, his pain hit Kyreen fully, causing her to sway slightly. Xarles steadied the woman with a hand to her elbow, his gaze never leaving Gautier's face.

Swallowing the lump in her throat and forcing her voice to come out steady, Kyreen asked, "Do we have a deal?"

"Oh, yes," the bandit leader murmured, his eyes blazing hatred at the beaten man now staring up at him. "We most assuredly have a deal."

The second and third spells almost completely healed Gautier. Kyreen supposed he might have some residual aches and pains, but all the lacerations had disappeared and all his bones had mended. The man still looked a mess. The healings had not erased the blood smeared across his naked body or caked into his beard and hair.

"How much more can you do? Will you be able to continue healing?" Xarles asked zealously, a bit of his stoic mask slipping away.

"I have held up my end of our deal," Kyreen shook her head. "Now it is your turn."

She felt the profound reluctance as Xarles turned away from Gautier to face Pierre standing by the tent entrance, switching back to elven as he spoke, "Take Bijou..."

Xarles paused at Kyreen's cough. With a glance at her stern expression, he gave her one of his boyish lopsided grins then turned back to Pierre, continuing, "Take Kyreen to the herd tent..."

"Excuse me?" Kyreen interrupted once more.

Xarles flashed her another easygoing smile. "Please, let me finish?"

Kyreen nodded, her expression reflecting her misgivings.

Xarles started over. "Pierre, take Kyreen to the herd tent where she may bathe, using their tub. Instruct Genevieve to find clothing for Kyreen. You are to stay with her. Make sure no one mistreats her. Any who have an issue with her status can speak with me. Do you understand?"

"Yes, Xarles," Pierre nodded, his gaze darkening slightly, obviously not liking the change in Kyreen's status. While he had not understood any of the words spoken between his commander and this strange woman, he had recognized the camaraderie in their tone and body language, thus was not surprised by Xarles' words.

Xarles glanced at Kyreen, switching back to common. "You look concerned."

"The herd tent?" she asked archly.

"It is either that or you bathe outside. I cannot permit you unrestrained access to my tent for that long without my presence. The other tents available would be Armand's or the men's, neither of which have a tub."

"Fine," Kyreen relented. "I specifically requested my clothes."

"Which are in my tent and, quite frankly, filthy," Xarles responded. "Allow me to have them laundered before returning them to you?"

Kyreen nodded her acceptance.

"As for your bath," Xarles remarked, "As you can well imagine a tub's amount of water is a precious commodity here in the desert. I trust you can produce your own bath water?"

"I can."

"Will it deplete you?" Xarles inquired. Kyreen knew his chief concern was not her personal wellbeing but what he needed her to do for him.

"I will meditate which will help," Kyreen responded. "I should be good for another five or six healing spells today, provided we reach another accord."

Xarles crossed over to a pile of clothing sitting in a corner of the tent. After a brief rummage, he picked up a sand colored cloak and walked back to Kyreen. Standing in front of her, he draped the garment over her shoulders, then worked to fasten the clasp.

"You are my guest now, not a prisoner nor a captive nor herd," he said in elven, presumably for Pierre's benefit. "I request you give me this day to ensure all in my camp have received my decree. If confronted, Pierre will ensure my word is relayed to any who may attempt to reprimand or restrain you. Once you have bathed and dressed, I would request you join me back here, to engage in further negotiations."

"Very well," Kyreen responded, inclining her head slightly.

Xarles rested his hands lightly on Kyreen's shoulders and gazed into her eyes. "I placed this cloak on you because you are now my guest. We do agree on this, correct?"

He nodded and Kyreen nodded back.

"Then," Xarles continued, explaining, "I would request that you allow Pierre to carry you to the herd tent. The sands outside would burn your feet if you attempted to walk without shoes,"

Kyreen glanced at the pile of discarded clothing behind Xarles. "Are there no shoes there?"

"Unfortunately, no," Xarles shook his head. "Gautier was in his tent, in his bedroll, asleep when Armand took him."

"Very well," Kyreen sighed. She moved to Pierre, flashing him a playful grin. "Shall we go, handsome?"

Without responding, Pierre hoisted Kyreen to his shoulder and the pair exited the tent, leaving Xarles alone with his prisoner. They managed the trip across camp without any opposition. In the herd tent, however, Genevieve challenged Pierre when informed that Xarles had freed Kyreen.

"Why would he mark her and then promptly free her?" Genevieve asked, her words clipped with anger.

"Because Armand marked me, not Xarles," Kyreen replied impatiently.

The Calanian gazed down at the diminutive woman glaring up at her, struck again by how petite these women of the herd were. Genevieve's face bore mementos from last night's punishment, a split lip, a swollen cheek and a partially closed black eye. Kyreen also noticed multiple lacerations crisscrossing the woman's naked body and wondered how many bruises were obscured by the pigmentation of the woman's dark brown skin.

"And because I can do this," Kyreen added, pulling the cloak off to stand naked, resolutely ignoring the discomfort of her nudity here in front of Genevieve, the women of the herd, and Pierre who stood with the other guard Orane just inside the tent entrance. Closing her eyes, she began to murmur the spell and move her hands. When she released the healing energies, Kyreen lifted her hands toward her own chest and shoulders.

A soft gasp rippled through the onlookers as Kyreen felt the wound on her chest close up and heal. Opening her eyes, she gazed looked down at the brand, the skin pink and puckered without any sign of a scab. Rubbing her fingers over the raised mark, a new flash of anger coursing through her veins, Kyreen renewed her vow to make Armand pay for this mark, for her shoulders, for Fanchon.

"You cannot do that!" Genevieve exclaimed softly.

Kyreen bent down to the cloak pooled at her feet, then straightening, pulled it back around her shoulders, taking her time in fastening the clasp. Once the garment had been positioned to Kyreen's liking, she turned her emerald gaze to the dark-skinned woman.

"You have no idea what I can do," Kyreen declared quietly. "Now be a good little girl and get me the items Xarles promised me."

Genevieve's gaze darted to Pierre standing behind Kyreen, but her eyes flew back to Kyreen when the taller woman asserted firmly, "Do not look to him. He is nothing here. I am the one you need to be obeying. I am the one you must please. I am Xarles' guest. If I am not happy, he will not be happy."

Kyreen watched as Genevieve gazed up at her, silently reflecting on Kyreen's words. Then Genevieve nodded and, even as the tiny woman spoke, her gaze dropping submissively, Kyreen saw the other woman's acceptance and knew she would have no further trouble from Genevieve or the herd.

"As you command, mistress," Genevieve murmured, taking a step back. Then, straightening, she turned to glare at the onlooking group of women, barking out orders which sent the women scattering.

A short time later, Kyreen relaxed in the tub. She could barely remember her last bath in the unnamed town on the edge of the desert. That, too, felt like a lifetime ago. Slipping beneath the softly scented water, relishing the sensation, Kyreen reflected on her current situation. Once Genevieve had decided to cooperate, she had been most helpful. When Kyreen filled the tub with water, the women had all exchanged looks of astonishment, but Genevieve had

clapped her hands, quickly driving them back into action. Bath oils
had been brought to Kyreen for her selection. Next soaps, shampoos,
and lotions. Kyreen had not wanted anyone helping her bathe but
Genevieve had insisted.

"As you yourself pointed out, you are Xarles' guest and we
are charged with assisting you," Genevieve had explained. "Then
permit us to perform our duties, although admittedly you are the first
woman any of us has ever served."

Therefore, reluctantly, Kyreen acquiesced to let one of the
women wash out her hair. Though she would be loath to admit it,
allowing someone else to deal with her unruly, tangled hair had been
rather pleasant. Later, after two women had toweled Kyreen dry and
wrapped her in a cotton robe, another woman had applied a fragrant
cream to Kyreen's curls and combed them out. Even more women
worked applying lotion to Kyreen's hands and feet. A plate of fruit
appeared and one woman's job consisted of feeding grapes and
berries to Kyreen. The entire experience had been relaxing until it
came time for Kyreen to get dressed.

Securing the robe around her body, the Calanian eyed the
brightly colored silks that lay out on the bed, an assortment of reds,
blues, greens, oranges, and purples. Some had adornments sewn
along the edges – tiny metal bells or silky tassels or colorful beads.
Kyreen could not figure how these bits of silk could be arranged as
clothing but really did not care to be informed. Instead she glanced at
Genevieve, asking dryly, "So you dress all of Xarles' guests in these
silks?"

"No, of course not," Genevieve quickly responded, shaking
her head while a few of the women giggled.

"Why, then, do you give them?" Kyreen inquired, struggling
to control her temper.

"The guests of Xarles provide their own clothing,"
Genevieve answered. "Sometimes, very rarely, if they do not have
adequate clothing, something will be procured. From the men's
tent."

Kyreen moved her gaze to Pierre, who still stood near the
tent entrance next to Orane. Now, in addition to his puzzling

nervousness, Kyreen felt Pierre's budding annoyance towards her. Pierre did not like being assigned to Kyreen, though none of this internal maelstrom showed on the man's face as he returned Kyreen's gaze with a bland expression.

"Not my job," he informed Kyreen.

"Very well," Kyreen responded good-naturedly, sitting down on the edge of the bed, the tent's single piece of furniture. Crossing her legs beneath the robe's folds, she smoothed down the fabric. "We will just sit here until Xarles gets tired of waiting for my return and comes looking for me. I will then let you explain why his guest was delayed."

After a few moments of silence, Pierre closed his eyes and sighed audibly. Without another word or even a glance at Kyreen, he turned and opened the tent flap to exit.

"Do not forget the boots!" Kyreen called after him as the flap fell back into place. Then she glanced at the women gathered around her asking chirpily, "Is there anyone here who could braid my hair for me?"

Pierre did well with the clothing, bringing back black trousers and a black tunic that fit Kyreen relatively well once Genevieve fastened a purple scarf about Kyreen's waist. As for the boots, he brought four pairs in varying sizes, and the smallest in size, a pair of black knee-high boots of butter soft leather, were only a smidge too big and not so loose that she would get blisters. Kyreen hoped that by the end of the day she would have her own boots back, even if she had to force Xarles to leave Gautier and return to his tent to fetch them. For walking about the camp, these loaners would suffice. Tugging on the boots, Kyreen stood up feeling almost completely refreshed. The healing spell she had performed had worked not only on the brand but also her shoulders, relieving any residual aches from Armand's punishment.

"Are you ready?" Pierre inquired, his impatience only visible in the feelings Kyreen could sense from him.

"Almost," Kyreen replied. She glanced around the tent, saying, "Genevieve, I need a little space here."

Executing her daily meditation with an audience proved challenging but soon enough Kyreen lost herself in the motions. After her second run through, the energies flowed freely once again without restriction and Kyreen knew she would be well enough to provide Xarles many more healings.

"My thanks to you all," Kyreen said, bowing at the waist as she swept an arm out, grinning first at Genevieve, then allowing her gaze to move over the rest of the women, many of whom giggled.

Spinning with a flourish, Kyreen ducked under Pierre's arm, out of the tent, and into the sunshine. Though the sun scowled down from directly overhead and the day's heat scalded, Kyreen paused outside to take a deep, centering breath. When Pierre, who had followed her out of the tent, moved to get by her, Kyreen put a hand on his arm to stop him.

"No," she said, without turning her gaze to look at him, her voice firm and quiet. "You may walk beside me, Pierre, or behind me, but not in front of me. I know where I am going."

Chapter 17

Without waiting for Pierre's response, Kyreen began walking towards the tent on the other side of the camp where Xarles and Gautier waited for her. She set her pace to be purposeful without hurrying and kept her gaze forward. The hardest part was making her walk look casual, like she was taking a leisurely stroll, when in reality her heart thundered in her ears as she waited for someone to confront her. No one did, though she felt some surprise from the handful of men who did notice her walking by. Standing before the entrance to the holding tent, as Xarles had called it, Kyreen took another deep, centering breath. Not only did she feel the need to focus on her continued charade but the emotions radiating from both men within this tent needed to be pushed away as well.

Pierre, however, having trailed behind Kyreen through camp, misunderstood her pause. With another audible sigh, he reached for the tent flap, pulling it up for her to walk inside.

Flashing Pierre a jaunty grin, Kyreen slipped into the tent. "Thank you, my dear."

Her sass was immediately rewarded by a spike in Pierre's irritation towards her. Kyreen allowed his emotion to wash over her, to boost her confidence, then turned her attentions on the scene inside the tent. Gautier now stood, his legs no longer bent and broken, with his hands restrained over his head to the center tent pole, water dripping from his body. From the waist up, the blood had been rinsed away from his skin. With his hair and beard no longer caked with dried blood, Kyreen could see liberal amounts of gray sprinkled amongst the light brown. Dried blood still covered the lower half of the man's body, although rivulets of water had streaked some areas clean.

Steeling her expression so as not to reveal the revulsion curdling her stomach, Kyreen moved towards Xarles who took a step back away from his captive. Kyreen noted the light pink tint of the water in the tub, no longer clear as it had been when she left. The emotions of terror and anguish, bordering on hysteria, rolled off of

Gautier, assaulting her senses, and she hoped none of this reflected in her eyes when she returned Xarles' gaze.

"I had begun to worry," Xarles commented in elven, dropping his eyes to scan her outfit.

"We had some miscommunications," Kyreen replied in common. "But I managed."

"Genevieve?"

"Most helpful."

Xarles' gaze moved to the V-neck of the tunic, the black so stark against Kyreen's pale skin. He reached out a hand, meaning to push back the collar so as to view the brand on her chest, but Kyreen took a step back out of his reach.

"Not without my permission," Kyreen stated calmly in common. "Not herd."

"Not herd," Xarles repeated, switching to common. "May I please see your mark?"

Kyreen nodded, stepping forward so that Xarles could hook a finger under the cloth, peeling it back to reveal the healed brand, the scar an angry pink against her pale skin. After a moment Xarles released the collar. Kyreen noted he was careful not to touch her bare skin with his.

"You healed yourself," Xarles stated.

"Yes," Kyreen nodded.

Xarles regarded her for a few moments. Kyreen returned his gaze without speaking, resolutely refusing to apologize or explain her actions. Finally, he turned to stand shoulder to shoulder with Kyreen as they both looked at Gautier, who stood with his eyes closed, head hanging down so it rested upon his chest. Trying to ignore the pain and shock exuding from the tortured man, Kyreen forced her face into a neutral expression and examined Gautier in order to decipher what had occurred in her absence. It did not take her long to see the unnatural angles of several of Gautier's fingers. The sight of his bloody fingertips minus fingernails curdled her stomach, but she managed to swallow the bile rising in her throat. Then she listened to the breath rattling in his chest. The man had water in his lungs. Her imagination filled in the details and she pushed back the shudder threatening to ripple across her body.

"Gautier and I have been reminiscing," Xarles remarked. Though Kyreen could feel the strong emotions of anger and sorrow emanating from the man, none could be detected in his level voice and neutral expression, "and I have decided I do not want him healed again until he has the opportunity to fully appreciate this round of memories."

"What does that mean for our negotiations?" Kyreen asked, pleased that her voice sounded as nonchalant and level as his voice had. Despite her discomfort, she kept her gaze on Gautier. She feared her repulsion might show in her expression were she to look up at Xarles.

"Do not fret," Xarles responded, flashing her a smile. "I still need your talents."

For a few more moments they stood there, gazing down at the still conscious man, who never moved. Then Xarles turned towards Kyreen, flashing another of his charming smiles.

"I invite you to my tent to pass the heat of the day," he said.

"And if I turn down your invitation?" Kyreen responded. "Where then would I go?"

"You do not wish to spend time with me?" Xarles countered, raising an eyebrow, his brown eyes twinkling.

"If indeed I have the freedom to choose," Kyreen replied, returning his smile, allowing it to reach her eyes, pushing away any residual negative feelings, "I merely wish to know my options."

"The same as before," Xarles remarked. "My tent. Armand's tent. The men's tent. The herd tent."

Kyreen could think of one other option—the tent with the pregnant mare–but she decided to hold that location in reserve for now. Going to Xarles' tent might gain her access to her belongings. So, she inclined her head towards the bandit leader, acquiescing, "I would be delighted to pass the time with you."

Xarles chuckled, his expression knowing, and she knew he knew her motivations. Without comment, he extended an elbow to

Kyreen, who did not hesitate in slipping her arm through his. As they crossed over to the tent entrance, Pierre held up the flap for the pair.

Once back at his tent, Xarles offered Kyreen a seat at his table. Gesturing towards the plate of fruit that had been placed on the table, he toed off his shoes.

"Please, eat if you are hungry," he said, sitting and reaching for the pitcher to pour them both a cup of water.

Feeling Xarles' eyes scrutinizing her, Kyreen reached for a luscious plump berry, pushing back the memories that threatened to well up. She popped the fruit into her mouth. She smiled and closed her eyes, hoping she appeared to be enjoying the taste instead of hiding the sorrow that she could not contain, the pain that she knew would radiate from her eyes. As the sweetness burst upon her tongue, the memories sprang forward, unwilling to be restrained any longer. She thought of her time in the wilderness with Lang, their complete immersion into each other, the laughter, the promises, the plans they had shared in their ignorance of the future. It all seemed so long ago.

"I thought you did not like berries," Xarles remarked, sliding a cup of water across the table towards her, bringing Kyreen's thoughts back to the present.

"No, I love them," Kyreen murmured, then mentally steeled herself before opening her eyes to flash him a smile absent of any sadness. "I was a bit distraught and overwhelmed the other night, what with the kidnapping and all."

Xarles watched her over the rim of his cup, his dark brown eyes thoughtful. Kyreen took a drink from her cup, mildly returning his gaze. The lack of emotions she felt from the man made her more nervous than his anger. It took all her concentration to contain her own anxiety.

Maybe because she had been actively searching for emotions or the absence of emotions from Xarles, but, whatever the reason, Kyreen sensed Armand's fury well before he exploded through the tent's entrance, startling both Xarles and Pierre. Kyreen, on the other hand, picked up another piece of fruit, a grape this time, and leaned back in her chair as the big man entered. Popping the fruit in her mouth, she met Armand's gaze with a broad grin that twinkled in her green eyes.

Armand halted just inside the entrance, his big hands balled into hammer-like fists. Pierre recovered from his surprise quickly, a grin spreading across his face. Maybe he expected Armand to put Kyreen in her place, or maybe he simply looked forward to a fight between the two men. Despite a slight flare of concern, Xarles' expression never wavered. He rose smoothly to his feet and Kyreen noted that he positioned himself between her chair and the angry man.

"Why is she dressed? Why does she sit at your table?" Armand demanded. "That woman is herd. She has been nothing but disrespectful and disobedient. She is responsible for five men's deaths."

"She," Kyreen interjected forcibly in elven, "only killed one of those men. I believe his name was Andre."

She glanced at the three men in the room, holding up a single index finger. "Just one."

"Kyreen, please," Xarles said quietly in common, his gaze never leaving his lieutenant's face. "If I may ask, stay out of this?"

Kyreen shrugged. Keeping her gaze on Armand, she took another piece of fruit. Plastering a saucy grin upon her face, she gave the big man a wink as she placed the grape in her mouth. To Armand that wink coupled with her impertinent expression was the final insult. With a growl he lunged forward, his vision tunneled on Kyreen. Xarles had no trouble intercepting the raging man, grabbing Armand's outstretched arms and using the bigger man's momentum to propel him away from the seated woman, who did not move, did not flinch, did not change her amused expression. Twisting Armand's arms behind the man's broad back, Xarles murmured quietly to his second, words Kyreen could not hear, but words that penetrated Armand's fury. The big man relaxed though Xarles did not release his hold on the other man's arms.

Kyreen watched, contemplating her next move. As she swallowed the grape, however, Xarles glanced her way. He must have seen something in her expression, for he shook his head, speaking to her in common. "As much as I desire the use of your talents, Kyreen, at some point you will either push him so far I will no longer be able to contain him or I will no longer feel the urge to protect you."

Kyreen's smile slid from her face, her eyes glittered angrily. She leaned forward, placing the front chair legs on the ground, so she could rise to her feet.

"You," she said in common, her voice flat and toneless, "do not need to protect me. This man here is nothing. You and he both need to realize that Armand is not the most dangerous person in this tent. Neither are you, Xarles."

She picked up her cup and, turning her back to the three men, moved away from the table to take a seat on the steps of the platform. Leaning her back against the side of the bed, she sipped, watching the room over the rim of her cup. Xarles relaxed his grip on Armand's arm and escorted the big man out of the tent. As the tent flap dropped behind the departing men, Kyreen set down the cup, turning her gaze to Pierre.

"Did you enjoy the show?" she asked in elven. "Or were you hoping for more?"

"What is your problem, bitch?" Pierre growled. He began stalking towards her but stopped when the woman held up her hand.

"You may want to give a thought, or possibly two, to your next actions, Pierre," Kyreen warned, her voice quiet and matter of fact as she pointed a finger to the tent entrance. "Neither of those men are my equal and I seriously doubt you are up challenging either of them."

She shook her head, gazing at the man as one would a petulant child. "No, Pierre, you have no hope of besting me, so your wisest path here would be to become my ally."

Any reply Pierre might have made was delayed by Xarles' return. Kyreen raised the cup to her mouth to hide her smile but her eyes still twinkled as she moved her gaze to Xarles.

"Pierre," the bandit leader commanded quietly, his eyes locked on Kyreen, "leave us. Return at sunset with our dinner."

"Yes, Xarles," Pierre replied.

Before he exited, Pierre gave Kyreen a triumphant smile behind Xarles' back. She felt his smugness, as though Pierre expected Xarles to be reprimanding Kyreen for her recent actions.

Kyreen, however, also felt the emotions rolling off of Xarles. She knew Xarles did not harbor any anger towards her. For the briefest moment, she indulged in the sensation, allowed it to roll over and through her, intoxicated by the emotions she picked up from the bandit leader. No, Xarles was not angry. Quite the opposite.

Once the tent flap fell into place behind Pierre, leaving the two alone in the tent, Kyreen rose to her feet, moving to stand before Xarles. Their bodies close enough for her to feel the heat radiating off of him, Kyreen reached behind her head to loosen the band holding her braid. Then, gazing into Xarles' smoldering dark eyes, she ran her fingers through the plait, releasing her still damp curls into a fragrant cloud around her face. When she lowered her arms, Xarles raised his hands to push her hair back, cradling her face as he leaned in to kiss her. Kyreen allowed him to continue the kiss several heartbeats before she pulled away, resuming her gaze into his eyes.

"Not herd," she murmured.

Xarles looked into her green eyes then smiled one of his charming, lopsided smiles before replying quietly. "No, definitely not herd."

"My choice," Kyreen remarked.

"Your choice," Xarles nodded.

She leaned forward, burying her nose against his neck inhaling deeply, allowing a quiet sigh to slip between her lips before pulling back to again stare into his face as Xarles' hands slipped to her shoulders.

"You smell so good, so tempting," she purred. "I worry you are a distraction I cannot afford."

For a few moments they stood, silently gazing into each other's eyes. Kyreen allowed his desire to wash over her again, pushing away the warnings her brain kept sending. Her body, on the other hand, awakened to the sensations, aching to feel his touch, vibrating like a starving person presented with a bountiful buffet, ravenous, greedy, impatient to assuage her hunger.

"It is the heat of the day," Xarles remarked. "Not much happens in the heat of the day."

"So, you are saying that maybe a distraction is in order," Kyreen replied quietly, closing the small span of distance between them to slid her arms around his body, his bare skin warm beneath her hands.

As their lips met again and Xarles' desire washed over her anew, Kyreen's internal struggle intensified. This man returned her kiss just as fiercely as she did, giving the impression that he too had abandoned caution, had succumbed to his lust, but under the heat of his desire lurked a coolness, a calmness, an indifference that gave Kyreen pause, created a germ of concern, and reinforced for her how dangerous Xarles was. She kept this in mind as her hands began slowly roaming his back, her fingers sliding across the ridges of scars marring his smooth skin, a testament to this man's violent history.

When their lips parted, Xarles led Kyreen back to the platform, sitting her on the edge of the bed. Then he proceeded to leisurely remove her boots, one at a time, carefully setting them aside before moving up to kneel between her legs, pulling her face to his to once again kiss her lips. Kyreen closed her eyes, allowing his intoxicating scent to invade her, savoring the feel of his touch, so deliberate, so unhurried, so sensual washing over her, until finally she succumbed to the bliss and all conscious thoughts drifted away.

Afterwards, her body loose, her bones like liquid, feeling more relaxed than she had in recent memory, Kyreen examined Xarles' face. They lay on their sides facing each other, his eyes closed, his expression soft, making him look even younger than he did when he flashed his lopsided grin. Kyreen marveled anew at his exotic beauty, the golden skin, the angular cheek bones, the neatly trimmed goatee. As though he felt her gaze, he opened his deep, dark eyes, his sensual lips lifting up into contented smile.

"Troubles?" he asked.

"Just enjoying the view," she replied.

The sun outside beat down on the tent, infusing it with a warmth, but not at all hot, the diffused light creating a relaxed ambiance, an intimacy that surprised Kyreen in its easiness. As they gazed silently at each other she felt an amusement from Xarles, something more rooted in a diversionary pleasure, rather than the emotional fondness she had felt in him towards Remy.

She registered his languid touch as his fingers grazed her shoulders before dropping to the mirrored crescent moon brand. His gaze moved to the mark, healed and pink. Some of his amusement gave way to annoyance.

"It is not too late for me to reprimand Armand," Xarles commented.

"As I indicated earlier, I will take care of him," Kyreen replied.

"And the person who gave you this?" he asked, his touch moving down to the scar from her fight the previous summer with Falk, the Faldorian mercenary who had led the Battle that had so completely changed both Kyreen's life and the lives of her people.

"He is dead," Kyreen stated, "by my hand."

"Of course," Xarles remarked. He slowly ran his hand across her skin, up and around to caress the cicatrix at the back of her neck, the impression of toothmarks that had magically bound her to Sten, the one usually hidden beneath her hair or clothes.

"And this one?" he asked. "Or perhaps this was a mark of pleasure?"

Kyreen's eyes narrowed, her smile fading away. "No, not pleasure, and, no, he is not dead, not yet anyway."

Xarles nodded, not doubting that Kyreen meant to kill the man who had inflicted this mark upon her skin. Xarles felt certain that the man's time in this realm was temporary, but wondered if the man knew this, or if he had dismissed Kyreen as so many men were apt to do with women. Armand surely had underestimated Kyreen, of that Xarles was sure. The big man thought this strange, dark-haired woman to be an annoyance, a temporary problem, someone he could bully into submission, but Xarles knew better. He suspected that Kyreen just might turn out to be Armand's demise, and the answer to Xarles' problem. Pushing away thoughts of his lieutenant and everything else, Xarles leaned in to kiss Kyreen.

Chapter 18

Kyreen and Xarles passed the rest of the afternoon exploring each other's body, oblivious to the outside world, inquisitive caresses escalating into urgent groping, their desires waxing and waning, their lovemaking a synchronized dance. By the time the shadow of the mountains washed the tent in twilight purples, Xarles had caressed every part of Kyreen's body, just as she had his body. Stretching languidly, she watched as Xarles rolled from the bed to pull on his pants, then walk over to pour himself a cup of water. Though they had just spent the last few hours together, as intimate as she had ever been with a man, Kyreen knew practically nothing about Xarles, felt no emotional connection.

Reluctantly, she ordered her body to move, slipping from the bed to begin drawing on her loaner clothes. Once she had tugged on her boots, she began combing through her hair with her fingers. The entire time she had been very conscious of Xarles' eyes watching her every move.

"Would you leave your hair down for the evening?" Xarles asked. "I wish to observe it loose."

"Would you share a story of yourself with me?" Kyreen responded. "I wish to learn more about you."

"I will answer one question," Xarles stated.

"Three questions and full answers, not a 'yes' or 'no'," Kyreen countered.

"Two questions answered to your satisfaction," Xarles remarked, "in exchange for your hair loose and your assurance that you will not cause trouble in the camp."

"I agree to your terms," Kyreen consented. "I will not braid my hair. As for trouble, I will not instigate anything."

As if on signal, Pierre and another man arrived with their dinner. Once the dishes had been set down on the table, Pierre shot a glance at the rumpled sheets, then at Kyreen sitting on the edge of the bed. She ruffled a hand through her curls, flashing him a grin with a quirk of one eyebrow. Pierre furrowed his brow as he and the other man moved to take up their post just inside the tent entrance.

"Wait outside," Xarles told his men as he sat down at the table.

Kyreen waited until the men had exited before she approached the table. Looking at the chairs she considered taking the one closest to Xarles, then opted to sit across the table from the bandit leader.

They dined in silence, their utensils the only sounds in the tent for several minutes. Kyreen could not have named most of the dishes but it all tasted divine. Following Xarles' lead, she scooped meat and rice onto a slice of flatbread. The spices burst on her tongue, so flavorful. One particular dish contained a sauce that exploded hotly in her mouth, causing her eyes to water, an experience Kyreen curiously did not find negative and she eagerly took another large bite. As she ate, she became aware of Xarles watching her with an amused expression. Finishing the main dish, she scooped up some of the thick paste to spread onto a piece of flatbread, giving him a questioning look.

"I am trying to remember the last time a woman sat at my table," Xarles remarked. "Mostly they kneel at my side."

"And I thought Hanoria treated women horribly," Kyreen muttered, taking a bite of the flatbread.

"Hanoria?" Xarles asked. "That is far south of here, yet you came from the east."

"Long story," Kyreen replied with a twinkle in her eyes. "And you owe me a couple of answers, not the other way around."

"Very well," Xarles said. "Ask your first question."

"What happened this morning to waken Armand in such a foul mood and have him send his plaything Fanchon away so suddenly? He has been on edge all day and, as much as I may want to think it is because of me, I can sense there is more to it."

Xarles leaned back in his chair, cup in hand, as he observed her. "How much do you know of this side of the Salandingar Desert, of the elf lands, as those in the Old Kingdoms call *Talamh sa bhaile Si*?"

"I can find them on a map," Kyreen answered honestly.

"Fair enough," Xarles chuckled. "You probably know that the most precious gems in the realm are mined from the desert."

Kyreen nodded. She recalled the pouch she had removed from the body of Falk after their fight in Myrddin. From the bag full of Salandingar gems, she had removed a single blood red gemstone, which she had given to Stian to buy back her herd from Markku's father. The rest of the gems had gone to Rhun and his guild. While coins were more common, they could be traced back to the province from which they originated. Gems were ideal for their portability and anonymity, having the ability to cross borders and factions with impunity.

"Several years ago, not long before I was born," Xarles said, "the mines along the eastern edge of the desert began to fail. The people of Old Kingdom had mined them empty. It was then that the miners moved west. Those who managed to survive the crossing found pristine untouched veins of minerals and gemstones. Amongst the ensuing rush of men dreaming to strike their fortune, chaos reigned. There were no towns, no communities, no laws to govern. The Salandingar was not, still is not, an annexed province of the Old Kingdoms, nor have the elves ever laid claim to it. So, in the ensuing chaos of the mining rush, small pockets of civilization popped up, sometimes overnight.

"I use the term civilization quite loosely here when referring to the desert communities," Xarles paused to refill his water and take a sip before continuing. "Where the mines are in the foothills, towns were formed and the men began creating councils to govern, but only with the permission of the elves, who were loath to see the human settlements. But out here in the desert, where the transportation lines control supplies in and the goods out, things were less structured, more unpredictable, constantly shifting like the desert sands. Controlling the water supply became quite lucrative. Looting and hijacking were the norm."

"And still are," Kyreen interjected thinking about her own ordeal just the previous evening.

"Your situation is unique," Xarles responded. "I have had my men looking for a single traveler for many years now. Had you been a part of a caravan you would have passed through unmolested, providing of course your caravan chief had paid the passage fees."

"Passage fees?"

"Tolls, if you may. All along this edge of the desert different camps control different parts of the route. Crescent Moons, this camp, controls a very integral section. The canyon out there leads not only to the largest human settlement along the western desert but also one of only two known thoroughfares into *Talamh sa bhaile Si'*. He who controls this particular oasis has a major power hold over the other camps," Xarles explained. "Armand is upset because this morning one of the neighboring camps, the Two Palms camp, attempted a takeover. A dozen or so men attacked before dawn. Though our men quickly squelched the attack, Armand is furious that anyone thinks themselves strong enough to beat Crescent Moons."

"You do not seem worried," Kyreen stated, thinking back to their afternoon of relaxation and pleasure. "Yet Armand continues to be upset."

"Armand takes an attack on the camp as a personal attack on him and his abilities as my lieutenant," Xarles said. "Me? I realize we will always be a target."

Kyreen finished eating the flatbread, contemplating Xarles' words as she chewed. Something about this morning's attack bothered her but she could not put a finger on why. The timing seemed suspect to her. Why now? Did it have something to do with her arrival, with Pierre's guilt, or was she being paranoid? Could the attack simply be a coincidence? Kyreen swallowed, pushing away her thoughts. The politics of this camp were of no concern to her. She needed to stay focused. She could not afford to get involved.

"You look as though you have something to say," Xarles commented.

Kyreen reached for her cup of water. She needed to hydrate but she also wanted a little time to think about how to proceed. What did she wish to reveal at this time? Setting aside her water, she decided it may be time to divulge one of her secrets.

"You mentioned interrogations to Armand," she remarked. "Thus, I deduce one or more were captured."

"One," Xarles responded.

"I would be interested in hearing about the invading group's strategy, their infiltration point, their timing," Kyreen asked without asking.

Xarles set down his own cup and leaned back in his chair once more. Though his expression never changed and his posture appeared relaxed, Kyreen sensed the change in his emotions. She had asked the right question. She now had Xarles' full attention.

"The bandits entered through the horse corrals and their timing corresponded with the early morning change in patrols taking place by the cooking tents," Xarles stated. "Armand is paranoid, always has been. Patrol routes are constantly alternated. Patrol changes are always scheduled at random times and at different locations. Armand constantly makes changes to make it more difficult for outsiders to…"

Kyreen watched silently as Xarles mind worked out where she had been going with her question. He looked at her with a new level of respect in his dark eyes.

"You believe the raiders had help from my camp, from one of my men," Xarles remarked. "And you know which one."

"I have my opinion," Kyreen replied with a shrug. "I know which one of your men has been extraordinarily nervous, even more so today than he was yesterday, the same man who took something of mine, something I was wearing when your men captured me, something I would like back."

"Pierre took one of your belongings?" Xarles asked.

"Something I would like back," Kyreen repeated.

Xarles regarded Kyreen a long moment, before nodding. "If I find said item on Pierre or among his belongings, I will return your item to you."

"Thank you," Kyreen replied.

Xarles wiped his mouth with his napkin. "Shall we take a walk?"

Kyreen drained her cup of water before standing and following him to the tent entrance. She looked forward to seeing how Xarles handled the confrontation with Pierre. A part of her, a very small part, felt bad for putting Pierre into Xarles' mind as the possible traitor, but she did not dwell on this. Pierre was hiding something else, something aside from her ring, and Kyreen looked forward to finding out what that something was.

Xarles held open the tent flap and, as she slipped by him into the evening, Kyreen murmured, "You still owe me one more answer."

"That I do," Xarles chuckled, following her outside, pausing to look at the two men standing watch outside his tent. "Jacques, stay here. No one goes in until I return. Pierre, you are with us."

Kyreen took the arm that Xarles held out for her. This man kept surprising her with little gestures like this. She reined in her mind as memories of their recent afternoon activities threatened to distract her from the task at hand. As though he knew her thoughts, Xarles flashed Kyreen a lopsided grin, full of mischief and knowing. Though she did not blush, Kyreen did return his smile, warmth infusing her body, as they began walking.

Once again, their evening stroll took them to the cooking tent, where Xarles left Kyreen outside with Pierre as he spoke with the head cook. Kyreen decided to take the opportunity to speak with Pierre.

"Have you thought on what we discussed earlier?" she asked, sliding up beside the bandit man so that their shoulders touched.

"What is your problem?" Pierre growled, casting her a dark look and taking a side step away from her.

"Me? I have no problems, Pierre, but you do," Kyreen replied, her voice and face suddenly devoid of mirth. "There is still time for me to save you, Pierre, but only if you can convince me that it is in my best interest to do so."

"You are demented," Pierre snapped, his facemask of indifference slipping away as his annoyance soared.

"Then you are a dead man," Kyreen replied quietly, moving away from Pierre as Xarles emerged from the tent.

The bandit leader looked between the two but held his tongue. Kyreen smiled innocently as she slipped her arm through his and they resumed their walk through the camp. She had expected their next stop to be the tent with Gautier, so was surprised when Xarles kept walking. They continued on pass the horse area as well, to the very edge of camp. Kyreen felt Armand with his anger and another man with his pain before she saw them through the evening twilight. A moment later, when he too saw the pair, Kyreen felt Pierre's surge of emotions, anguish, panic, shame. This last emotion intrigued her as she turned her attention to the scene before her.

A small, temporary structure, canvas stretched over four tent poles, had been erected, but the man staked to the ground had not been under the tent's protection during the day. Kyreen gave silent thanks to the lack of light as what she could see made her recent meal turn in her stomach.

"Please refrain from antagonizing Armand, if you can?" Xarles murmured quietly as they approached. "The distraction would be most annoying."

"I can behave if he can," Kyreen responded, her tone implying the big man would start the trouble without any prompting from her.

Though Xarles sighed, she felt his amusement. For all his complaints, Kyreen's actions did not annoy or upset Xarles in the least. She grinned as he turned his attentions to the big man and the prisoner.

While Xarles and Armand discussed what had not been discovered through Armand's interrogation techniques, Kyreen turned her own attentions to the man staked out on the desert sands. He had been positioned on his back, all four limbs stretched and secured so he made an 'X' on the ground. Unlike Gautier, this prisoner had been left with his trousers on, though his torso and feet were bare. As the evening breeze picked up, Kyreen smelled the blood from this man. The scent matched the pain he radiated. Though conscious, the man lay motionless with his eyes shut.

In the few heartbeats it took Kyreen to take in the prisoner's statistics, Pierre's emotions also began to assault her. His nervousness had spiked and she could not help wonder if he knew this bloodied man. When, with her brow furrowed, Kyreen turned to face the anxious man, Pierre's anxiety mutated into full-fledged panic. He pulled out a dagger and grabbed at Kyreen, who made the decision mid-grab to permit the man to continue. She could not be sure her attempt to stop him would not kill him, and then where would she be? If Pierre died, she may never recover her ring.

Armand and Xarles stopped speaking as soon as Pierre began his move. When Pierre wrapped his arm around Kyreen, with his dagger to her throat, Armand took a half step forward, only to be stopped by Xarles. The bandit leader shook his head, his gaze on Kyreen's face.

"Pierre, Pierre, Pierre," Kyreen sighed melodramatically in her most disappointed tone of voice. "I thought maybe we might be able to work together. Are you sure you want to do this?"

"Shut up!" Pierre screamed in her ear, spittle spraying from his mouth, to hit and drip down her cheek. "Shut up! Shut up! Shut up!"

Kyreen trained her gaze on Xarles, whose eyes had never left her face. The bandit leader gave her a small nod, silently encouraging her to handle the situation.

"You want him alive I suppose," she said calmly, as though she did not care whether the man holding her lived or died.

"Yes," Xarles replied. "Conscious if possible."

"You already owe me one answer," she stated. "And we have not even started negotiating Gautier's healing."

"I said shut up!" Pierre said, his voice sounding more like a whiny child than a man holding a knife to a woman's throat, and he did have the dagger's tip pressed quite firmly against Kyreen's jugular. She felt Pierre's entire body, pressed up against her backside, trembling. The man was excited, but not like he had been earlier in the day during her branding. Lust she could have manipulated, but panic was another matter entirely. If she did not hurry, Kyreen feared Pierre may puncture her jugular by accident and actually kill her. She had deduced from his emotions throughout the day, that, under normal circumstances Pierre would not harm her or kill her, not on his own. Pierre harbored plenty of anger towards Kyreen and would willingly participate in violence towards her, but the man holding a dagger to her throat was a follower. That he had taken the initiative to grab Kyreen and hold the weapon to her throat spoke volumes about his deteriorated mental wellbeing. Kyreen did not have time for further negotiations with Xarles.

"Fine," Kyreen mumbled. "Let us call this a good faith gesture."

Before Pierre could react to her words, Kyreen grabbed his wrists to push his hands away from her even as she slammed her head backwards, driving her skull into Pierre's nose. As he yowled in pain Kyreen twisted around, both hands now clamped on the wrist of Pierre's hand holding the knife. With a soft grunt she pressed his arm back until something snapped and the dagger fell from his hand. Stepping aside, Kyreen aimed a swift hard kick to the man's knee, which resulted in another crack of bone and a howl from Pierre.

As Kyreen bent down to pick up the dagger, Armand stepped forward to grab Pierre. Only Xarles' quick movement to her side, strategically placing himself between Kyreen and Armand, kept the woman from burying the knife in the big man's neck.

"None of that," Xarles murmured quietly, steering Kyreen away from the man writhing on the ground in pain and Armand.

"He should not have done that," Kyreen murmured into Xarles' ear. She allowed him to gently pry the dagger from her hand. She would not have stabbed Armand, but she wanted Xarles to think she would have. She knew when she took care of Armand she would need to be stealthy. Right now, the big man was too alert.

"No, he should not have," Xarles replied once he had the dagger out of Kyreen's grip. She suppressed a grin at the worry the bandit leader exuded. It seemed she had broken through some of his emotional defenses.

"Wait here," Xarles told her before walking back to where Armand supported Pierre standing on his one good leg.

Kyreen had no intention of waiting anywhere, especially when Xarles stood with his back to her as he and Armand quietly conversed. Slowly, so as not to attract Armand's attention, since she stood within the big man's peripheral vision, Kyreen began moving away from the trio, back towards camp, into the horse area. As soon as she had backed around a corner, out of view of the men, she turned and began walking quickly towards her destination, silently giving thanks to Pierre for bringing her dark clothing.

When Kyreen reached her destination, she did not pause. Lifting the tent flap, she ducked quietly into the tent, careful not to startle the tent's lone inhabitant. The lantern hanging by the entrance had been set low, but still shone enough light that Kyreen did not feel the need to raise the flame.

Crossing over to the gray mare who watched the woman with those dark intelligent eyes, Kyreen murmured quietly, "Hey, girl."

The mare, obviously used to receiving treats from Xarles, nuzzled at Kyreen's clothes. Finding nothing of interest, the gray snuffed quietly before returning to finish her drink of water. She did not react when Kyreen placed a gentle hand on her distended belly.

When Xarles arrived a while later, after having looked several other places, he found Kyreen sitting in the straw beside the mare, now reclining on her side. His irritation at Kyreen dissipated when he saw the mare was in labor.

"I had felt her when we walked by earlier," Kyreen said as greeting, her voice quiet and level.

"You could have told me where you were going," Xarles responded, walking over to squat beside the mare.

"After you ordered me to stay like a good little pup?" Kyreen commented, allowing a sardonic grin to temper her words.

"My apologies," Xarles chuckled quietly. "I deserved that."

"I am not herd, Xarles, nor am I one of your men," Kyreen reminded him, the humor leaving her voice. "As much as I enjoyed this afternoon's activities, I think I may have made a mistake in indulging you, in indulging myself. You still treat me like your captive, not your guest, escorting me around, ordering me to stay put. You are smothering me, Xarles."

"Do you blame me for being cautious?" Xarles asked. "After verbally poking and mentally abusing a man all day and driving him into a severe lapse in judgement, you incapacitated him as quickly and efficiently as I have ever seen a woman, no, anyone ever do except maybe Armand. And your execution, my dear, was far more elegant than anything Armand has ever done."

"Did Pierre confess?"

"Yes," Xarles nodded, concern radiating from him, "in a way."

"You look worried," Kyreen prompted him to continue.

"Pierre has been with the camp several years. He is, was a good, reliable man, a hard worker. He never was going to rise in the ranks, never was going to be a leader, but he got along with everyone and was well liked," Xarles shook his head, standing to pace. "If you had asked me to guess who the traitor was among my men, I would have easily named eight or nine others before even considering Pierre."

"Damn," Kyreen muttered. "What exactly did Pierre confess to? What were his words?"

"He is not doing much talking thanks to the multiple broken bones," Xarles remarked. "Mainly he has nodded to Armand's questioning. Why?"

"I smelled magic on Pierre earlier," Kyreen commented. "At the time I thought it was from Pierre playing with my property. What if he were being compelled magically to spy on the camp?"

"That would be highly unlikely," Xarles said.

"But not impossible?"

"No," Xarles shook his head. "Not impossible, but magic is not common out here in the desert."

"That is what I was told at home," Kyreen remarked, her hand moving reflexively to rub the scar at her neck. "Right before a mage enthralled me."

Xarles' eyes followed her hand's movement, but he did not comment. Instead he turned and he headed for the tent entrance. "Maybe I should try providing a different set of questions for Pierre and our other guest."

He paused to glance back at Kyreen, still sitting in the straw beside the quietly laboring mare. "Will you be here when I return?"

"Yes, Xarles," Kyreen answered, smiling at his wording. "I will be here when you return."

Inclining his head with a smile, Xarles ducked out of the tent, leaving Kyreen alone with the gray mare. Soon, however, the mare moved into active labor, chasing away all thoughts of Xarles and Pierre and desert politics, and Kyreen concentrated on the mare.

Chapter 19

Kyreen had no idea how long she had been watched before she noticed the form standing amongst the shadows in the corner of the tent. All of the Calanian's attention had been focused on the colt as he struggled to his feet while his anxious mother licked at him. Even had she not been distracted, Kyreen could not have sensed the presence anyways.

When the form wearing Tyra's body and face finally stepped forward, Kyreen gave the spirit a glance saying, "Lakwen'dil."

Ignoring Kyreen's greeting, the spirit approached the newborn foal slowly, carefully placing a hand on the colt's back. Neither the foal nor its mother gave notice to the spirit's presence. After a few gentle strokes on the colt's back, the spirit turned Tyra's gaze to Kyreen.

"You seem better this day," she said.

"It has been better than most in recent memory," Kyreen confessed. "I am most grateful for the sleep you gave me last night."

"You have been casting today," the spirit observed.

"Yes," Kyreen nodded. "Is that an issue?"

"Only if the wrong one notices," Lakwen'dil responded.

Kyreen took a flake of alfalfa from a stack in the corner of the tent to give to the mare. Then she stood by her mother's figure to watch the coal black colt as he nursed.

"The wrong one?" Kyreen asked.

"The one who keeps the elves safe, who keeps their magic flowing, who keeps you and the humans from casting," Lakwen'dil replied.

"And who might that be?" Kyreen inquired. She gazed over the mare's back at Lakwen'dil, who had moved to again softly stroke the nursing foal. Resolutely Kyreen refused to glance towards the tent entrance behind the spirit's back, although she did cast out with her empathic senses. The mare's labor and the foal's birth, while routine and uncomplicated, had taken a good part of the evening, and Kyreen expected Xarles to return at any time. She had no desire for the bandit leader to meet this spirit.

"I would do well not to speak her name," the spirit answered, moving away from the foal, taking an aimless stroll across the tent. Kyreen's gaze followed her as the spirit continued to speak. "Though she has been withdrawn from this realm and the other for some time, it would not be good for you to know her name. She is not as benevolent as I for you."

"Oh?"

"She hates you," Lakwen'dil stated, gazing at Kyreen, the expression on Tyra's face inscrutable.

"Me?" Kyreen asked. "What did I do to her?"

"You exist. You question. You do not conform. You cannot be controlled," Lakwen'dil shrugged. "She did not like that you are mine."

"I am not yours," Kyreen asserted.

Lakwen'dil barked that humorless laugh then said, "Of course you are, my child. You and that friend of yours both. You are *Tepla'Hini*, a gift given me by my father when I came into my powers in the Time Before Time. Just as *Yeste'Hini* were given to her and *Numenore'Hini*, the humans, were gifted to my brother."

"*Yeste'Hini*?" Kyreen asked, though she had many more questions. It seemed every conversation with this spirit left the Calanian with more questions than answers.

"The First Children. The elves. They are hers and she guards them fiercely, so fiercely she had you banished and magic outlawed among the humans," Lakwen'dil remarked.

"Speaking of humans," Kyreen said, allowing her gaze to drift towards the tent entrance. "I am expecting the camp's leader back any..."

"Do not fret," Lakwen'dil interrupted with a wave of her hand. "I do not manifest for *Numenore'Hini*. Your human has not started back this way. He will soon, but I thought you should know about her, especially since you will soon be going into *Talamh sa bhaile Si'*. Her magic taints this camp so she may already know you have returned."

"Her magic taints this camp?" Kyreen asked, silently wishing that she could get a straight answer from the spirit. She also thought, not for the first time, that Brigit or even Synnove might be better mentally equipped to have these conversations with the spirit.

"The human you injured?" Lakwen'dil said. "He smells of her magic, though it is faint and faded. The one in the sand? He has a second-hand taint of her magic. Most likely both humans have been spelled by her elves to watch for elven artifacts. It is something she has done in the past."

"Her magic? Spelled to watch for elven artifacts?" Kyreen asked, attempting to be patient. The spirit had information, important information, if only Kyreen could pull it out.

"Yes, when the humans took you in the desert," Lakwen'dil answered, appearing oblivious to Kyreen's frustration. "When the elven items were discovered, the quiescent spells activated. Though the elves know these humans have elven items, her children may not know about you. There is still time."

"Still time?" Kyreen asked.

"For you to enter *Talamh sa bhaile Si'* undetected," Lakwen'dil responded, her tone implying Kyreen should already have known the answer.

"I have a plan to get out of here," Kyreen commented, "but it will take me a day or two."

"That is unacceptable," Lakwen'dil shook Tyra's head. "You must move more quickly. That human leader sent word to *Talamh sa bhaile Si'*, to his former House. I managed to redirect the message to a more suitable elf, but stories travel swiftly on the desert sands. At some point someone will speak of you and her children will hear. That will ruin the surprise for my dear sister."

"The one who hates me is your sister?" Kyreen asked. "Why am I not surprised."

"Did one of the humans damage you, hit your head?" Lakwen'dil inquired, tilting Tyra's head to gaze at Kyreen. "You seem addled, unable to comprehend."

"I suppose I am a bit mentally exhausted," Kyreen confessed, running a hand through her curls. "It has been a long couple of days and I am playing at a game I am not familiar with."

"You should rest, then. Because what you experience out here is a pittance to what you will face in there," Lakwen'dil advised, pointing in the direction Kyreen knew to be the mountains and the elf lands beyond.

"I am ready for rest," Kyreen said, glancing over at the colt, now lying in the straw near his mother. "As soon as Xarles shows up."

"He is on his way," Lakwen'dil said stepping up to take Kyreen's hands in Tyra's hands. "Remember, my child, you must be wary of her. Do not trust the elves, not even the one I sent you."

Kyreen looked down at her mother's hands holding hers. "I will keep that in mind."

"Good," Lakwen'dil remarked.

Then, before Kyreen could react, the spirit shifted her appearance, donning the figure of a tall, bearded Calanian with twinkling green eyes. With her gaze downward, Kyreen witnessed only the shift in the hands that held hers but could not pull back fast enough to escape the spirit's grasp as Lang's hands tightened around hers. Trembling, Kyreen slowly raised her gaze to look into the excruciatingly handsome face of her dead love. Pain exploded in her chest as Lang leaned in, his lips pressing against her mouth. Absently Kyreen registered that Lakwen'dil even smelled like Lang. Then the spirit faded away, leaving Kyreen alone with the mare, the foal, and her tears.

When Xarles entered the tent, he first saw the mare dozing, her head hanging near the tiny black colt asleep in the straw. He paused just inside the entrance to gaze at the pair, then turned his head to look for the woman, noticing the soiled straw and cloth stacked near the tent door ready for disposal. He did not worry that he did not see Kyreen immediately. She had said she would be here, and, for some odd reason, Xarles believed her. Still his heart jumped a bit when he finally located her sitting on the ground in a shadowy corner of the tent. Something in the way she sat with her legs drawn up, her chin resting upon her knees, gave the bandit leader pause.

"He is beautiful and healthy," Kyreen spoke, her voice quiet without revealing any of the emotions that swirled inside her at the moment. "The birth was long but nothing out of the ordinary."

Xarles moved to squat before the Calanian. He noticed the moisture on her cheeks but did not comment. "Thank you for staying with her. This is her first foal. I do not usually breed my horses, but an unusually fortunate opportunity presented itself so I took the chance."

"I did nothing. As someone once told me, mares have been giving birth without my help since the beginning of time. Foals will come whether I am there to deliver them or not," Kyreen commented flatly. The interaction with Lakwen'dil had left her drained, both mentally and emotionally.

She lifted her gaze to Xarles' face. "I believe I falsely accused Pierre of treason. I no longer believe he is to blame for his actions."

"How did you arrive to this?" Xarles asked, not hiding his surprise. "I, too, believe he has been used, but only after listening to his story and the other man's as well. Neither have any memory of knowing each other, let alone ever speaking or corresponding, yet the Two Palms man had in his possession a letter from Pierre, written in Pierre's hand. And Pierre claimed no knowledge of this I found in his pocket."

Xarles opened his hand. In his hand rested the lumpy silver ring with the dark red stone. Kyreen hesitated before reaching out to take the ring. Xarles closed his hand around hers, then placed his other hand on top of their clasped hands, but not to keep her from claiming the ring. Instead he wanted to get her attention.

"The hour grows late," he said quietly. "Shall we retire for the night?"

Kyreen shook her head, pulling her hand away from Xarles' hands, leaving the ring in his palm. "I cannot rest until I have healed Pierre and, with your permission, the other man."

Shame at her actions, at how easily she had crippled Pierre, at how little thought she had given to inflicting pain, coursed through Kyreen. She forced back the tears but could not keep the disgust from her face. Two days in this camp and already she was becoming as ruthless and violent as these bandits.

Without comment, Xarles nodded, leading her out of the mare's tent and towards the outer edge of the camp where Armand stood watch over Pierre and the other man. When he saw Xarles return with Kyreen, the big man glowered, but he remained quiet. In addition to the injuries Kyreen had inflicted upon him, Pierre's face reflected the damage from Armand's fist. Both eyes were swollen shut, his nose obviously broken, his lips bloodied.

Taking a deep breath, Kyreen attempted to center herself so as to cast the first of the healing spells that would alleviate the man's suffering. It took her three tries to finally calm her own emotions enough to complete the four spells, two for each of the injured men. The spells drained Kyreen, but not nearly as much as the self-loathing coursing through her veins. Kneeling beside the man from the other camp, Kyreen lowered her hands after the final spell and swayed slightly, dizziness overtaking her momentarily. Xarles placed a gentle hand on her shoulder to steady the Calanian.

Holding out his hand, moonlight glinting off the silver ring, the ruby black in the night, Xarles repeated in common, "Shall we retire for the night?"

"Are you certain you wish me to sleep in your tent?" Kyreen asked, gazing up at his face, hidden in the shadows, her own face sorrowful in the pale moonlight. "Could you sleep? Do you trust my presence while you slumbered?"

Xarles nodded. "I believe if you say you will not kill me in my sleep, then you will not kill me in my sleep. Are you planning on killing me?"

"Not tonight or even tomorrow," Kyreen responded truthfully. "Tell me though, why me? Why do you not spend your nights with the one you truly desire?"

Her question startled Xarles enough that for one fleeting moment she felt his uncertainty. When he attempted to pull his hands away, Kyreen placed her other hand atop theirs, holding him there as she felt his emotions flicker through his shields.

Finally, Xarles sighed. "As I told you earlier, I cannot afford to be sentimental or become attached to anything or anyone."

"But you have," Kyreen remarked.

"No one can suspect that I have or that attachment will be used against me. I will not allow that to happen," Xarles snapped. "Not ever again."

For a long moment, they gazed at each other. Then Xarles pulled at Kyreen's hands, drawing her to her feet. Staring into each other's eyes, he wrapped her hand around the ring then lifted both his hands to push back her curls and cradle her face.

"Would you share my bed with me this night?" he asked in elven. Kyreen felt the surge of anger from Armand, standing out of the way, observing the interaction between Xarles and her with disgust.

"You do owe me one more answer," Kyreen replied in common, a small smile playing about her lips. She slipped the ring on her finger.

"If you can wait until we are settled for the evening, I will answer anything you ask," Xarles said.

"Deal," she answered, leaning in to kiss him softly on the lips, more to anger Armand than from affection.

When they parted, Xarles extended his arm for her and they strolled into the shadows, leaving Armand, Pierre and the stranger behind them.

Passing by the campfire, Kyreen noticed the festivities. Bodies, only shadows against the flames, danced and cavorted, music and sounds of merriment wafting through the still night air. The mood from the area exuded celebration. Noticing her glance, Xarles gestured to the full moon overhead.

"It is the harvest moon festival," he explained. "Tonight anyone not on patrol duty or out on a caravan, is given the night off. The cooks made special food. That was our dinner tonight."

"It all tasted divine," Kyreen remarked. "I thought it was your normal fare."

Xarles shook his head. "My head cook is very good, but no, the days of lunar festivals are special menus. The rest of the month is rather bland."

A small figure, shrouded in shadows, darted out from between two tents, scurrying across the path in front of the pair. A moment later three other shadows, slightly bigger, followed. Kyreen managed to catch an impression of the four shapes.

"Children?" she said in disbelief. "You have children here?"

"There is always a small pack hanging around," Xarles replied.

"Small pack? Hanging around?" Kyreen asked. "Who care for them?"

"Mainly they care for themselves," Xarles stated.

They had reached the entrance to Xarles' tent but Kyreen paused, her gaze trained on the spot where the shadowy figures had disappeared. Her brow furrowed.

"It felt like the first child was afraid," she said. "As if the others were chasing her."

"Him," Xarles corrected. "None of the wild children are females."

"If you say so," Kyreen commented. "I do not know if I want to hear the reasoning behind that piece of information."

Xarles chuckled then nodded to his man guarding the tent. "Jacques, you may go join the festivities."

"Thank you, Xarles, but Armand instructed me to stand watch over your tent for this evening," the man said, his nervousness washing over Kyreen.

"No worries, Jacques," Xarles said. "The tent will not be unprotected. If Armand has an issue, he may discuss it with me in the morning."

The man radiated doubt, but he inclined his head respectfully before disappearing into the night.

As they entered the tent, Kyreen gave Xarles a glance. "What was that about?"

"I was thinking on our walk over, how best to make you feel at ease," Xarles remarked, turning to fasten the tent flap. "I thought if you were permitted to place your wards upon the tent, then you would feel safer, more at ease, less inclined to act out."

"You have given this some thought," Kyreen stated, thinking but not saying much more thought to it than she had.

"Also, I am curious to see how your protection spells work," Xarles admitted, moving over to the platform to toe off his shoes before ascending the steps to sit on the edge of the bed.

Feeling more than a little self-conscious Kyreen faced the tent entrance to begin casting the basic protection spell that would alert her if anyone attempted to enter the tent. The now familiar energies coursed through her, combining with the wonder she felt radiating from the man watching her, helped to push away her reticence. When Kyreen finished the simple protection spell, she continued into a silencing spell so no one outside the tent walls would be able to hear what happened inside. Even as she cast, Kyreen thought about asking Brigit if there were other defensive or trap spells that she could use for camp protections.

Finishing up the second spell, Kyreen turned to face Xarles who had not moved from his spot on the edge of the bed. The look on the bandit leader's face stoked the flames of power coursing through Kyreen. All her fatigue melted away. She felt invincible, capable, potent. Xarles' emotions echoing his expression bolstered these feelings. The energies of her spells, of Xarles, of the camp, flowed through her, filling her, rejuvenating her. For the first time Kyreen felt the full power of magic, the pull of its allure, felt it calling her to delve deeper into its mysteries. She craved more of the feeling even as it swam through her veins.

"Kyreen?" Xarles voice brought her back to the tent. From his expression that had not been the first time Xarles had spoken her name. When she leveled her glittering emerald eyes on him, he asked, "Is everything alright?"

"Yes," she said, surprised that her voice sounded so level, so calm, so normal. "Everything is very much alright."

"Are you ready to ask your question now?"

Kyreen shook her head slowly as she began stalking towards the bed, towards Xarles. She quickly ascended the steps to pounce on the man, his surprise only stoking her desire as she pushed Xarles onto his back, her body dropping to cover his, her lips greedily claiming his. Even as they kissed, she began toeing off her boots, while his hands tugged at her shirt. Raising up, her knees straddling his hips, allowing him pull the shirt over her head, her eyes devouring his naked torso, Kyreen growled softly, "Later."

Xarles had just enough time to nod and say, "Later," before she once again claimed his lips with hers.

Chapter 20

Kyreen stretched out languidly on the rumpled sheets, not dozing yet not fully awake, relishing the feel of the linens against her bare skin. Beside her she felt Xarles resting in a similar state. She had just begun to formulate her final question for him when the perimeter spell went off and she felt the first waves of anger from the person clawing at the tent entrance. Without conscious thought, Kyreen rolled off the bed to the low-lying table upon which her sword lay. Grabbing the tri-colored hilt and pulling the blade free, she turned towards the tent entrance even as Armand cut through the fastenings and charged into the tent. With her sword in one hand Kyreen extended her other hand, the one upon which the ruby ring glinted from her middle finger. The words she mumbled forced the sand that made the floor of the tent to rise up and around the big man's feet. Armand, forced to stop as the sand enveloped and hardened around his feet, encasing him up to his ankles, glowered at Kyreen.

"Armand, hold!" Xarles commanded quietly as the big man moved a hand to the vicious dagger sheathed to his belt. Then he added, just as quietly, in common, "Kyreen, please stop."

Kyreen glanced over at the bandit leader, who now sat upright in the bed, sheets pooling about his hips, lamplight glistening off his bare torso, saying in common, "He should not have done that."

"No, he should not have," Xarles agreed.

Kyreen lowered her hand but kept her sword ready. She stole another glance at Xarles before returning her gaze to Armand. "You knew he would show up tonight."

"I thought he might if he noticed Jacques at the festival," Xarles responded. "Could you release his feet? Please?"

"Once you make sure he does not come after me," Kyreen replied. "Or I may have to kill him now instead of later and ruin our pleasant evening."

"Armand," Xarles said, speaking in elven, "Kyreen is going to release your feet, then you are going to turn around and leave this tent. We can discuss this in the morning. As you can see, I am very well guarded."

"But who is going to protect you from her when she turns?" Armand growled, his dark eyes boring into Kyreen.

Xarles rose from the bed, pulling on his black pants before moving to stand before Armand. The bandit leader man murmured something to the big man, something that Kyreen could not hear, but which made the big man relax and turn his gaze away from Kyreen, focusing now on Xarles, who continued speaking for a few short moments.

"You may release his feet," Xarles finally said in common.

Kyreen complied, but stood with her blade at the ready, although she did not need to. With a curt nod to Xarles, Armand turned and exited the tent without another glance towards Kyreen.

When the tent flap fell back into place, Xarles turned to face Kyreen. His smile widened as he took in the view of her standing there, naked, her blade in hand. Kyreen returned his smile. Nothing in his emotions was derisive or scornful. Only admiration and respect flowed from Xarles, the warmness of his feelings enveloping her.

"I think it is safe for you to put that away," Xarles commented, motioning towards the sword.

Kyreen sheathed the sword, leaving it on the table, then moved over to recast the protection ward on the tent's entrance. While she worked Xarles poured them each a cup of water. When Kyreen finished the spell, he brought her the cup which she took gratefully, and drained, watching Xarles watch her as she drank. When she finished, he took the cup from her, returning both cups to the side table.

"Shall we try this again?" he asked gesturing to the bed. "I believe you were about to ask a question of me when Armand interrupted."

Kyreen slid back onto the bed, lying on her side to face Xarles as he lay on his side. In the low light, she gazed at him while her mind struggled to formulate her question.

"Are you having trouble thinking of a question?" Xarles asked, smiling. He reached up to brush her hair back from her face.

"No," Kyreen replied. "I have several questions and am trying to decide how best to word it so as to encompass all my questions."

Xarles chuckled softly, twirling one of her curls around his index finger.

"My question is about your history—how a man such as yourself has such knowledge of the Old Kingdom's language, has a history with a man such as Gautier, and becomes leader of Crescent Moon camp?"

He remained quiet for several long moments, continuing to play with her curl. Though his face remained neutral Kyreen felt his swirling emotions. She determined to remain quiet herself, not moving, resisting the urge to nibble at her lip, quietly observing him in the dim light.

"I was born in the Old Kingdom, in Labeck," Xarles finally said, naming a province to the south, not far from Hanoria. Kyreen recalled lying about this province being her home when she introduced herself to Kare and his family, when she left Hanoria for Calan and thought to pretend to be a man. So many lifetimes ago. Looking back Kyreen barely recognized the girl she had been. Mentally shaking her head, she shoved away the memories and concentrated on Xarles' words.

"My father came from a farming family with seven sons. He was the middle child, without many prospects for prosperity. The farm was not large enough for all the sons to work and make a profit, and his father did not think to send his younger sons out as an apprentice to learn a trade. Then a drought hit, making the farm even less productive."

Xarles paused to roll onto his back, his eyes staring up at the tent's ceiling. Kyreen remained where she lay, watching his face in the shadows as he spoke. Though they had shared many intimacies earlier and she felt comfortable here in his bed, Kyreen felt no pull to snuggle against his side, still felt no emotional attachment to Xarles, nor him for her.

"With the drought, my father found himself to be a husband and father without means to sufficiently support his family. News of the mining boom in the eastern Salandingar Desert had reached their little province and my father grasped at the opportunity. Selling everything he had and taking out a loan to cover the rest, he bought mules and a wagon and equipment then headed to the desert with his wife and two children."

Because he paused, Kyreen quietly asked, "How old were you?"

"Five. My sister was two," he answered, his sorrows washing over her in waves.

"At first our trip was a big adventure," Xarles continued. "Labeck had easy access to the desert right near the foothills so our journey was not nearly as desolate and dangerous as your trek across from Pembroke. Additionally, there were many other men making the same journey with their families, same as my father."

This time when Xarles paused, Kyreen felt his emotions turn. First, he exuded frustration, then the deep burning anger. She placed a hand gently on his chest, her finger tips softly stroking his skin, soothing. He picked up her hand, bringing it to his lips for a brief kiss, then held it as he continued.

"My father had to have been the unluckiest man in all the realms. Every time we pulled up to a potential claim, someone had just beaten him there. Day after day, week after week, we traveled north, always just missing out on a fresh mining claim. As the crowds thinned out so too did the opportunities."

Xarles shook his head with a harsh laugh. "Looking back, it is easy for me to criticize my father, but he was young and naïve and desperate, a dangerous combination."

He released her hand to rest upon his chest and put both his hands behind his head, staring up at the tent ceiling.

"We had been on the trail several months when we came across a man traveling alone, with just a donkey. He had all kinds of tools and gadgets in his pack. He called himself a peddler. My father, with Old Kingdoms hospitality, invited the man to camp with us and to join us for dinner. It did not matter we had very little food left, my father felt it his duty to share what we did have. During dinner this man regaled us with stories from the desert, about riches to be found. He told my father about an unmined stretch just north of our current location, but that we would have to hurry to get there before anyone else."

Xarles paused again, his anger burning so vehemently Kyreen struggled to remain still. She did not know if she wanted to comfort Xarles or pull away so she waited, unmoving.

When Xarles resumed speaking, none of the anger Kyreen felt from him reflected in his voice. "Our camp that night was not too far from where we are right now. My parents had already decided to turn out of the desert the next morning, to head up into the foothills, to go to Derby Run, the town just over the hills. After listening to this man, however, my father changed his mind and decided to make one more run for a mine. My father pushed the mule hard that day. When we made camp at dusk, I remember my father being so excited. He was so sure he would make his fortune in the dawn when he found that promised mine.

"We were all asleep when the bandits struck. My mother's scream woke me up. I had taken to sleeping in the wagon under the stars, instead of in the tent with the rest of the family. At five years of age, I had no idea what was happening. When I woke, hearing my mother screaming and the sound of many strange men's voices, I did not know what to do. I did not hear my father or my sister. When I looked over the edge of the wagon, I could not see anything. It was so dark. I think it was the new moon. Then my mother yelled my name, telling me to hide, so I curled up in the back of the wagon under a tarp."

Xarles paused once again before continuing. "As an adult I have been able to piece together the events of that evening. A dozen men entered our camp. One of them sliced open the tent so as to surprise and immobilize my father. They knocked him unconscious, then dragged my mother outside. My mother screaming as the first man raped her was the scream that woke me. When she yelled for me to hide, one of the men struck her hard enough to daze her but not to make her unconscious. I lay under that tarp and listened to her as each of those men took a turn at her. I am fairly certain one of them held my sister, my two-year-old sister, during this but I do not know how much she witnessed. There is no way she could have slept through such an ordeal and I also know she was not harmed that night."

Xarles sat up suddenly, swinging his feet around to stand up. Without speaking he moved to the table to pour himself some water. Kyreen watched him, allowing his conflicting emotions to wash over and through her.

Setting the cup down, Xarles moved back over to sit upon the edge of the bed. Kyreen resisted the urge to stroke his scarred back, choosing instead to remain inclined on her side, as he picked up his story.

"When they were done with my mother, she was placed in the wagon where I was hiding and given my sister. Then they hooked up the mules and began the trek to this very camp. I do not know how they transported my father. I never saw him, but he was not left behind. When I peeked out from under the tarp at one point, my mother shook her head so I hid back down. Eventually my mother managed to scoot towards me unobserved so she could whisper. She told me to run as soon as the wagon stopped and to hide away from these men. So, I did as she instructed. No one noticed me when I slid over the edge of the wagon and darted in between the tents. I had always been small and quick and agile, but I was only five. It was inevitable that someone would find me. I had no idea how to scrounge for food or find a hiding place during the heat of the day."

Xarles paused again, running a hand over his dark hair. Kyreen resisted the urge to verbally comfort him. She had asked the question and did not want to give him an out to stop before he finished his story.

"I was fortunate that it was the cook who caught me stealing food from the kitchen tent. He was a decent fellow, not inclined to beat a vagrant boy, or worse, like some of the other men. He put me to work chopping vegetables and helping out with the meals. Other boys helped out as well. In exchange for a meal, we would work for the cook. Cut vegetables. Feed the fire. Pick herbs. Whatever little chores he could devise. That lasted a few weeks before one of the men, one of the not so nice men, saw me and decided he wanted to have some fun with me.

"That afternoon as I slipped out of the back of the tent, he was waiting for me. He threw a bag over my head and picked me up. Again, as a naïve five-year-old, I had no idea what this man had planned for me but I was scared. Though I struggled and put up a fight, it was no use. I was too small. He carried me for a while, taking us away from camp, before setting me down. My leg slipped free and I kicked at him, connecting with his groin, which made him angry. Without removing the bag, he punched me so hard I blacked out. When I woke up the bag was still on my head but everything around me was quiet. I was lying on my back, with my trousers pulled down around my knees. I sat up, yanking the bag off my head and saw the man stretched out, unconscious, face down on the sand beside me, his trousers also down around his knees, his arse glaring white in the sun. One of the boys from the kitchen stood over him, a frying pan in his hand.

"That boy was Armand. He saved me that day, and although he only spoke elven and I only spoke the language of the Old Kingdoms, our friendship had been forged. We have been looking out for each other ever since."

Xarles glanced over his shoulder at Kyreen reclining in the bed, watching him. "Armand was born to one of the women in the herd. To this day I do not know how he survived early childhood. He was almost ten when we met. If not for him I doubt I would have survived those first couple of years."

He turned to sit cross-legged on the bed facing her. "My father was sold to one of the commercial mining companies, one of those big operations that went bust several years ago, but my father died long before that. He and a group of other indentured miners – that is what they called their slave labor, indentured—were caught in a cave-in only a year or so after he was sent to the mine. My mother..."

Xarles paused and Kyreen felt his internal struggles though nothing showed on his face. She admired the control he had on his external features. Even his voice remained calm as he continued. "My mother was placed in the herd. I managed to sneak in to visit her occasionally. She had become pregnant shortly after we entered the desert. The baby, too many months premature, was born and died a few weeks after we were attacked. Between that and losing my sister, my mother never really recovered. She simply faded away until one day when I went to visit with her, the women told me she had died. Later I learned she had taken some poison that she had stolen from a tanner who had rented her for an evening. After that it was just me and Armand."

"What happened to your sister?" Kyreen finally asked when it appeared Xarles would not be continuing. "Do you even know?"

"Yes, I tracked her down when I became leader of this camp. Felina was sold away, to one of the other desert camps as most girls are. The desert camps will raise girls within the herd but never with their mothers, which is why a two-year old was..." For the first time, Xarles exhibited some of the emotion Kyreen could feel boiling inside him. "It turns out the leader of the camp she was sold to had an appetite for very young girls. By the time she was of an age to be married in the Old Kingdoms, just barely a teenager, my sister had already miscarried two pregnancies. Once she had fully developed, stopped resembling a young girl, the camp leader lost interest in her, put her with the rest of the herd. Women in that man's herd did not last long. My sister died long before I found her. My only solace is that I did avenge her, though now I wish I had had access to your skills when I finally took that man. Anything I have in store for Gautier is nothing compared to what I would have done to the man who bought my sister."

"You tell me this story, yet you continue the practice of abducting women from their camps?" Kyreen could not keep the question from slipping out, nor could she keep the scorn from her voice.

Xarles looked at Kyreen, some emotion finally seeping through to shine in his dark eyes. "My herd is not typical. I do not keep girls in my herd. My women are cared for and are not mistreated. These women are adults and they make their choice. It may not be ideal, but everyone knows how hard it is for a woman out here in the desert and even in the foothills. They have very few choices. Even if a woman is fortunate enough to find a good man and choose to toil through life as a miner's wife, she will always be at risk to be captured and enslaved by another camp, one whose leader does not care for his herd.

"Those who carry my brand earn it and they do so willingly. What Armand did to you this morning was premature. He knew better, but I told you not to goad him. I told you he was clever. Technically he did nothing wrong."

"The evening I arrived in camp, I was told I would be the reward for the men," Kyreen said, "and I felt fear from the women at the main fire."

"One of the girls is new. She has only been with us a few weeks. This was her first time with the men, at the fire that night. Of course, she was nervous," Xarles said. "Some women never get over that. But my women do not get beaten, unless they have transgressed like Genevieve did with disobeying Armand's direct order and lying to him. Believe me, that is not the case in most camps."

Kyreen made a soft sound of disdain. "Armand has taunted me several times about how he was going to enjoy breaking me in."

"Armand rules through intimidation and he had no reason to think you would not be joining the herd. Most women who come into this camp do," Xarles remarked. "I, on the other hand, after hearing of your performance when they took you, knew there was no way you would ever be herd. Had you been destined for the herd, be assured you and I would have worked out an agreement and signed a contract, before you went to the men."

"What about Fanchon?" Kyreen asked.

"That woman," Xarles growled softly. "I never should have allowed her to sign on. Finial, Fanchon's sister, a wonderful woman, had joined the herd and asked me to also take on her older sister. Fanchon, though, came in with an attitude, always pushing authority, always talking back, always testing the boundaries. She willingly signed on, which meant she forfeited her freedoms for the protection of the herd. With her poisoned attitude, however, Fanchon could not be sent out on caravans, which is the herd's main function, both to bring in revenue and information. Then she started antagonizing Armand. No, I cannot feel sorry for that woman. Fanchon brought her troubles upon herself."

"So, your women have all willingly joined," Kyreen conceded, though her tone reflected her doubt. "What about when girls come through, what do you do then?"

"I do not buy or deal in girls," Xarles lied.

Kyreen's surprise at how easily she detected his lie must have shown on her face for Xarles asked, "What is wrong?"

"You lied to me," she stated bluntly and immediately felt his embarrassment. "Why would you lie?"

Xarles contemplated her a few moments before replying. "You are correct. I lied. Whenever a girl is available, I buy her."

"Why?" Kyreen asked again. She did not think she had misjudged Xarles. He did not strike her as the type to abuse young girls, not only after his proclamation the other night about only sharing his bed with willing partners, but after feeling his emotions about his sister.

"I have a contact in town," Xarles remarked. "She takes the girls and places them with families back in the Old Kingdom, gets them out of the desert. It is the least I can do to honor my sister, who never had the opportunity at a regular life."

"And Gautier?" Kyreen asked, fairly certain of the answer, knowing Xarles had more than answered her question, but hoping he would continue speaking.

"Gautier, yes," Xarles remarked quietly. He looked down at his hands loosely folded in his lap lost in his thoughts so long Kyreen wondered that he might not answer her, then he looked up. "Gautier is the peddler who came into our lives, shared our camp, ate my mother's cooking, told us stories, then led us right to the bandits. That was his trade, more than selling his wares. He made money guiding unfortunate travelers towards the bandit camps. If not for Gautier, my family would have gone into town that final day. That man killed my family. His actions made me into the man I am today. Now that I have him, I will make him pay for what he did to me, to my family, and to who knows how many other families over the years."

Just like that Xarles' barriers fell away, leaving him open to Kyreen's empathy. She felt the depth of his pain, his sorrow, his guilt, and his anger. So strong were the emotions that she struggled to catch her breath as they stared at each other in the semi-darkness.

After several moments Kyreen took Xarles' hand and pulled him back down onto the bed. Once he lay beside her, she wrapped her arms around him, his head resting upon her shoulder. She held his body close to her, his emotions washing over her until he fell asleep and then, eventually, she too slept.

Chapter 21

Every morning, in that timeless moment rising out of sleep, just before coming fully awake, before reality set in, she had a moment of anticipation. This morning the weight of an arm across her body only added to that experience. But then she took a breath, inhaled another man's scent, and she remembered. Lang did not sleep beside her. The arm pinning her to the bed was not his. Only this morning when Kyreen opened her eyes in the gray shadows, the pain did not overwhelm her. It still hurt but it did not cripple her, it did not draw tears, it did not consume her waking thoughts.

After reflecting on this change, Kyreen slid out from under Xarles' arm and out of the bed. At the foot of the bed she collected her clothes and began dressing. As she drew on her boots, Xarles rolled over in the bed.

"Breakfast should be here shortly," he said quietly. "Will you be back?"

Kyreen nodded in the direction of her sword resting on the low table. "As long as that remains here, you know I will be back."

Standing, she deactivated the protection ward and stepped into the early morning. Her exit startled the young man dozing by the entrance. Evidently Armand had posted another guard after he left last night.

"Xarles is fine," Kyreen told the sentry. "He is awake if you would like to see for yourself."

Without waiting for a response, Kyreen strode away. She did not have a destination in mind, just an urge to move, to be outside, to enjoy the new day. She breathed in the cool morning air, relishing her freedom. Overhead the sky glimmered gray and pink, the tiny full moon still visible, a pale disc hanging over the mountain peaks.

Kyreen thought about visiting the mare and her foal, so set out in that direction. As she walked closer, however, she found herself drawn to the tent where Gautier was being held.

The stench of human waste assaulted her senses when she first entered the tent, then the emotions of the man hit her. Gautier had been left restrained in a sitting position, his arms over his head.

At some point he had released his bowels and sat in the mess, his knees and ankles dislocated, painfully swollen. Standing back, a hand over her nose, Kyreen gazed down at the man, who although conscious had not acknowledged her entrance. Confronted with this bloodied and broken body, Kyreen felt a new twinge of guilt at her part in his condition, for having healed him so these new injuries could be inflicted. Then she thought about a young family traveling through the foothills, innocently searching for a new start, for livelihood, for survival. She thought about a husband trying to provide for his family. She thought about a young wife, pregnant, ravaged, torn from her children. She thought of a little boy thrown into a grownup world too soon. She thought about a baby sold and abused, and Kyreen's anger flared hot.

"Just kill me," mumbled the man, his voice cracking, barely audible.

Kyreen stared down at Gautier and thought about Xarles' anger. He said he had been looking for this man for years. She thought about the mercenary Falk whom she had fought and killed last summer. Would she, had she had the chance, have preferred a prolonged torture for the Faldorian? She doubted it. Her anger towards the man had not been stoked for years. Though years in the making, her confrontation of the Faldorian mercenary had happened so quickly, coming to a head with Engla's kidnapping. Kyreen had not had the opportunity for her hatred to fester.

Then her thoughts turned to Sten, her hand drifting to the spot on her neck where the indention of his teeth marred her skin. The memories, though only vague and indecipherable images, continued to leak through, sending her the wrong message in their attempt to convince her that what Sten had done to her was love. Most of the time, after months of work, Kyreen could thwart off the guilt and regret she felt from the enthrallment. When she thought about the mage, however, about what he had done to her, about what he had done to Lang, about what all he had stolen from her, she felt the those smoldering, tentative sparks of hate. Yes, given enough time and thought, Kyreen's hatred for Sten could definitely fester and grow. But, she wondered, would she be able to torture him as

Xarles tortured Gautier? Maybe. Maybe not. A part of her still feared Sten's power. He had proven himself to be an accomplished mage and a ruthless one at that. Given their history, Kyreen planned to follow Rhun's sage advice and simply kill the mage the instant he showed himself to her.

"Kill. Me," Gautier said again, his voice ringing off the tent walls.

Kyreen turned back towards the tent entrance. Before ducking out, she looked back at the man and replied, "Your life is not mine to take. You forfeited it to Xarles years ago. You have earned your punishment."

She let the tent flap fall back into place, silencing the man's shouted obscenities but not blocking the hatred he exuded. For all his time in the tent, Gautier did not seem to feel remorse for his actions. Kyreen wondered if he ever had or if he ever would before Xarles killed him.

As she began strolling towards Xarles' tent, Kyreen turned her thoughts towards the bandit leader and her quest. At breakfast she would begin negotiating in earnest. She had entered the desert near summer solstice and lost track of time. Last night had been harvest moon which meant three months had passed. Only six more months before she had to be back in Calan. If the elves moved as slow as she had been told then it could be that long before she even made it to the elf lands if she waited for Xarles' negotiations. Lakwen'dil had said she sent for someone, but it made Kyreen uneasy to rely on the spirit.

Though she thought as she walked, Kyreen also took in her surroundings, becoming aware of the person following her before she had cleared the horse area. Speeding up slightly, without giving the appearance of hurrying, Kyreen managed to pull out of her follower's line of sight and slip between two tents.

A moment later the figure passed by Kyreen's hiding place. The Calanian popped out and grabbed the figure from behind and retreated back into the shadows between the tents. The small body erupted into a flurry of hands and feet flailing out aimlessly.

"Shh! Stop that!" Kyreen hissed as the child's foot caught her shin and she ducked barely missing a hand in her face. "I will not hurt you! I just want to know why you are following me."

By the time Kyreen finished speaking the child had ceased struggling. Kyreen set the child down keeping a hand on one of the child's shoulders just in case the urge to bolt became too strong.

The dark brown eyes that stared up at Kyreen were wide, fringed with thick black lashes, and set in a round face, capped with a cap of tight curls as black as Kyreen's hair but much coarser, more compact, bouncier. The child's skin was tawny brown, a smattering of freckles across high cheekbones and a broad flat nose. She appeared to be about ten, not tall, mainly skinny arms and legs.

"I wanted to see you," the child said. "They says there was a woman walking around camp, a woman without no escort."

"Well, you have seen me," Kyreen remarked. "And I have seen you, twice now. You are the girl from last night."

"Keep quiet! No one can know!" The child exclaimed quietly, her eyes growing wide. "Hey! How did you know?"

"Part of my magic," Kyreen replied. "How can no one know? How did you get here? Where are your parents?"

The child crossed her arms and clamped her full rosebud lips tightly together. Kyreen sighed. She did not have time for such a distraction. As she contemplated her next words, Kyreen felt Armand's presence approaching. His underlying fury shone like a beacon, one she could sense a far distance away. He was moving in her direction. Drawing the child close, Kyreen stepped farther back into the shadows. Both looked out onto the path in the sunshine, both tensing when the big man stalked by. After Armand had disappeared Kyreen squatted down to address the child.

"I do not know your story," she whispered. "But this is not a safe place. You should have Xarles help you."

"He will sell me like he does all the girls. No way I am going to be herd. Not ever never," the child responded.

Belatedly Kyreen realized Xarles' way of handling girls must not be common knowledge. Of course, it would not. For him to remain the leader of these men, in this place, he had to appear to be ruthless. Kyreen sighed quietly.

"Do not worry about me. I get on fine enough. No troubles," the child remarked. "Long as they think I am a boy."

Kyreen arched a brow at the child. "How much longer will that be an option? How about when your breasts come in? When you start bleeding every month? What happens then?"

The child shrugged but Kyreen felt the surge of fear. Kyreen pinched the bridge of her nose. While she thought, Kyreen became aware of the child examining her closely.

"What?" Kyreen asked, the question coming out harsher than she had expected.

"You are not hideous," the child replied honestly. "You are very tall and rather skinny but still quite pretty. Why did they kick you out of the herd?"

"I was not kicked out of the herd," Kyreen retorted, stunned that she found herself upset by this child's comments. "I removed myself from the herd. I have certain talents that Xarles wants."

"So, you are his," the child nodded knowingly. "An exclusive. He has not done that before."

"No," Kyreen shook her head. "I do not belong to anyone. I am free."

"Free means you can leave anytime you want," the child commented. "Why are you still here? Why would you remain? We saw the men bring you in the other night. Word in camp is that you killed seven men before they got that toxin in you."

"Yes, I was brought here unwillingly but it was a misunderstanding," Kyreen explained patiently. "And it was only one, one man died by my hand. Just one. Why is everyone blaming me for the others?"

"Seven sounds better. Makes you seem more powerful," the child said. "If you want to stay free, you should claim them lives. Men get scared and nervous when a woman is powerful and beautiful."

Kyreen shuddered hearing that phrase from this young child. Not only did it bring up uninvited memories of Sten, it concerned

Kyreen that someone this young could be so starkly cynical about the world.

"I do not need to kill people to be powerful," Kyreen remarked, happy to hear her voice did not skip at the word 'powerful' like her heart did.

"And if you are so powerful and free why did you hide from Armand?" the child asked, her voice and her expression both reflecting her doubt.

"Because I have not had breakfast and I do not like to fight on an empty stomach," Kyreen quipped, only half joking. She was not sure how Armand would have reacted to her out without an escort. Considering Kyreen was looking to negotiate her exit and safe passage to the mining camp, her injuring or killing Armand probably would not put Xarles in a very generous mood.

"Speaking of breakfast," Kyreen remarked. "I need to get back to Xarles' tent. What is your name?"

The child looked back at Kyreen, her mouth once again tightening into a thin line.

Kyreen sighed and started over. Standing up and releasing the child's shoulder, she extended her hand. "I am Kyreen."

The child's dark eyes stared at Kyreen's hand as though it were a snake that might strike out. Not knowing the child's history, Kyreen thought she probably had a good reason to be wary of the adults in her life. Eventually the child reached out, grasping Kyreen's proffered hand in her own, lifting her eyes to gaze directly into Kyreen's face. "I am Aston."

Kyreen shook the small brown hand. "Aston, well met."

"Well met, Kyreen," Aston replied. Her somber expression and solemn tone reminded Kyreen of a similar introduction she had gone through with Lang's daughter Jetta at Spring Festival, just a few short months ago, yet a lifetime away from here. Resolutely Kyreen pushed back the memories and her questions about the little girl with the ebony braids, the chubby baby with Lang's sparkling green eyes, and their beautiful mother.

"I am heading to breakfast. Would you care to join me?" Kyreen asked.

"In Xarles' tent?" Aston shook her head vehemently, the tight spiral curls bouncing about her head. "Uhn-uh! No way I be going in there. Tents are not safe. No escape. Only brings trouble."

Looking down at the child, so defiant, so fiercely independent, so alone, Kyreen suddenly realized how very fortunate she had been as a child. She had never been so completely alone or abandoned like this girl appeared to be, like Xarles and Armand, like Rhun. This world was not soft. It was actually very dangerous. When they first left Calan, Kyreen had been shielded by her mother, had been naively unaware of their predicament, of what could have, would have happened had they been caught. Then, when her mother had been killed, her Hanorian foster parents had sheltered Kyreen from the worst of the world's violence and danger.

Chasing away the melancholy thought of how many orphan children there must be, Kyreen said, "I understand my words are not enough to convince you. If you change your mind, however, you know where the tent is. If you do decide to trust me, then I say Xarles would be an ally. He can help you. But only him. No one else. That is all I can say on that. Alright?"

Aston nodded, her face serious. "I will think on it."

"Do not wait too long," Kyreen advised. "I know how tiring it is to always be on alert. Those boys may catch you one day and inadvertently discover your secret. That would not be good."

Resisting the urge to tousle Aston's hair, the thought reminding Kyreen too much of Armand and the way he had ruffled her own hair, the Calanian instead gave the child a curt nod and walked towards the early morning sunshine. After checking that Armand had not doubled back, Kyreen made her way towards Xarles' tent, mentally girding herself for negotiating her exit. After her discussion with the child, Kyreen decided she would not call it negotiations for her freedom. The implications that her unfettered stroll was an illusion did not sit well with the Calanian.

Xarles sat at the table pouring himself a cup of coffee when Kyreen entered the tent. Though he merely gave her a mild smile, motioning for her take a seat, Kyreen felt his surge of relief, quickly followed by anger. She briefly wondered if her empathic abilities were getting stronger or if she was simply using them more here in the desert where she did not have to worry about being detected. Probably the latter she thought as she slid into a chair across the table from Xarles. When had she lived in Hanoria, before her return to Calan, she had been very adept at discerning emotions.

Shaking her head at Xarles' offer of coffee, Kyreen reached for the water pitcher saying, "No thank you. I have never developed a taste for coffee."

Xarles placed a hand over hers on the pitcher handle. Kyreen gave him a questioning look, noting for the first time the firm set of his mouth and the anger glittering in his dark eyes.

"I am capable of pouring my own drink," she remarked. Already on edge from her conversation with Aston, Kyreen's tone came out a bit sharper than she intended.

Xarles lifted his hand away and sat back in his chair, regarding Kyreen, his expression once more neutral. "Did you have a nice stroll?"

Kyreen finished pouring her water and sat back. Watching him over the rim of her cup, she drank before answering. "It was lovely. Did you send Armand out to fetch me?"

Even maintaining eye contact, Xarles did not reveal his surprise at her question, though she felt it. 'Good,' she thought. Now it was her turn to keep him off balance.

"No," he lied, leaning forward to scoop a spoonful of yoghurt. "Did you have a confrontation with Armand?"

"Why would you send him for me?" she pushed back, ignoring his question. "Did you not trust I would return? Do you want him dead? Any confrontation between Armand and me cannot end well. I have lost count of how many times you have saved that man in the last day. I doubt he is even aware of your interventions."

Leaving her questions to hang between them, Kyreen turned her attention to the food before her. For the first time in a very long time her stomach rumbled, not from hunger, but anticipation. Gazing at the assortment before her, Kyreen's mouth watered. She dished up yoghurt, fruit, and flat bread, upon which she drizzled honey, very aware of Xarles watching her every move, his anger seething as he calculated his response.

"Yes, I sent Armand to check on you," he finally admitted, some of the anger dissipating with his words. "I was being petty and I apologize for that. I am unaccustomed to people leaving my bed. It is I who usually kick them out. You did not hesitate to abandon me this morning."

Kyreen took a bite of food to conceal her surprise. She had not considered the ramifications or implications of her actions this morning. She could feel that Xarles had no emotional attachment to her, but she had forgotten to consider the man's ego. Instead of giving in to her initial instinct to apologize and explain she meant no harm, Kyreen took another bite of the flat bread, savoring the sweet explosion of honey on her tongue. Swallowing, Kyreen impulsively slipped from her chair and moved to stand beside Xarles. Leaning down, slipping a hand behind his head, she kissed him, long and deep.

As their lips parted, she murmured, "Apology accepted."

Then she moved back to her seat. Exchanging smiles, they continued their meal in silence, the tension between them broken. Kyreen appreciated Xarles' penchant of dining without talking. It allowed her to concentrate on her newly awakened interest in the food, the textures, the flavors. She found the experience to be almost meditative.

Once their plates were empty, Xarles leaned back with his second cup of coffee.

"Growing up constantly hungry, I have learned to relish my mealtimes. Many people cannot sit with silence, especially when eating. So, I thank you for that," Xarles remarked, lifting his cup up with a nod to Kyreen before taking a sip.

Kyreen pushed away her plate and picked up her cup, asking, "Is this a good time to resume negotiations?"

At Xarles' nod, she continued. "Instead of dancing around, I would appreciate getting to the big issues. Is that agreeable with you?"

"So direct. No games. So unlike a woman," Xarles commented, his eyes twinkling. "I agree. What are the big issues?"

"For you, Gautier. For me, getting to the elf lands," Kyreen replied. "You have been the most delightful distraction and my sojourn here has been surprisingly restorative, but I do need to be on my way."

"What do you propose?" Xarles asked.

"I offer to stay this day giving you the gift of my skills to be used as you see fit. Then, in the morning, you will give me supplies and grant me safe passage to town. I believe you called it Derby Run. From there, I am sure I can find my way to *Talamh sa bhaile Sí'*."

Kyreen could feel his resignation. He would acquiesce. She sensed no duplicity from him so she relaxed.

Xarles sipped his coffee.

"Your skills?" Xarles remarked, a playful smile adorning his face. "As I see fit to use them? Any of them?"

His expression and suggestive tone made Kyreen smile. She had no way to stop the color that crept into her cheeks, her blush deepening when Xarles' smile widened. Maybe she had relaxed too soon.

Then Xarles leaned forward, setting his empty cup on the table so as to extend his hand to Kyreen. "You have yourself an accord."

Kyreen took his hand, grateful and relieved. After they shook, Xarles rose, pulling her to her feet with their clasped hands. Tugging her body against his, he kissed her. When they parted he whispered, "You do have some particular skills I would like to make use of later. Right now, however, it would be your magical skills that I desire. Shall we visit Gautier?"

Chapter 22

As the sun hit midpoint in the sky, Kyreen exited the holding tent for the fourth or fifth time. She had lost count. All morning she had healed Gautier, then strolled around the camp. While Kyreen had resigned herself to her role in Gautier's ordeal, she could not remain present as Xarles reinjured the recently healed flesh and bones. Not only did the sounds of flesh rending and bones cracking turn her stomach, the emotions of the men, especially Xarles' hatred, overwhelmed her Connate senses. Once Kyreen had explained to Xarles how her empathic abilities were being assaulted, he had been agreeable to her leaving the tent. Kyreen could not help but wonder if her absence also permitted Xarles to indulge in his revenge even that much more ruthlessly.

On this, what was actually her fifth trip around camp, the sun overhead beat down mercilessly, only recently having begun its downward descent. The heat caused her tunic to stick to her back. The activity that had been bustling in the earlier hours had diminished. It was about the time that everyone retired to the shade of their tents until dusk. Fabrice, the blacksmith, appearing impervious to the heat, continued to work his forge in the increased temperatures. They exchanged cordial nods as Kyreen strolled by. When her path once again took her by the herd tent, Kyreen finally gave into her urge and ducked inside.

All conversation ceased upon Kyreen's entrance. Just as when she had spent the afternoon here, the women lounged about the room in small groups. Fanchon lay on her pallet alone and separate from the rest of the herd, her scarred back to the room. She did not stir when the Calanian entered. Genevieve, who had been reclining on the mattress, rose immediately and approached Kyreen.

"Greetings, mistress," the petite dark-skinned woman said, her gaze and comportment deferential. "How can the herd be of assistance today?"

Kyreen ruffled a hand across her braided hair. Her trip here had been impulsive. She had not thought through how to ask what she needed to know. Finally, when her silence had begun to drag on uncomfortably long, she blurted out quietly, "What do you use for contraceptive?"

A short while later Kyreen exited the herd tent relieved to have learned that the procedure Genevieve had performed on her the other day had been the administration of a contraceptive tonic that was effective for multiple days. So not only could she stop worrying about pregnancy, Kyreen would not need to return to the herd tent ever. Though Xarles claimed his women voluntarily joined his herd and Kyreen accepted that life could be very difficult for a woman all alone in the desert, she still could not be comfortable with the practice.

Entering the holding tent, Kyreen found Xarles standing away from Gautier. The bandit leader wiped his bloodied hands on a cloth. Kyreen wondered if she should heal Xarles' hands. Before she could ask, Xarles said, "One more healing before caesura should do it. Can you manage more healing this evening and maybe once more in the morning before you leave?"

Kyreen nodded. "That should be no problem."

As she lifted her hands to begin, Xarles raised a hand. "Wait. One more before you start."

Before Kyreen could react, Xarles pulled back his leg and kicked at Gautier's body. Ribs cracked audibly as the leather boot connected with Gautier's side. Kyreen grimaced, the force of Gautier's emotions causing her to stagger back. Immediately Xarles moved to her side, steadying her with a hand to her arm.

"My apologies," he murmured. "I got caught up in the moment."

"I will be alright," Kyreen said, waving him off. "Just give me a moment."

Once her head stopped spinning Kyreen healed the wounds on Gautier's body. This round took three spells. After casting the third, Kyreen decided she needed to do some centering meditations to replenish her energies. She also needed to address the guilt that continued nagging in the back of her mind.

Xarles frowned at the unusual pallor of Kyreen's naturally pale face. "Are you alright to walk back to my tent alone?"

Kyreen nodded, touched by his genuine concern, especially as it held no pity. "I will be fine. Let me I heal your hands?"

"How about when I get to the tent?" Xarles replied, his gaze drifting to Gautier. "I need to give him something to think on as we rest."

Kyreen nodded once again, biting her tongue to suppress her regret and sorrow. Tomorrow she would be free of this place, of these deeds, of these people. This was the price for her freedom. She had already committed herself. She could not back out now. With a soft sigh, she headed back out into the midday heat. She paused momentarily just outside the tent to steady her breath, breathing deeply to clear her head. The scorching dry air singed her nose and lungs as she inhaled, eyes closing. Slowly she exhaled. Then Xarles was at her elbow, his concern washing over her. Opening her eyes, she frowned to see the man's furrowed brow.

"What are you doing here?" Xarles asked, his worry clouding her senses.

"I just needed a moment to clear my mind before I walked back to your tent," Kyreen replied. "Go finish with Gautier. I will be alright. I do not need an escort."

"Kyreen," Xarles responded solemnly, "I am done with Gautier for now. You have been standing out here for a while."

Without another word, Xarles took Kyreen's arm and began the trek back to his tent. Whether it was the midday heat or her exhaustion from the spell casting, Kyreen found the walk interminably long. Only her sheer determination not to lean on Xarles kept her feet moving forward. By the time they reached the tent she could only shuffle.

Xarles led her to the table where he sat her down and poured her a cup of water.

"Drink," he instructed. "I need to meet with Armand before caesura. I will be back shortly. I should not meet with him here."

"Too late," Kyreen mumbled as Armand entered the tent. She forced her body to sit up straight, hoping the big man would not notice her fatigue and try to act on his anger. This would not be an ideal time for Kyreen to need to defend herself.

Thankfully Armand focused solely on Xarles, who took the meeting outside of the tent. Kyreen drank two cups of water while Xarles was gone. When he came back inside, she was pouring her third cup of water.

"Are you better?" he asked, walking over to pour himself a cup of water.

"Yes," Kyreen nodded, her eyes following his hand with the swollen, bloodied knuckles. Something inside her twisted at the sight, knowing how the injuries had occurred, realization welling anew of her role in the morning's events.

Xarles noticed her look and flexed his hand. "Nothing bad. You do not need to heal me."

"I would like to," Kyreen replied, standing up. "It will only take lesser healing, nothing major."

"Very well," he agreed, setting down his cup so she could hold both his hands in hers.

When the spell had been completed and Xarles' knuckles healed, Kyreen swayed as the room swam before her eyes. Xarles led her to the side table where he carefully removed her clothes then bathed her from the basin of perfumed water on the table. Kyreen wanted to protest but she felt too tired and his ministrations felt so good. Once Xarles had dried her skin, he tucked Kyreen into his bed. The last thing Kyreen saw before sleep took over her was Xarles removing his bloodied pants in preparation for his own bathing.

When she next opened her eyes, Kyreen felt Xarles' body nestled up against her backside, his arms cradling her gently. From the soft light infusing the tent, she could tell she had not slept long but she felt refreshed nonetheless. As she turned her head, Xarles' arms tightened, pulling her body closer against his.

"How are you feeling?" he whispered into her ear, his hand lightly running down the side of her naked body.

"Better," she answered quietly, turning in his embrace so as to face him. "But I know what would make me feel even better."

She kissed him, letting the sensations of their lovemaking carry her away, pushing away all conscious thought for the remainder of the afternoon.

When the sun dipped behind the mountains, casting purple shadows inside the tent, Kyreen slipped from the bed to perform her daily ritual. Running through the meditations two times, she finished feeling freshly renewed, her energies replenished and completely rejuvenated. Opening her eyes after drawing center, she glanced towards the bed where Xarles watched her, his expression and emotions invigorating her further. She had just slid back into bed to kiss him when a chime sounded at the tent entrance. Having never heard the sound before, Kyreen had no idea what it meant. Xarles rolled onto his back, keeping an arm tight around her as he glared at the tent entrance.

"What is it?" he called, his voice too loud to be considered a growl.

"The elves are here," a voice, a man's voice tinged with nervousness, replied.

Xarles sighed, his eyes on the ceiling. "Very well. Bring me their scroll."

"No, sir," the voice remarked. "The elves. They are here. At camp. Asking for you."

Xarles sat up abruptly. Then swiveled his legs around to stand up. He moved towards the entrance, pulling on his pants as he walked. Kyreen watched him, admiring his grace in such an awkward move. By the time he reached the flap, Xarles had the drawstring tied. He lifted the opening, speaking in soft urgent tones. Kyreen could not hear the words, but she detected Xarles' uneasiness as the messenger repeated his message.

When Xarles turned away from the entrance, he did not head back to the bed. Instead he went to a low chest and began pulling out clothing.

"Your clothes have been laundered. Your tunic was ripped beyond repair so you will have to make do with one of mine," he said, gesturing to another table. "They are there with your boots."

Kyreen slid to her feet, moving toward her clothes. "What is the matter?"

"I do not know," Xarles shook his head even as he changed from his loose-fitting pants into a fitted black pair of trousers with intricate red embroidery down the pant legs. "The elves rarely venture out of their realm, let alone here into the desert. That in itself is concerning. That I only sent the message about you two days ago is doubly concerning."

"Is it possible they are here for the artifacts?" Kyreen asked, recalling her conversation with Lakwen'dil.

"No," Xarles shook his head. He fastened a sash about his waist, the red fabric a stark contrast to the sky-blue of his tunic, the color stunning against his tawny skin. "Your name was specifically mentioned. I did not include your name in my missive."

Xarles ran a hand across his black hair, fastening a pony tail at the nape of his neck. Then he smoothed down his goatee before sliding on black boots. He next strapped a knife sheath over the sash, sliding an ornamental black handled dagger into the sheath before opening another drawer.

He glanced over at Kyreen, who had just finished tugging on her boots. Standing she relished wearing her own boots and trousers. The tunic was a tad big but she enjoyed the fact that even freshly laundered it smelled like Xarles, who now nodded towards the low-lying table upon which Kyreen's belongings set.

"I think you will be leaving me this evening. You may want to pack up," he suggested, turning his attention back to the drawer. Withdrawing a flat steel knife, Xarles tucked the weapon into a hidden pocket of his trousers. Kyreen watched him do this a few more times before turning her attention to packing her bag. Strapping on the sword something deep inside of her relaxed. Kyreen had missed its weight upon her back.

"Are you ready?" Xarles asked, already standing by the tent exit.

"What about Gautier? I owe you another healing," Kyreen asked, walking to stand beside him.

"No," Xarles replied, opening the flap and gesturing for Kyreen to precede him. "It is never wise to keep the elves waiting."

"It will only take a moment," Kyreen commented.

Xarles paused outside the tent and Kyreen felt his indecision. "You are not of the desert. You do not understand. Even though they are not present in the towns, the foothills, or the desert, the elves control everything here. They are the lords here. To cross an elf is to invite your death."

He turned to gather her hands in his, peering at her through the early evening dusk. "If you truly learned your perfect elven language from an elf, you would also know more about their culture."

Xarles shook his head when Kyreen opened her mouth to reply. "No, we do not have time to quibble and it does not matter. Just listen to me. Our time is short."

Kyreen nodded, closing her mouth. His anxiety continued to roll off in waves, though no agitation was reflected in the dark eyes that bore into hers or the cool hands cradling her hands. That these elves so deeply concerned Xarles, the leader of these bandits, the man who could control Armand, moved her to listen and heed his words.

"The elven culture is very structured, steeped in ritual and protocol," Xarles began. "They are a rigid and controlled people. It makes predicting their reactions much easier than with humans. That a contingency physically traveled outside their borders to my camp in lieu of a formal communication? Highly irregular. That they responded in two days? Very unusual, unheard of actually.

"I spent many years inside the elven lands, indenturing myself. The money, the training, and the contacts I gained in their realm helped me become the leader of this camp," Xarles paused to glance towards the palm trees that marked the public section of his camp before continuing to speak in a quiet, rushed voice. "Now I cannot guess what reaction we will get when we enter the tent. Humans are lesser beings in the eyes of the elves, just barely higher than livestock in their minds. How they will receive one of the Banished I cannot predict. You could be prized or feared or both. Do not expect them to greet you warmly or as an equal. They would not expect you to know elven. It may be to your advantage to keep that from them for as long as possible."

"It did not work that well with you," Kyreen reminded him with a wry grin.

"True," Xarles admitted, allowing a soft chuckle before sobering once more, "but the elves typically are less observant than I. Humans are inferior creatures so they tend to give us less notice as it takes all their attentions to guard against their own kind."

"You make them sound so sinister," Kyreen commented.

"Devious. Ruthless. Cruel. Calculating. Yes," Xarles nodded. "But all done within the confines of their laws and customs. Do not trust them. Not even one you consider a friend. Especially not a friend."

Kyreen nodded, remembering Lakwen'dil's warning, murmuring, "That I have been told."

Xarles narrowed his eyes and she felt his curiosity. Instead of asking his thoughts, however, Xarles turned, tucking her arm against him to begin walking. "One last thing before we get there. Time moves differently once you cross the bridge into the elven lands."

"Differently? How?" Kyreen inquired as the cluster of trees she had noticed during her earlier reconnaissance came into view.

"I do not know exactly," Xarles replied, his voice lowering as he halted once more. "I spent ten years in *Talamh sa bhaile Si'* yet when I returned barely five years had passed here."

Xarles inhaled deeply, a full centering breath, then exhaled quietly. "Their hearing is excellent. We probably should not talk beyond here. Though they are loathed to speak it, most elves are fluent in the language of the Old Kingdoms."

The tent Xarles paused in front of was located in an area of the camp Kyreen had not visited. She had noticed the clustering of tall palm trees along one side of the camp under which this tent stood and had speculated that this must be the public side of the camp, while she had been sequestered in the residential area.

The sun had disappeared behind the mountains, leaving the desert shrouded in purple shadows. The air still hung heavy from the day's heat, but a breeze ruffled through her loose curls with the promise of the cool night temperatures.

Kyreen glanced at the two horses standing off to the side, their reins draped over a hitching post. In the shadows, she could only discern that they were large beasts with dark coats, their mane and tails flowing long and wavy.

Xarles' eyes also saw the pair of horses. He turned to face Kyreen, drawing her to him, hugging her tightly. His breath warm against her ear, he spoke so softly in common she barely heard the words.

"Only two horses," he commented. "I have never known them to travel with less than five when they venture outside of *Talamh sa bhaile Si'*. One will be designated the speaker. His status is lower than the one who remains silent."

At a signal from Xarles, one of the men standing guard lifted up the tent's entrance, a spill of light cast upon the ground. Xarles entered the tent with Kyreen following. Walking to the middle of the brightly lit tent, Xarles dropped to one knee, his head bowed. Kyreen chose to pause just inside the entrance, her internal anxiety escalating as the flap fell back into place behind her. Blinking against the bright lights, her eyes quickly adjusted and she turned her focus onto the pair of tall, slender figures standing on the far side of the tent.

Both wore traveling cloaks that shimmered silver in the lamplight. The one on the left had skin as pale as Kyreen's while the one on the right had skin as dark as night, darker than anyone she had ever seen. Their white hair hung long and straight over their shoulders, pointed ears peeking out. Both pairs of eyes gazing down at Xarles glimmered violet.

While Kyreen had been examining the elves, Xarles had been greeting his guests with a long, wordy span of sentences, a formal welcome she supposed. When his voice faded away, the elves' gazes moved to Kyreen.

"Bring her forward," the dark skinned one commanded, his voice deeper than Kyreen expected from such a slender form. The elven he spoke sounded richer, clearer, more precise than she had heard from the humans. He spoke in a flat emotionless tone without inflection. He spoke as Lakwen'dil spoke. Kyreen wondered if these were the elves the spirit had sent and that was why he sounded like the spirit or if all elves spoke this way.

Xarles turned his head to glance back at Kyreen. "Come forward," he said to her in common.

Tentatively she took the steps to stand by Xarles' side. Though nothing registered from either elf, their essence a blank spot, Kyreen saw the slight widening of the pale elf's eyes as they took in her face, her hair, her eyes.

"She looks like the Banished," the dark skinned one commented.

The pale skinned elf nodded once, his eyes boring into Kyreen's. Not being able to gauge any emotions from him or his companion disconcerted Kyreen greatly.

"You said she had a mark," the dark-skinned elf stated, not exactly asking.

Xarles nodded and turned to Kyreen to translate. "They wish to see your tattoo."

"What if I do not wish to show them my tattoo?" Kyreen remarked, keeping her tones level but her eyes glittered as she gazed at Xarles. "I have not been introduced."

"One does not introduce the livestock," Xarles commented quietly. "You were warned. Please comply."

"I. Am. Not. Livestock," Kyreen stated, still speaking to Xarles in common. "Ever since I entered this dismal, wicked desert people, men, have been treating me as such. That ends now."

Chapter 23

Abruptly, Kyreen took a step towards the elves. Switching to elven she stood tall and, looking directly at the pale elf, she spoke. "I am Kyreen, first daughter of Tyra, only child of Rolf, middle son of Arvid, youngest daughter of Ebba, first daughter of Nanna, middle daughter of Rasmus, first son of Evo, only child of Malin, first daughter of Ynquie, father of all, created by Lin, Mother of Life. I journeyed across the Salandingar Desert from my home, Calan, located in the far north reaches of the Old Kingdoms, in search of one I hold dear to my heart."

As her voice faded, Kyreen bowed before stepping back to stand beside Xarles. Though he did not move or look her way, she felt his anxiety.

The dark elf opened his mouth, his expression unreadable though his eyes had narrowed. The pale elf, though, held up a hand to silence his companion.

"She is impertinent like the Banished," the pale skinned elf said, his voice not nearly as deep as his companion's.

Kyreen bit back an angry retort. She had acted on instinct instead of logic. No need to compound her gaffes.

At some unseen signal, the dark-skinned elf inclined his head towards Kyreen, then gestured towards his pale-skinned companion. "Kyreen, first daughter of Tyra, I present to you Al'phage of the House of Al, the arm of the House of Al, the prolocutor of the High Council, gerent of this region. I am Hagan."

"Well met," Kyreen acknowledged his words with an incline of her head. She wondered at the title of the pale-skinned elf, while the dark-skinned elf had only his name. Not for the first time, she realized how little she knew of the elf lands, the elves that lived there, and their culture.

"Now," Hagan continued, "introductions have been completed. Might you show us the mark?"

Kyreen had deposited her knapsack by the tent entrance when she had moved up to stand beside Xarles. She had not, however, removed the sword strapped to her back. Remembering the spirit's and Xarles' reactions to seeing it, she now shrugged off the leather straps, shielding the blade from the elves' view. Turning around, so her back faced the pair, she held the scabbard close to her body with one arm, before reaching back to lift the hem of her tunic with the other. After a long silent moment, she asked over a shoulder, "Seen it?"

"Yes," said Hagan. "You bear the mark."

Kyreen lowered her shirt, pausing for a slow centering breath. When she did turn around to face the two elves, she pulled out the sword, allowing the sheath to drop to her feet.

"I also bear this," she remarked, holding the sword in her palms, the tricolored hilt resting in one hand, the flat of the rune engraved blade in the other. Though she appeared relaxed, Kyreen could, if necessary easily shift her grip to wield the weapon.

Neither of the elves flinched when she pulled the sword, though she felt Xarles' tense. The elves' eyes, however, gazed upon the weapon in her hands for several moments. When no one seemed inclined to speak, Kyreen made to sheath the blade but Al'phage held up a pale hand. She paused raising a single inquiring brow towards the silent pair. Without her ability to sense emotion, she tried to gauge their actions on body language but the elves sat completely still, neither giving anything away. Xarles had said he spent years among these people. Now she knew where he had learned his stillness and how to mask his feelings and reactions.

"You have brought *Megil tel'kaane* back," Hagan commented. "Do you plan to wield it against *Tel'quessir?*"

Kyreen considered the question. She knew so little about the history between her people and the elves. She could, however, discern that her people's leaving may not have been their choosing. Much like the Galorian's recent relocation across the Great Sea, Kyreen's people leaving their homeland had not been their preference.

To buy herself a little more time to think, Kyreen bent down, picked up the sheath, then spun the blade around, sheathing it with more flourish than necessary. Deftly slinging the sheath over her shoulder, she strapped the sword in place before once again lifting her gaze to the pair of elves regarding her. Besides the blankness of emotions, their eyes – glittering violet, devoid of reaction – boring intently upon her, very much disquieted Kyreen.

"I do not come to *Talamh sa bhaile Si'* for aggression," Kyreen finally answered Hagan's question. "I will defend myself as necessary but I will not initiate the fight."

Xarles did not move or react, standing still as a statue by her side, his face carefully neutral, as Kyreen felt a burst of humor from the camp leader. His reaction made her smile as she gazed at the elves.

"Your words bind you," Hagan replied. "We shall escort you to our zupan."

Kyreen inclined her head, but before she could speak, Xarles' surprise stilled the response on her tongue. Hagan had not said what Xarles expected him to say. She recalled Xarles' earlier words about the predictability of the elves.

"That seems irregular," she remarked, forcing her voice and expression to remain unchanged, neutral.

"All will be revealed in time," Hagan responded.

Kyreen recognized a dismissal in the words. Indeed, Xarles at her side made a small bow.

"Denizens of the House of Al," the leader said, "your presence honors this camp. Might I offer you refreshment, simple food and beverage from my kitchen before you depart?"

Hagan nodded, though his eyes and Al'phage's as well, never left Kyreen's face. "Make it so and secure a beast for this one's journey."

"By your command," Xarles replied. As he began to back away Kyreen glanced at him and he mouthed, 'Come with me.'

Following Xarles' lead, Kyreen inclined her head and began backing towards the entrance. The instant she was through the doorway, standing outside, Xarles let the flap fall back into place and grabbed her arm, steering her away from the tent. While they had been inside, night had fallen though the moon had not yet cleared the horizon. Overhead millions of galaxies twinkled though not shedding much light.

Kyreen opened her mouth to speak but Xarles shook his head, his grip on her upper arm tightening.

"Not yet," he muttered quietly through gritted teeth.

They had not walked far when a group of four appeared in the shadows. Kyreen did not need light to identify Armand and his anger. The other man she did not recognize, while the other two Kyreen belatedly recognized as women from the herd. The women were clothed in pale loose-fitting robes, their hair lightly bound in a bun at the nape of their neck. One carried a tray with pitchers and goblets and the other held a tray of food.

Xarles looked at the man. "Take them to the tent. Hold the door for them, but do not enter. They have served elves before and know what to do. Do not allow anyone besides myself to enter."

As soon as the man nodded and walked away with the women, Xarles resumed walking, his hand at Kyreen's elbow. As Xarles motioned for Armand to walk with them, Kyreen noticed Xarles had placed himself between her and his second-in-command.

"Armand, go to the corrals," Xarles commanded. "Bring Mariah back, saddled."

"Are you leaving with the elves?" Armand asked. Though he never glanced in Kyreen's direction, she felt his anger intensifying.

"Armand, please," Xarles said, his tone quiet and firm.

The big man growled softly but took off without a reply. Their walking had brought them back to Xarles' tent. Xarles and Kyreen stood in silence for a moment watching Armand stalk away. Once the big man was out of hearing, Xarles turned to Kyreen.

"We do not have much time," he said not for the first time this evening. "Those elves are not taking you to the High Council, as would be protocol. Everything about this is irregular."

"You seem overly agitated," Kyreen remarked. "If you worry about my well-being…"

"No!" Xarles interrupted quietly, running a hand across his hair. "You have demonstrated your ability to protect yourself more than adequately these last couple of days and, as I think on it, in that tent just now."

He peered at her in the shadows. "I worry about releasing you to this pair because I sent my message directly to my former zupan who now sits on the High Council. If this pair do not represent the High Council, then how did they know of your presence here?"

Kyreen could guess but did not wish to reveal all of her secrets. "You are certain they are not from your, what did you call him, zupan?"

"Her, and no," Xarles shook his head. "They represent the House of Al. My lady commanded the House of Je. The one called Al'phage. That is not his given name, it is his title. Whatever name he had before ascending has been erased. His title is his life, his sole purpose. He has sworn fealty to the head of the House of Al, to do the zupan's bidding until death, either his or the zupan's."

"Who is the head of the House of Al?" Kyreen asked.

Xarles shook his head. "As a servant of House Je, I was never privy to such politics. The elves guard their houses' privacy, especially from humans."

With that he turned and entered his tent, pausing in the entrance for her to join him. Once inside Xarles strode to a chest from which he withdrew a garment of silver silk. Walking back to where Kyreen had paused by the entrance, Xarles held it out to her.

"Though you have not seemed eager to follow advice," he remarked, the twinkle in his eyes and smile playing about his lips lessening the sting of his words, "please allow me to offer one final piece. The Banished are only a myth to the humans, but the elves remember your people and not fondly. Most were alive when the Banishment occurred. Your travels amongst the elves may be smoother should you not be recognized. This was my cloak, when I served House Je."

Kyreen reached out to stroke the rich fabric. Her reluctance must have shown in her face for he pressed the cloak forward. "I have no use of the garment anymore. I will not be returning to the *Talamh sa bhaile Si'* ever again."

Something in Xarles' tone made Kyreen lift her gaze to the bandit leader, who smiled at her.

"Truth be told," he confided, "I am not certain how long I will be here in the desert."

Kyreen took the garment, holding it up between them. Her eyes examined the elaborate decoration of fine silver embroidery stitched along the edges of the garment but her attention remained on Xarles. "Why would you be leaving? Where would you go?"

Xarles reached out, reclaiming the cloak so as to settle it upon Kyreen's shoulders. Without looking up at her face, he fastened the filigree clasp, and smoothed down the fabric.

"My only reason for becoming leader of this camp was to track down those responsible for my family's suffering. Revenge has been my life's goal," he said, drawing the hood up over her head. "Gautier was the final one I needed to find. I grow weary of this desert. I would like to see Nowles again, maybe settle there, in a village or on a farm."

Kyreen hid her surprise in the shadows the cloak's hood cast on her face. She had difficulty imagining this man settling on a farm. She had even more trouble reconciling the image of Armand settling in a village, and she did not think Xarles would leave the big man here.

Xarles chuckled, more to himself than Kyreen, "Somedays I believe that dream has passed me by."

"I do not believe that," Kyreen replied, leaning forward to place a gentle kiss upon his lips. "Thank you for the cloak. I will attempt to blend in."

"Attempt maybe," Xarles joked, his tone and expression conveying his opinion that she would fail.

"Armand is back," she announced turning towards the tent entrance.

Outside Armand held the reins to a small dark coated horse. When he saw the pair exit the tent with Kyreen wearing Xarles' cloak, Armand snorted. "She takes your cloak. Takes your horse. She goes to *Talamh sa bhaile Si'* without restraints. They are as foolish as you, Xarles. Have you even received recompense? From the elves, I mean, not her. From her, you seem to have received plenty of benefits, though I still wonder about your judgment with regards to this one."

Kyreen bit back a comment, her hand under the cloak resting upon the pommel of her dagger. The cloak might be useful to disguise her looks, but, with her sword hidden beneath the fabric, it was not ideal should she need to defend herself.

"Thank you for your opinion, Armand," Xarles remarked, taking the reins from his second. "Do you not have evening tasks to which to attend?"

Armand nodded, his dark gaze never straying from the cloaked woman. "Yes, my captain."

The big man appeared to want to say even more, but he held his tongue. A wise decision thought Kyreen as Armand turned to stalk away. Xarles' temper had risen at Armand's words though his voice had remained calm. She watched the big man disappear into the dark night, knowing she would be returning someday to finish what he had started. She would, she knew, kill that man for the pain and suffering he had so gleefully inflicted upon her.

Once Armand had vanished, the pair turned back towards the copse of palm trees where the elves waited. They walked in silence, the mare plodding between them. Excitement and anxiety fluttered in the Calanian's breast. As different and exotic as the desert had been, the elf lands were completely foreign. She looked forward to finding her brother and Arvis.

As they approached the receiving tent, Kyreen realized she knew nothing about the geography of the elf lands. She glanced at Xarles, wondering if she should ask.

"You have a question?" Xarles asked as they came to a halt before the tent entrance.

"No," Kyreen replied, casting away her worry. "Nothing important."

Xarles handed the mare's reins to Kyreen, giving the mare a fond parting pat on her neck, whispering, "Take care of her."

Kyreen could not be certain whether he addressed her or the mare, but before she could wonder more, Xarles gathered her hands into his, holding them lightly. Kyreen returned his gaze with a fond smile. Then he leaned in to press a chaste kiss to her cheek.

"Safe journeys," he murmured into her ear, pausing just an instant before adding, "Bijou."

The anger inside Kyreen flared instantly at the mention of his pet name for her. That single word reminding her vividly of everything that had transpired in this camp, of the events of the past few days. Kyreen jerked back quickly, but before she could pull her hands out of his, Xarles tightened his grip. His brown eyes, now hard and cold, searched her face. Then he nodded slowly.

"Yes," he murmured, "there she is. The fierce warrior. Do not lose that feeling, Kyreen. You will need it and all of your talents in there. *Talamh sa bhaile Si'* is ever so much more dangerous than the desert."

His message delivered, Xarles lifted Kyreen's hands to his lips for one final kiss before turning and disappearing into the tent, leaving Kyreen and her anger to wait outside while he conducted his farewells to the elves. By the time Xarles and the two elves appeared in the tent entrance, Kyreen had lashed her gear, sword included, to the back of the saddle. Her anger she kept close, a tight ball resting in her core, though none of the emotion reflected in her posture or face. Gathering up the reins, she swung up into the saddle.

Without speaking Al'phage and Hagan mounted and turned their horses away. Viewing the elves from behind, with their hoods drawn up, Kyreen could not discern between the two. As she nudged the mare to follow, Kyreen glanced one final time at Xarles, smiling as he gave her a small salute.

The moon, having continued its ascent, shone bright in the star-jeweled sky. As the trio exited the camp, Kyreen felt the presence of the humans fall away, leaving her in the silence of her thoughts. Were she to close her eyes, she could imagine she once again traveled solo. Her eyes instead looked for the bright blue star upon which she had been navigating for months, but it lay hidden behind the mountains.

Now as the mare's hooves began traversing the rocky trail that led into the foothills, Kyreen allowed herself a small self-satisfied smile. She had conquered the desert. Feeling both healed and marked from her time in the burning desert, Kyreen squared her shoulders, leaving the known behind her and journeying towards her next destination without a backwards glance.

The End

Kyreen's journey continues in
Banished, Chronicles of Calan: Book IV.
Coming in Fall 2018!

Follow Nikki on Twitter and Facebook for the latest updates
or check out her website at moore-books.com.

www.ingramcontent.com/pod-product-compliance
Lightning Source LLC
Chambersburg PA
CBHW051240250626
47155CB00009B/3108